ROBIN JARVIS

With illustrations by the author

EGMONT

EGMONT

We bring stories to life

First published in Great Britain in 2017
by Egmont UK Limited
The Yellow Building, 1 Nicholas Road, London W11 4AN

ISBN 978 1 4052 8024 2

61957/1

A CIP catalogue record for this title is available
from the British Library

Typeset by Avon DataSet Ltd, Bidford on Avon, Warwickshire
Printed and bound in Great Britain by the CPI Group

A colour a day to brighten our play.
But once begun can't be undone,
till all are gone and washed away.

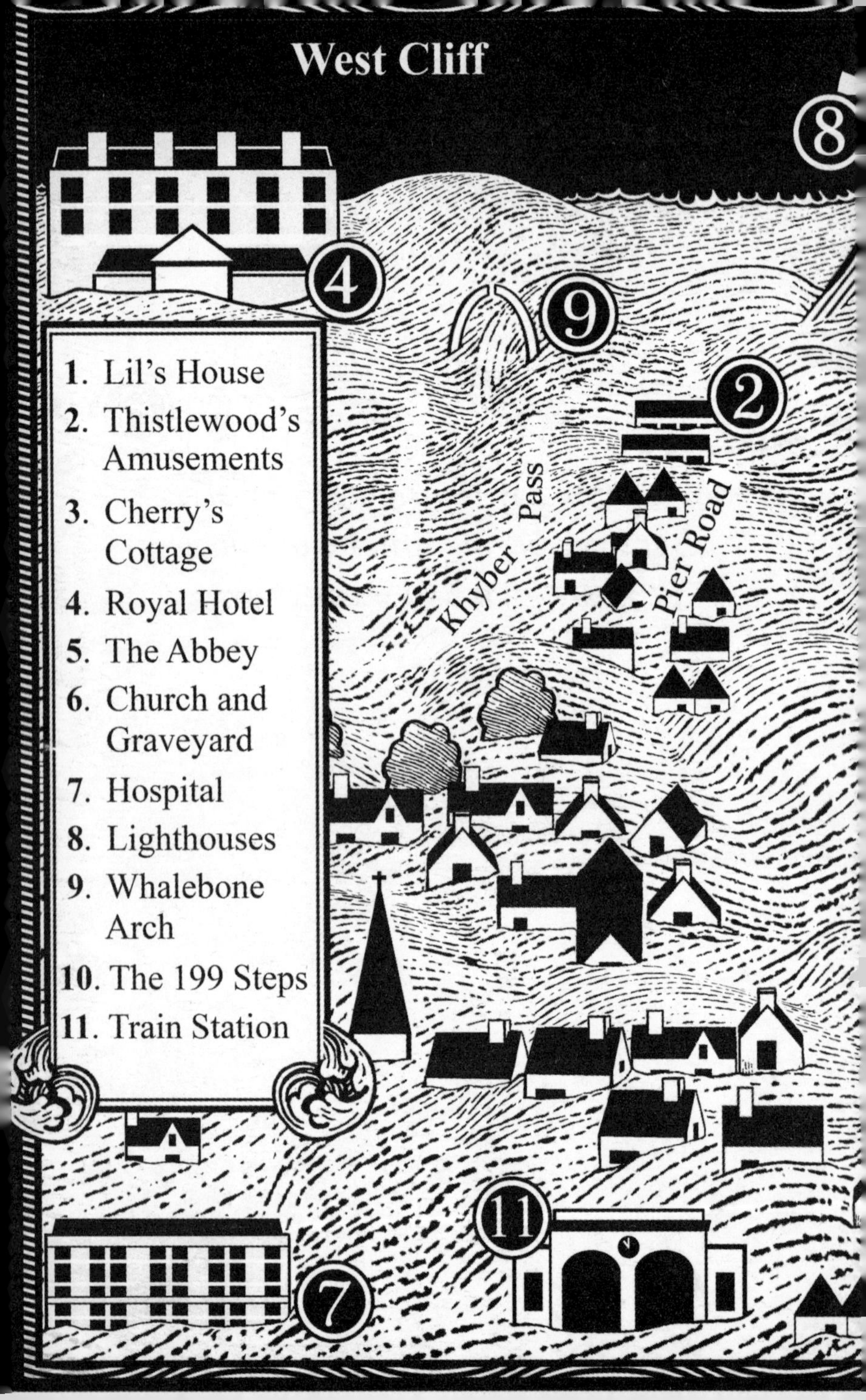
West Cliff
1. Lil's House
2. Thistlewood's Amusements
3. Cherry's Cottage
4. Royal Hotel
5. The Abbey
6. Church and Graveyard
7. Hospital
8. Lighthouses
9. Whalebone Arch
10. The 199 Steps
11. Train Station
Khyber Pass
Pier Road
4
9
2
8
11
7

East Cliff
8
1
6
Henrietta Street
10
3
5
Harbour Desert
Church Street
Bridge
Whitby

TRIALLUM

Indistinct shapes, blacker than the eternal night that reigned over this furthest region of the sea, guided the shadowy figure to the place appointed. A pale luminescence glimmered from the mouth of an unseen cave and a monstrous terror of the uncharted abyss, with a forest of teeth, swam forward. The glow emanated from countless growths on its grotesque head and by that ghastly radiance the spirit of Mister Dark found he was standing upon a finger of rock at the edge of an immense trench that no light would ever reach.

The creature circled him and he could feel many hostile eyes spying from crevices in the surrounding stones. Foul voices, thick with slime, were gargling and whispering; distorted shells scurried and barbed tentacles reached towards him. The water seethed with resentment.

If Mister Dark had been a living man he would

have been paralysed with terror, for beyond these attendant courtiers he could sense he was in the presence of *Them*.

The Lords of the Deep were watching.

Mister Dark's nerve almost failed. Malignance crashed over him in violent pulses. Dropping to his knees, he waited for Their judgement.

He could feel Them invading his mind, shredding through the intricate plots and schemes and laying bare his most secret desires.

'Forgive me! I humbly beg you!' he cried. 'Indulge me this one more chance. I swear this time I shall succeed.'

Shuddering, he shrieked in pain as he felt Them withdraw sharply from his thoughts and he fell forward, nearly plunging into the trench.

The sea grew even colder and he waited for a pronouncement.

In that remote region there was no concept of time, no way to measure the hours. He did not know how long he remained on that perilous outcrop.

Eventually he heard sounds approaching. Something was scuttling up the rock. Rising, he saw two crab-like claws rear over the edge, followed by the helmet of a Roman gladiator.

'Emissary,' Mister Dark greeted it. 'What is the decision?'

The creature within the helmet poked its stalk eyes through the visor at him.

'You are fortunate,' came the gurgling voice. 'Your scheme has found favour. The terms are agreed. If you succeed, your requests will be granted.'

'Thank Their exalted Majesties!' Mister Dark called out.

The helmet bobbed up and down on spindly legs and the pincer claws snapped in irritation.

'Know this,' the emissary warned. 'Should you fail, there is no returning. You will suffer Their full wrath and endure torment – forever more.'

Mister Dark smiled grimly. 'I shall not fail. I too have scores to settle with Whitby and its witch. When she is defeated, and I compel her to watch the destruction of everything she is pledged to protect, I shall offer up her overwhelming despair unto Them as sacrifice. Whitby's doom is assured.'

'It had better be,' the emissary hissed.

The girl on the bicycle squeezed the brake and slid off the saddle when it halted sharply. Tracy Evans hadn't ridden one of these since she was ten years old and she hadn't enjoyed it then. She cursed under her breath. It would have been easier – and a lot less exhausting – to have stolen a car.

So here she was, twenty miles out of Whitby, at half past one in the morning, breathless with the exertion and pale from the anaemia that had afflicted her since the spring.

Shivering and sweating on this warm summer night, Tracy wiped her dripping face and looked at the stretch of road ahead. She was on a remote tract of countryside at the edge of the moors. There were no street lamps and the moon was behind clouds, but the lonely road was not featureless. Her destination was close and lit by stark bulbs.

McKenzie Metals a large sign declared near the

wide, gated entrance. FERROUS AND NON-FERROUS SCRAP & END-OF-LIFE VEHICLES SPECIALISTS.

It was a sprawling plot of urban refuse surrounded by fields and hedgerows. The large scrapyard was fenced by high corrugated iron sheets topped with barbed wire, snarled with dirty tatters of old plastic bags that fluttered in the light breeze. Tracy and her cronies had always called rustling rags like that 'witches' knickers' and the memory brought a sad smile to her face. She hadn't spoken to Bev and Angie for months. She had been told she didn't need them any more: only one person mattered in her life now.

Tracy grunted at the momentary stab of regret. It was a mark of weakness and she despised that. Clenching her jaw, she concentrated on the matter in hand.

Beyond that forbidding perimeter she could see irregular hills of rusting cars, battered cookers and dirty washing machines. The skeletal arm of a crane towered above everything and its shadow cut deep across the road.

She took a phone from her pocket and stroked the screen that was sticky with drying blood.

'Dark?' she spoke urgently. 'Dark, are you there?'

The screen glimmered pale green and a pair of eyes appeared, as hypnotic and powerful as the first time she had beheld them and fallen under their spell.

'I am never far from your side, my sweetest heart,' a reassuring voice answered.

Tracy pressed the phone to her lips and kissed it.

She believed the voice belonged to the ghost of the most gorgeous lad she'd ever seen. For several months he had been the ultimate secret boyfriend, communicating via her phone when she smeared the screen with her own blood. He had told her he was the agent of mysterious ancient beings and they were going to grant him new life once he had completed a task for them. But the weeks had dragged by and her heart's one dream was still only a phantom.

'Tonight we'll finally be together, yeah?' she asked uncertainly. 'Proper like you promised, not just on my phone or a shadow. It's been so long. Sometimes I don't believe it'll ever happen. I can't stand it!'

'It is no simple matter to cross the bridge from death to life. Special measures must be in place, and this time there must be no resistance, no interference from the witch of Whitby.'

'That Cherry Cerise is a mad old bag, everyone knows it.'

'And yet she managed to hinder our previous endeavour – she and her acolyte.'

'Lil pigging Wilson!' Tracy spat. 'She's nothing. I'd love to smack the smug smiles off both their faces.'

The voice chuckled softly.

'Together we shall do so much more than that.'

'Makes me heave, seeing them lord it, thinking

they're better than everyone else. Hope they suffer, real bad.'

'Oh, they shall, do not doubt it. They dared to obstruct the will of forces far beyond them and such insolence is never forgiven.'

'I'm so gonna snog your handsome face off, the first second you're here for real!'

'Not before I kiss the life right out of you, dearest girl. Now make haste. Go to the entrance.'

'It'll be locked.'

'Do as I say. You have brought the coins?'

Tracy shook the other pocket of her jacket. It was heavy with change.

'Every ten pence I could find,' she said. 'Went through my mum's purse, our Liam's money box and I pinched the charity tin from the post office, about seven quid's worth. What's it all for?'

There was no answer. Leaning the bicycle against a hedge, Tracy approached the wide double gate. Another sign warned of guard dogs. Tracy eyed it and chewed her lip. Close by there was a metal door set into one half of the entrance and she gave it a testing push.

'Told you it was locked.'

'Hold up the device,' the voice ordered.

Tracy raised her phone. The green light shone brighter and she heard bolts being dragged across on the other side of the metal. With a rusty squeal the door swung inward. Immediately, ferocious barking broke out. Two large Rottweilers with chests like barrels came tearing across the yard from a dilapidated lean-to.

Tracy lunged for the door to snatch it back again, but the voice forbade her.

'Do not fear the beasts. I shall shield you from their bite. Trust me and enter.'

The girl stepped inside. The savage dogs rushed towards her, their great jaws snapping. Instinctively Tracy froze and squeezed her eyes shut. A stream of black smoke poured out from her phone and took shape behind her. The barking grew fiercer and closer – and then, abruptly, it ceased. She heard large paws skidding on gravel, followed by a frantic, tumbling scramble.

Tracy opened her eyes to see the dogs cowering, staring fearfully at something over her shoulder. Their ears were flat and they were whimpering. Then, timid as lambs, they bowed and rolled on to their backs, exposing their throats. Cold laughter mocked them.

'Rise and dance the jig of Dark for me.'

The Rottweilers flipped over. With a grunting effort they reared their hulking bodies on to their hind legs, and pranced around each other like circus poodles.

Tracy felt the hairs on her neck bristle and a chill breath blew across her shoulders.

'You're here!' she cried excitedly. 'Dark! You're here!'

'Do not turn around,' the voice warned, close to her ear.

'Why? Why can't I see you?'

'No questions. We have not yet claimed what we came for.'

A slice of yellow light cut a diagonal across the yard as a door in a Portakabin opened. A grizzled nightwatchman in a vest and wielding a baseball bat descended the steps.

'Kong! Tank! What were that racket for? What's up with the pair of you?'

He cast a cautious glance about the towering stacks of twisted metal. The cigarette he was smoking dropped from his lips when he saw his fearsome dogs capering in a circle, performing before a sickly-looking teenage girl.

'Hoy!' he yelled, striding forward. 'Who the 'ell are you and what you done to my dogs? Tank! Kong! Down! Get here!'

The man's urgent, angry stride faltered when he saw the sinister, curdling shape of mist and shadows behind Tracy.

'What's that?' he blurted. 'W– What . . . what is it? Get out! Get out of here! I'll call the police, that's what I'll do!'

Backing away, he spun around and started running for the refuge of the Portakabin. As he fled he flung the bat from him, knowing it would be no use against what he had just seen.

'Supper time, my sprightly ballerinos,' the shadow said.

The Rottweilers dropped to all fours and bolted after their owner. They caught him just as he reached the steps and dragged their former master under the lean-to.

A silly smirk lifted Tracy's mouth. Her own will was so crushed by the domination of her ghostly boyfriend that she felt no shock or revulsion and, when the terrible sounds ceased, she had forgotten there had ever been a nightwatchman.

'That small lodging,' the shadow said. 'What we seek is in there.'

Tracy dutifully crossed the yard and stepped up into the Portakabin. It was the firm's office, but it was a chaotic tip. The desk was buried under heaps of invoices and unfiled mail, and Post-it notes covered every spare surface. In one cluttered corner was a toaster, kettle, radio, pyramid of dirty mugs and a small fridge. A portable DVD player had been placed on top of a tool chest, and the movie it was playing had been paused mid-explosion.

Tracy's eyes flicked over the more unusual items rescued from the heaps outside: old enamel signage, Victorian brass bath fittings, mismatching golf clubs, a dented saxophone, a variety of antique lanterns hanging from the ceiling, assorted trophies and ornaments that included three Eiffel Towers, a box of spoons and tangled costume jewellery.

'To your left,' the voice said to her.

The girl looked quizzically at a coat stand smothered with overalls, scarves and parkas.

'Over there,' she was urged.

Tracy began pulling the garments clear, then let out a snort of surprise. Underneath was a man-sized figure made from bits of scrap. A vintage fruit machine formed the chest, on to which was bolted a pair of bellows. It wore a leather tailcoat and a pair of baggy trousers over metal, chain-operated legs. The drooped head was made from old tins, cut up and shaped into a rudimentary skull, and the face was an adapted hockey mask with a brass tea-strainer mouth and torch lenses for eyes.

'This is what we came for?' she asked. 'It's just a load of tat.'

'It is an automaton, built by one deep in the thrall of the Nimius, at the very epicentre of its influence.'

'What – one of those mad machines the West Cliffers cobbled together when the town went mental? I thought they fell apart when it wore off?'

'This splendid gentleman was special, and he has held the golden Nimius in his metal hands.'

'But it's broken.'

'Look to the side of the head, my love.'

Tracy saw a coin slot and realised why she'd been ordered to bring the ten pences. When she had fed in a handful of money, she stood back and waited.

A small green indicator light began to flash on the tin skull and the bellows wheezed in and out. The reels of the fruit machine lit up in the robot's chest and spun around slowly until three cherry symbols juddered to a stop on the centre line. There was a snap of electricity and the eyes flashed on. The bicycle chain that ran from the head into the shoulders grew taut and the contraption raised its hockey-mask face.

'What has occurred?' a perplexed metallic voice asked. 'What is this untidy midden? Where have the glorious forces of Melchior Pyke gone? I was busily serving refreshment when my coin time ran out. Have I missed the entire battle? Has the genius creator of the Nimius defeated the ragged witch and her unholy army?'

'The soul of Melchior Pyke has departed this sphere,' the shadow informed him. 'Never to return.'

'My master is gone? Then what is the purpose of Jack Potts now? My principal function is to serve the Lord Pyke. I was granted sentience for that alone.'

'Do you know me?'

The torch lenses shone past Tracy's shoulders at the shifting shape behind her. An amber light on the side of the tin skull flickered in recognition.

'You are the wraith of Mister Dark,' the robot

declared. 'In life you were my master's manservant; you aided him in his great endeavour.'

'Aided be damned! I was more than mere assistant. Without Mister Dark he would not have been able to complete a tenth of the work on the Nimius. My hand fashioned it as surely as his and therefore I claim ownership. There can be no dispute of this and you, who were born of its power, owe me, its true master, your allegiance.'

The reels in the robot's chest revolved again.

'Your reasoning is sound,' he said after a short, considering pause. 'Henceforth, Jack Potts shall serve Mister Dark. What is your bidding? You wish me to fetch the Nimius from its present keeper?'

'Not yet. There is still a task ahead of us. In the town of Whitby there remains the last in a bedraggled line of insolent witches that has plagued this coast for far too long. I am charged by the Lords of the Deep to bring it to a humiliating end. You, my servant, will aid me in this. We have an elegant web of deceit to weave and, at its conclusion, not only shall I possess the Nimius, but I shall be a living man once more.'

'As you command. But first I would very much like to flick a duster around and organise these bills and papers into alphabetical order. Can you direct me to a damp cloth and a ring binder?'

Tracy had been listening to this with mounting impatience and confusion.

'Hang on,' she interrupted. 'Dark, what are you wasting time on this thing for?'

'Dearest truculent, tractable Tracy.' The shadow mocked her in a harsher, more callous tone than he had used before. 'You truly are the slowest-witted creature in creation.'

'Don't say that. I love you.'

The voice laughed cruelly. 'Love? What use have I of love? Obedience is all I desire.'

'I do everything you tell me.'

'You have completed your task well enough, but your usefulness is limited. To fulfil my pact with the Lords of the Deep, I require a servant who can venture into places barred to you, with more cunning than you possess.'

'Servant? What do you mean? What about us? What about the future we planned together?'

There was an edge of steel in the voice that answered.

'Look at me, Tracy.'

'What?'

'Turn and look at me. It's what you craved earlier, only this time you shall see my true self – not the boyish mask I have worn to deceive and dangle you. I release you from all such bonds; awaken and view me with a clear, unfogged mind.'

'Stop it.'

'Look at me – see the face of Mister Dark, whom

Melchior Pyke once cut down from the gallows and revived by unnatural means. Gaze into these eyes that have stared on the coldest wastes of oblivion and beheld the terrors of the world.'

Tracy felt dread creep over her.

'Why are you trying to scare me? I won't turn round. I know what you look like. You're lovely!'

'Must I order Jack Potts to compel you?'

The robot straightened and the metal fingers that were made of kitchen utensils twitched in readiness.

'Is it blood?' Tracy asked. 'You need some? I can cut my hand, give you loads – more than ever. You won't get any of that from a robot!'

'True, but Château Tracy is bitter, cloying and tart, bordering on vinegar. Fortunately I have a fresh veinyard in mind – someone from whom it will be a smooth delight to sip, someone with enough full-bodied vintage in them to form the bridge from one plane of existence to another. Someone who will make my new flesh strong.'

'You seeing someone else?' Tracy cried and her fear flashed to anger. 'You . . . you dumping me?'

Spinning around, she glared at the writhing clot of shadow and let out a scream. The churning black cloud revealed a spectral figure, tall and lit with a ghastly radiance. His hair was lank and his head was held at a strange angle on his twisted, kinked neck. A horrific scar ran down his right cheek and through his lips, but it was the pitiless hate that shone in those foul, dead eyes that really terrified her.

'Who are you?' she protested. You're not my lovely Dark!'

Cruel laughter banished the last fragments of his hold over her and Tracy staggered as though she'd been physically kicked. Panicking, she blundered back towards the door.

But the two Rottweilers were waiting by the Portakabin steps, and they snarled threateningly at her.

'I shouldn't try to get past them if I were you,' Mister Dark warned.

'Let me go!' Tracy begged. 'Let me go! Please!'

'That would be . . . untidy of me. The meticulous arrangements must not be spoiled in any way.'

'I won't tell anyone. Just let me get away.'

'I believe you. Then let us part on a sweeter note. One final kiss?'

Tracy shuddered. Stepping up to the hideous apparition, she swallowed her disgust and held her breath.

Mister Dark's ghostly face bent down and the scarred lips lifted in a repugnant grin as he gave a signal to Jack Potts behind her back.

The reels in the robot's chest ceased spinning and three skulls stopped on the winning line. Metal hands were around Tracy's throat before she knew what was happening.

'Gullible to the very end,' Mister Dark said. 'Such a pity you'll miss the entertainment. The final humiliation of the Whitby witches will be spectacular. You'd have enjoyed that, you unpleasant, stupid girl.'

As Tracy slumped to the floor, he added, 'You really did have a very pretty neck.'

Jack Pott's left eye was flickering erratically.

'What more would you like me to do, Master Dark?' he enquired.

'Firstly, find a shovel. And then – oh . . . so many things.'

2

Verne Thistlewood lay on his bed, staring up at the ceiling. He'd jammed pillows against his ears, but could still hear his parents rowing.

That's all they did nowadays: argue and stress about their finances. The Thistlewoods owned an amusement arcade, but back in the spring most of the machines had been dismantled to make ludicrous gadgets and weapons when an ancient feud had magically possessed the entire town. The people of Whitby had come perilously close to destroying one another in a bloody battle.

The arcade never recovered after that. The insurance company wouldn't pay out to replace the damaged amusements and Verne's parents had sunk into debt. The summer season was already here and the town was thronged with tourists, but with only a dozen machines still working the arcade simply wasn't earning enough. It was desperate.

The front door slammed and the vibration travelled through the apartment. One of his parents, probably his mother, had stormed out. Always practical, she had taken a job as a cleaner in the very gym she could no longer afford to be a member of and that morning was her first shift. Verne let out a long and dismal breath. He imagined that, unless some miracle occurred, they were going to have to sell up and probably live in a tent – if they could find a cheap, second-hand one.

The boy glanced at the chest of drawers across from his bed. Miracles *were* possible, he knew that better than anyone. He had his very own mini miracle-maker hidden away among his socks.

Getting to his feet he opened the top drawer, reached into a corner and pulled out a bundled-up T-shirt. Pausing a moment while he listened to make sure his father was still downstairs, he carefully unwrapped the precious object within. The morning sun blazed over the richly engraved golden surface. It hurt his eyes to look at it. This was the Nimius, the most incredible magical device ever created. Verne placed it gently on his pillow and sat back on the bed. He never tired of looking at this amazing treasure. It was breathtakingly beautiful and there always seemed to be some new detail to see.

The Nimius had lain dormant since that crazy week in the spring. Verne didn't know how to wind the secret mechanisms, and none of the levers or symbols would push or slide. He and Lil had spent many patient hours examining and testing it, without success. Verne suspected it was broken.

The Nimius was his great secret. Only two people knew that he still had it: one was his best friend, Lil Wilson; the other was the town's resident witch, Cherry Cerise.

'What's driving me round the bend,' he muttered, 'is that you're probably the most valuable thing in the world and here we are, barely scraping by.'

Taking it up once more, he let out a squeak of surprise as he felt an internal movement and a series of delicate clicks. Then, to his delight, some of the many symbols began to rise.

He and Lil had made a pact that if and when the Nimius became active again, he would let her know straightaway. His first thought was to call her, but then he stopped himself. Placing the Nimius back on the pillow, even more gently than before so as not to accidentally press anything, he opened another drawer and took out a notepad.

Turning the pages, he consulted the secret list he and Lil had made. They had studied the magical device very carefully, researching every one of its symbols and trying to figure out what they signified. The Wilsons owned a witchcraft-themed shop called Whitby Gothic over on the East Cliff and the reference books in there had proved very helpful. They had identified several astrological and alchemical signs, including the one for 'air', which had once enabled Verne to fly. Some others were easy, like the little hand inscribed with the lines important in palmistry – that was obviously something to do with fortune telling. Then there was a circle engraved with a strange compass-like pattern that Lil recognised as 'the Wyrding Way', which was supposed to keep the bearer from getting lost. There was the Eye of Horus, which was protection against evil, a scarab that represented rebirth, an owl that might be to do with wisdom, and some Viking runes.

Other symbols were more ambiguous and had question marks next to the drawings Lil had made of them. Lil and Verne had spent a long time discussing the ones with less obvious meanings. There was an oak leaf, which had remained a puzzle, although they knew that oak trees were important in Celtic mythology. (Verne had wondered if it might grant enormous strength and he had posed like the Incredible Hulk to demonstrate, which had sent Lil into hysterics because he was the absolute opposite.)

Verne scanned the list and turned to the Nimius to see if any of the newly risen symbols were of the obvious variety.

There was a rune inscribed on to an oval button: a vertical stick with two branches to one side. He found the corresponding entry in the notes, then grinned and punched the air.

It was the rune for wealth.

Without a moment's hesitation, he pressed it. There was a click and the Nimius trembled. The other levers and switches sank slowly into the golden casing once more.

Verne waited eagerly, hardly believing how lucky it was that the very miracle he needed had been supplied so readily. But as the minutes ticked by his joy faded and he began to grow doubtful. He had half expected everything in the room to magically transform into solid gold, or diamonds to fly in through the window. Suddenly uneasy, he reached for his phone again, then decided to go and see Lil and tell her in person.

Rewrapping the Nimius in the T-shirt, he slipped it into his rucksack and hurried downstairs.

'That you, Verne?' his father called from the living room.

'Just going over to Lil's!' he called back as he ran past.

Dennis Thistlewood appeared in the hallway, just in time to see the kitchen door close.

'Hang on!' he shouted. 'Take this!'

He had pulled out his wallet and the last of his precious ten-pound notes were clutched in his outstretched hand. For some time Mr Thistlewood stood there, waiting. After a while, when Verne didn't return, he shook his head in confusion and wandered back into the living room, letting the money fall from his fingers to the floor.

Verne cut through the amusement arcade. With only the front section in use, it was a sad place. The area at the back had once housed vintage automata, but was now filled with broken machines. In this dimly lit area, with its deep shadows, they looked melancholy and neglected. The boy quickened his pace and was soon surrounded by the familiar noises of the working slot machines near the entrance.

Only a handful of holidaymakers were playing them, spending whatever change they had rattling in their pockets. Clarke, Verne's older brother, was sitting in the change booth, absorbed in a cheeky text conversation with Amy, his girlfriend.

Just as Verne passed by, every machine went crazy.

Lights and buttons flashed, buzzers blared and bells rang in a cacophonous riot. Clarke looked up, startled. Even the amusements that weren't being played were going nuts. Jackpot after jackpot was clunking into position. There was a rush of silver as each machine spewed out a heap of money. Coins gushed down with such force they overshot the payout tray and cascaded to the floor. It took only moments for each amusement to empty, but the mechanisms continued to chug long after.

At first the bewildered customers backed away in alarm. Then they gave elated yells and were on their knees, shovelling the cash up with their hands.

'What the . . .?' Clarke shouted, as he leaped from the booth. 'Wait, you can't have that! There's been some technical fault. Put it down!'

The holidaymakers laughed at him. This was brilliant! There were hundreds of pounds here, just waiting to be scooped into their pockets.

Clarke looked around wildly and saw Verne by the main entrance.

'Don't stand there gawking!' he roared. 'Get over here, or call the police.'

The people were like greedy seagulls going berserk over a discarded bag of chips. Clarke tried to stop them, but it was impossible. Passing between the spent machines and slipping on the coins, Verne ran to help.

'Stop it!' he pleaded. 'It isn't yours, you know it isn't.'

To his surprise, they halted and turned to him, with faces drained of all expression. There was an eerie silence, broken only by a last coin falling from the push-and-drop. Then, as one, they advanced towards Verne.

The boy watched them nervously. They looked weird, with silly grins on their faces. He began to edge away.

The holidaymakers grabbed hold of Verne's rucksack.

'Get off!' he cried. 'You can't have that. Let go!'

Afraid they were after the Nimius, he lashed out and stamped on a flip-flopped foot. The person didn't flinch. Verne was about to kick the nearest shin when he realised that they were actually trying to give him all the money they had taken.

The rucksack dragged on his shoulders as each new load of coins was tipped inside.

'All for you,' they told him in flat, empty voices.

Verne struggled and managed to pull himself away. He ran to Clarke who bundled him into the booth for safety. The customers followed, their vacant smiles frozen in place, holding out hands that were still dripping with change.

'What do you think you're doing?' Clarke demanded. 'Get out, go on!'

'We'll leave it here for him,' they said, casting the coins on to the floor in front of the booth. 'We wish there was more.'

The crowd wandered from the arcade, blinking groggily when they reached the sunshine outside.

'What. Was. That. About?' Clarke uttered, shaking his head in disbelief.

'They were like money zombies,' Verne said with a shudder.

'Always zombies with you, isn't it? Look at the state of this place. I'm going to have to close up till I can sort it. How do I explain this to Mum and Dad?'

'It's like the machines were all hacked or got a virus or something,' Verne said. 'That's not possible though, is it?' He began tipping out the looted change from his rucksack.

'Here, you'd better have this too,' Clarke said.

When Verne looked up, his brother was holding out a wad of notes from the change booth's till. Clarke was smiling vacantly.

'What?' Verne muttered faintly.

'Take this money,' Clarke told him. 'There's eighty quid. I can get more.'

Verne felt a knot tighten in his stomach, beginning to understand. This was the power of the Nimius. The wealth button was working, but not in a way he had expected or hoped for.

'No thanks. You go sit down for a while. I need to see Lil – pronto.'

'Do you want my phone then? It's better than yours.'

'No, really – I have to go.'

Swinging the rucksack on to his shoulder, Verne ran from the arcade.

It was a glorious summer morning. Pier Road was busy with tourists and a fresh salt breeze was blowing in from the sea.

Verne hurried along the quayside, dodging families who stopped in their tracks as he passed, staring then reaching for their wallets and purses. A corridor of unnatural silence formed in his wake as their gabbling voices and laughter were stilled. Keeping his eyes fixed on the way ahead, he ignored the unsettling attention, stopping only when he barged into a small girl who ran into his path.

'This was for ice cream!' she shouted up at him, thrusting out two pound coins. 'I have to give it to you instead.'

'No you don't,' Verne told her. 'Go get your ice cream.'

'Can't!' she replied fiercely and tears began to splash down her face. 'It's your money now.'

Verne shook his head and strode past her. The girl let out a desperate wail and tried to stuff the coins into the back pocket of his jeans.

Verne pushed her off and would have run, but the way was blocked by a huge red-faced man in a vest, whose bulging arms were sleeved in tattoos.

'What you doin' with my little Rebecca?' he barked.

'My ice cream money!' she cried before Verne could answer.

'You snatched her money off her?'

'No!' Verne protested.

'He won't take it, Dad,' the girl sobbed. 'Make him!'

The man's fleshy face scrunched up and the veins bulged at his temples as he bent down to glower closely at Verne, his mouth twitching into a silly grin.

'Her money not good enough, is that it?' he asked.

A large hand grabbed Verne by the shirt while the other took the money and shoved it into his pocket. Then the man tore a thick gold chain from his own neck and tucked it in as well.

'I got no idea why I just did that,' he snarled through the fixed smile, 'but you'd better get out of my sight before I change my mind and give you a slap you won't forget.'

Verne didn't argue. A large group was forming around them.

'Scuse me!' he shouted, barging through. 'Got to go!'

'Wait!' urgent voices called after him. 'Take this!'

Verne ran along New Quay Road, towards the swing bridge. His friend Lil lived across the river on the East Cliff and, at this hour on a Saturday, would undoubtedly be at the shop her family ran in Church Street.

Before he set foot on the bridge, squeals of astonishment broke out behind him. Glancing across the road he saw two cashpoints pumping out a blizzard of crisp banknotes. Thousands of pounds were spraying on to the pavement, faster than anyone could catch. Eager hands grabbed up fistfuls, then everyone turned to face the boy with the rucksack and started moving towards him.

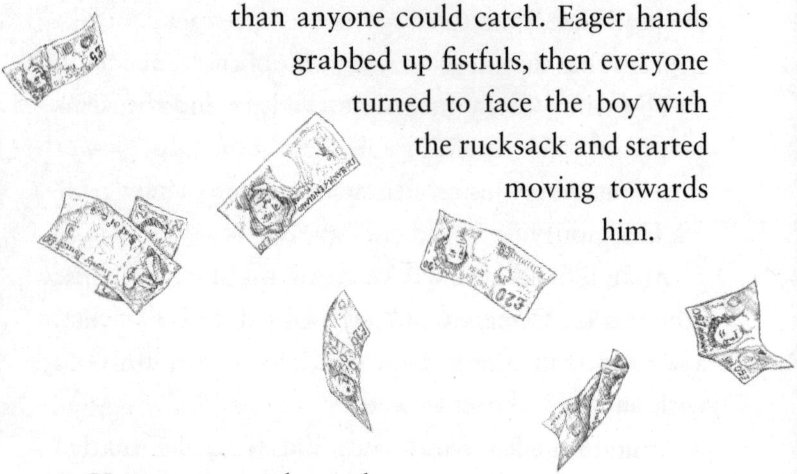

Verne groaned and, as he did so, a gust of wind came funnelling down Flowergate and caught up the rest of the notes. They whirled like autumn leaves in a tornado, then came swirling over the road, heading straight for him.

He spun around and ran across the river. The vortex of cash pursued him, catching up before he was even halfway across the bridge. Next minute he was encased by a violent storm of money. When he tried to yell, some flew into his mouth. Spluttering and thrashing his arms to clear a space in front of his eyes, he lurched into Church Street.

In Whitby Gothic, Mike Wilson was unpacking a stock delivery.

'Plastic pumpkin baskets?' he exclaimed. 'There must've been a mix-up – we never have tacky tat like this. I'll ring the supplier and send it back.'

His wife, Cassandra, was sitting behind the till, removing black varnish from her fingernails.

'I ordered it,' she told him. 'Punters expect it so we might as well flog it.'

Mike looked at her with concern. Ever since their schooldays, Cassandra had professed to be a witch and dressed accordingly. But lately she hadn't bothered with her usual elaborate eye make-up and had started wearing baggy T-shirts and stretch leggings instead of the Victorian-style gothic dresses she loved.

'You all right, Cass?' he asked.

'I'm fine,' she said with a vague shrug.

'Because you'd never normally allow a pumpkin in the shop. You've always said you can't stand the Disneyfication of All Hallows' Eve. We've always had traditional turnip lanterns.'

'No one makes plastic turnip lanterns,' she answered flatly. 'And most of our customers couldn't care less anyway. Don't think I do any more either.

Does it matter? It's just junk for the tourists. I'm giving in to consumer demand.'

Mike thought she'd given in to more than that, but he kept quiet and took the box to the storeroom. As he returned to the main shop, a commotion in the street caused him to look out of the window.

'What's going on out there?' he wondered. 'Cass – come look at this. It's snowing money!'

Church Street was choked with swarming banknotes. Shoppers and holidaymakers were leaping to catch them, pausing only to stare at the bizarre spectacle that came staggering over the cobbles. It was a churning cloud of money, reeling clumsily from one side of the street to the other.

A fifty-pound note blew against the shop window and Mike peered closely at it in amazement. A twenty joined it, then another cluster of fifties.

'Them's genuine!' he exclaimed. 'There's a fortune in jumbo confetti flapping about out there. Has a bank exploded?'

The light dimmed as more notes papered the glass, and a small hand slapped the pane, right in front of Mike's nose, making him jump. Then a familiar face thumped against the window and howled for help.

'It's Verne!' Mr Wilson cried, wrenching the door open and plunging into the freak windstorm outside.

The strings of bells and charms that hung around the door frame rang and clattered madly as the tempest burst in, along with Verne. Cassandra hurried from the till to help. It took all their strength to slam the door shut as the screaming wind focused its full fury against it. For long, anxious moments it juddered and quaked, then all was suddenly quiet. The bells stopped jingling and the money that had flown inside with Verne fluttered gently on to the floor. Outside, the wind dropped to a soft breeze and three hundred thousand pounds went dancing down the street.

Verne sagged in Mike's arms, gasping and shaking.

'You OK?' Mr Wilson asked.

'Been better,' he panted, trying to sound as casual as possible. 'Having a bit of a peculiar morning.'

'No kidding. Your face and hands are bleeding.'

'Paper cuts.'

'I'll get the first-aid kit. So what just happened – that wasn't normal. Was it, er . . . was it . . . umm, you know?'

Smoothing her storm-lashed hair, his wife moved away from the door. She looked with disdain at the money littering the shop.

'He wants to know if it was supernatural in origin,' she said tersely. 'You'd think, owning a witchcraft shop, my husband wouldn't be so coy about it. Was it something to do with our Lil?'

Verne shook his head.

'No, but it wasn't a natural thing.' He squirmed. 'I, er, can't say any more.'

'I see,' she said, bending down to pick up the notes. 'More mysteries and intrigue we're excluded from.'

'Where's Lil?' Verne asked. 'Isn't she here?'

Before Mike could respond, his wife snorted.

'Course Lil isn't here. She's with *her.* Where else would our daughter be these days?'

'Go easy, Cass,' Mike said. 'So, Verne, how's your mum and dad?'

The boy gave an awkward shrug.

'Noreen still behaving like a two-year-old throwing a tantrum?' asked Mrs Wilson. 'She always did cut her nose off to spite her face.'

Verne frowned. She and his mother had fallen out. The Wilsons' shop had made a large profit from the trouble back in the spring. In a moment of stress, Noreen Thistlewood had made a comment about it and a row had flared up that had not been resolved.

Mrs Wilson was about to say more when there was a *beep* from the counter, followed by the sound of the till drawer sliding open on its own.

Verne winced. The Nimius's power was still exerting itself.

'Take this,' Cassandra said in a far-off voice as she pushed the cash she'd collected at him. 'Mike, get the takings as well.'

Her husband went to the till, but Verne made a dash out of the shop.

Church Street was a lot emptier than it had been five minutes ago. Verne pelted over the cobbles, nervously hoping the supernatural gale wouldn't return. He knew where Lil was now. There was only one '*her*' who was that important to his best friend these days – Cherry Cerise.

Racing to a narrow entry that led to one of the yards behind Church Street, the boy rushed up to a cottage with a brightly painted yellow door and a letter box framed by garish red lips.

Verne rang the bell with one hand and knocked with the other.

'Hey!' a brash voice called from inside. 'Get your sticky digit offa my ding-a-ling! What is this, a raid? I'm warnin' you, I go from nought to riot real quick.'

The door was opened by a slender woman in her sixties, wearing a neon-blue wig and a minidress covered in large orange circles. She stared at him through yellow sunglasses.

'For a puny stick insect,' Cherry Cerise said, 'you sure got a heck of a knock, kid. Say, you been messin' with your dad's razor? What gives with the face?'

She was about to usher him inside when the door of the adjoining cottage opened and a frail lady in her seventies hobbled out with a stick.

'Wait!' the neighbour called. 'Don't disappear just yet.'

Cherry braced herself. Mrs Gregson was not the

most agreeable of neighbours.

'What is it this time, Joan?' she began. 'My breathing keepin' you awake at night again? And I can't help it if I yelp when I wax my particulars. You'd know what that felt like if you let me take care of that moustache for you.'

The woman ignored her and jabbed a finger at Verne.

'Saw this lad go by,' she said, 'and I have to give him something.'

She pulled out a purse. 'Here's what's left of my pension this week,' she said, tipping out a paltry seven pounds. 'This was supposed to last me another five days.'

She thrust it at Verne, but he stepped away.

'Stand still!' she demanded. 'I can't catch you with this dodgy hip. If I fall and end up in hospital, it'll be your fault.'

Verne could tell she was deadly earnest, so he took the money, intending to post it back through her letter box later.

Mrs Gregson hadn't finished. The pensioner leaned heavily on her stick and twisted her wedding ring off.

'Worn this over fifty year,' she said. 'But here, have it. You want me to get on me knees and grovel?'

Verne shook his head and took the proffered ring without resistance.

'What's goin' on?' Cherry demanded.

'Witchery!' Mrs Gregson spat back, and tears were coursing down her face. 'What else would it be, with the likes of you next door – and her what lived there before you? Always been a witch's cottage that one. When will you leave us ordinary Whitby folk in peace? When?'

Kissing her naked finger, she returned to her own home.

'You got an Everest of explainin' to do,' Cherry told Verne. 'Get inside.'

Clutching the wedding ring and the seven pounds, the boy obeyed.

The hallway of Cherry Cerise's cottage was a delicate pink and smelled of roses and berries until she closed the door behind them. Then the walls dipped into a shade of violet.

Verne had grown accustomed to the interior changing colour to match the witch's mood. What he wasn't expecting was to find his best friend Lil sitting cross-legged and perfectly still on a chaise longue, with filaments of faint amber-coloured light threading and tangling around her raised hands. A stream of the same glimmering energy flowed from the centre of her forehead, slowly forming a halo around her.

'Whoa!' he exclaimed. 'What's all that?'

Lil grinned at him and the shifting lattice of light flickered.

'Quick, take a photo with my phone!' she urged,

directing him with her eyes to a nearby cushion, where her mobile lay. 'Mum'll choke when she sees this.'

Verne did as he was told, but repeated his question.

'It's Lil's aura,' Cherry answered, following him into the parlour. 'As a rule, they're invisible, even if you've got the sight, but I gave it some zizz and lit it up so we could see how she's progressin' and maybe get a clue as to what kind of witch she might be. Her own powers are kinda weak and trembly right now, but they'll get stronger the more she uses them and grows in confidence. Witches' auras express themselves in different ways. Mine looks like my own personal disco – like a huge psychedelic Afro.'

'Cherry thinks the way it's forming knots around my fingers shows that it's connected to my knitting,' Lil told him. 'Might be where my gift is strongest, which isn't exactly the most fearsome or ostentatious deal ever.'

'Knot and cord magic is an ancient form of the craft,' Cherry chided. 'Goes way back to the earliest practitioners. If done right, a charm created by a knot witch can store a crazy amount of force and be stronger than most of the later flashy spells and complicated hexes. Trouble is, I don't know much about that kind of hoodoo so Lil's gonna need a better guru than me.'

A bright blue star sparkled from Lil's forehead and

swiftly travelled the path of the halo before shooting into one of her ears.

'What was that?' Verne asked in surprise.

'We think it might be psychic energy Scaur Annie left behind,' Lil told him.

'I s'pose being possessed by a seventeenth-century witch must leave its mark,' the boy said.

'Either that or it's puberty kickin' its heels,' Cherry cackled. 'But that's all, folks. The light show is over. This old broad needs her twinkles back. Feelin' kinda angsty already; a colour witch requires every drop of her spectrum inside of her.'

Moving her hands as if winding in a kite, Cherry drew the amber glow away from Lil's aura and absorbed the light back into herself. She breathed in deeply as if refreshed, then turned to Verne.

'Now then, kid, fess up. What've you been up to? Why'd old grumpy Gregson throw her dough and wedding band at you?'

The boy shifted unhappily and stared about the parlour, ashamed to meet the witch's severe gaze. He noticed that since he was here last week, decorations of bright, crocheted flowers had been sprinkled around the seventies-themed room. They were Lil's handiwork and demonstrated just how close she and Cherry had become.

'I've done something really stupid,' he blurted. 'I just didn't think!'

He pulled the rucksack from his shoulders and unzipped it with trembling fingers.

'The Nimius!' Lil exclaimed. 'You got it working again? Brilliant! I told you it was just tired, not broken.'

'You make it sound like it takes batteries,' Verne said. 'It's not a phone that needs recharging. And no, it's not brilliant actually, not at all.'

'Lots of things need recharging,' Cherry interrupted, easing herself into the egg-shaped wicker chair suspended from the ceiling. 'What else do you think you're doing when you're in the land of snooze? Even magic can get exhausted – seizing control of half a town would drain anything. Or did it occur to you that your pimped-out gizmo might've just been waiting?"

'Waiting for what?' Lil asked.

'Hey, I'm not the one who had Melchior Pyke's avenging spirit squatting inside my wig stand,' Cherry answered. 'If anyone knows the answer to that, it's the Twiglet Kid here. If a witch can leave her mark in your noodle, so can a magician.'

Verne shook his head. 'You know, as soon as everything got back to normal, I forgot how to work it.'

'*Normal*, he says,' Cherry scoffed. 'Kid, this town weren't never what you call normal. Hate that word anyways. But that glittery little doodad should've been gotten rid of months ago, somehow. I keep tellin' you – it's way too powerful and we don't know what it's really capable of. Pyke didn't write a user manual, or if he did it got burned up with his workshop.'

Verne's brows creased. 'But I'm sure I was meant to be its guardian.'

'Oh brother, why has everybody got to be the chosen one these days? You seriously think you can keep that thing safe in your apartment, nestling in your skivvies? I'm surprised your mom's not found it already, hawked it on eBay and jetted off to Vegas. Flattered though I am that you told me about it, you really should've clued in your folks as well. Secrets in families only do harm.'

Cherry stopped abruptly and stared at her own hand. Without realising, she had removed a bracelet studded with three ammonites from her wrist and was holding it out to him.

'As the Whitby witch in residence,' she began, 'this is my symbol of office and is pretty darn priceless to me. So why am I giving it to you right now? Just what did you do, kid?'

'I clicked the symbol for wealth,' he confessed.

The violet-coloured walls shifted through different hues of red and the carpet turned tangerine.

'Were you always this dumb?' Cherry asked. 'Everything you get through this mysterious force we call magic has to come from someplace, 'specially if it's the in-your-face, heavy-handed macho kind like what's in the Nimius. Masculine forces follow two basic principles – control and grab.'

'Female energies are the healing and nurturing ones,' Lil added.

'And the smuggest,' Verne said. 'Look, I'm really sorry, honest. It's just that everything's so bad at home. Mum and Dad are at each other's throats the whole time. Since they fell out with your folks it's got so much worse.'

'Wait,' Cherry interrupted. 'Your moms and dads have had a row?'

'They're not speaking to each other,' Lil said, embarrassed.

'My mum doesn't even like me hanging out with Lil now,' Verne continued miserably. 'But she knows she couldn't stop me. When the Nimius woke up earlier, I thought it was answering my wishes. I just wanted to make everything better.'

Cherry let her annoyance out with a long breath and the parlour dipped into softer tints of pale green, accompanied by a refreshing waft of peppermint and freshly mown grass.

'Hey, I was gonna fix Lil and me a shake when you knocked,' she said, nipping to the kitchen and returning with three tall glasses of milk, topped with creamy froth and impaled with straws. 'What's your favourite flavour?'

'Chocolate,' Verne said without hesitation.

'And I know Lil's is butterscotch, so here we go.'

Setting the tray down, she waved a hand over it. There was a pulse of pale light. The milk in one glass turned a rich velvety brown and the other a pale caramel.

'It's how I first realised I weren't quite like everyone else,' Cherry said, passing the glasses round.

Verne took an experimental sip. It was the most delicious milkshake he'd ever tasted.

'On my sixth birthday,' Cherry continued, 'my daddy took me to a diner for a treat. I'd put on my prettiest new dress, candy pink with a white sash, pearl buttons, bobby socks and the dinkiest red shoes you ever saw. I was so proud to be out with him. He was shame-the-devil handsome, with his Sunday church suit and pomade in his hair. But even back then I was a contrary gal and, by the time the banana malt that I'd asked for arrived, I'd changed my mind and wanted strawberry instead. My daddy, who was just as stubborn as me, wouldn't get it switched. So I held that glass in my hot little hands and glared at it like it was the worst calamity that ever befell a human being. Didn't take long for that evil yellow malt to turn pink and start bubbling like a tar pit. I couldn't stop it and I screamed. Then the glass exploded and there was strawberry gloop all over the diner. Ruined the dress and my daddy's best suit. Never touched a banana since – but strawberries I forgave.'

She had taken up her own glass. It was now shot through with deep pink swirls and she applied her fuchsia-painted lips to the straw.

'My daddy never took me no place again,' she said presently. 'He vamoosed soon after and it was just me and Mom and our daily war of wills till I ran away at thirteen.'

'That's so sad,' Lil said.

'It's part of being a witch,' Cherry warned her. 'It'll turn your life inside out and sometimes you lose those dearest to you. They can't handle what you really are, but if you try to stifle it, pretend you're somethin' you're not, you'll make yourself miserable.'

'We're OK here though,' Lil argued. 'Everyone in Whitby knows you're a witch now, and how we ended the curse.'

'Oh sure, they know,' Cherry agreed. 'And they was real grateful at first, but folks don't like being beholden. Gratitude wears thin real fast.'

'I haven't noticed anything like that,' Lil said.

'That's the way it goes. You'd better get ready for the backlash.'

'They can say what they like,' Lil declared. 'I've been laughed at all my life because of Mum and Dad. A bit more won't hurt.'

'I'll always be Lil's friend,' Verne said. 'I think it's fantastic she's a witch now!'

'You've got a chocolate moustache,' Lil told him.

Cherry smiled. The bond between those two was beautiful and strong.

'Real friends are the truest treasure,' she said. 'They're the family you choose and will be there when the real thing lets you down.'

'I'm lucky with my parents,' Lil countered. 'They've been playing at being witches since they were kids themselves. Their idea of a date night was getting in the car, finding some remote spot and dancing round a bonfire in the nuddy.'

'They don't think they're playin',' Cherry reminded her. 'It's a serious deal for them.'

'Well, they don't need to pretend any more. Their daughter is a proper witch.'

Cherry wasn't so sure. She felt that Lil was being a bit blind to what was happening in her own family. Changing the subject, she tapped the Nimius with her straw.

'So,' she asked Verne, 'how strong d'you reckon this wealthus-pocus is?'

'Very,' he answered firmly. 'I was chased across the bridge just now by a furious cloud of money that the bank spat at me. The cashpoints vommed it out and I couldn't get away.'

Lil started to laugh. 'Like Winnie-the-Pooh and the honeybees?' she cried. 'Or money bees! I wish I'd seen that!'

'Wasn't funny!' Verne protested. But his friend's

laughter was always infectious and he couldn't help joining in.

Cherry bit her lip and tried to stay stern, but the walls were shimmering pink and gold, betraying her amusement, which made Lil laugh all the louder.

'What if it never stops?' Verne giggled. 'What if the queen comes knocking – with the crown jewels in a wheelbarrow?'

They all laughed at that and were only stopped by an urgent banging on the front door. Looking at one another with shocked faces, they burst out laughing again.

The insistent, battering summons continued.

'It better not be Her Maj,' Cherry said, going to answer it. 'This Biba minidress weren't made for no curtseys – *ooh la la*!'

Verne turned the Nimius over in his hands. 'Seriously,' he groaned to Lil, 'what am I going to do?'

In the hall Cherry gave a yell. They heard the front door smash against the wall and a tall figure came stomping into the cottage.

The face was hidden in the hood of a parka, fastened as high as the zip allowed. He wore trousers so baggy they were comical, but they were caked in mud and so were the shoes.

Striding into the parlour, the intruder took his hands from the parka's pockets.

'Can't be!' Verne gasped.

The walls and ceiling turned an angry scarlet as Cherry came storming after.

'Just who d'you think you are, bustin' in like this?' she demanded.

The figure unzipped the coat and pulled the hood down, revealing his tin skull and torch-lens eyes.

'Pardon this unseemly intrusion,' Jack Potts apologised. 'I could not help myself.'

The reels in his chest spun around and three oranges clunked to a stop. The ten pences that had been fed into his head earlier came gushing from the payout tray above his waist.

'This is for you, Master Verne,' he said, bowing formally. 'How pleasant it is to see you again.'

And the left eye flickered.

'But you fell to pieces with all the other impossible gadgets, months ago!' Verne declared. 'How can you be here now?'

'Begging your pardon, young master,' the automaton replied, 'but I did not fall to pieces; that would have been most undignified. Whilst the Nimius exists, so shall I. The coins that trigger my consciousness and motion ran out, that is all. The next thing I was aware of, I found myself in a scrapyard in the early hours of this morning.'

'Who revived you?' Cherry asked suspiciously. 'And why'd they wait so long?'

The chains in Jack Potts's neck rattled and he turned his hockey-mask face towards her.

'There was a bent coin jammed in the slot at the side of my head,' he answered smoothly. 'Something must have jarred me and dislodged it.'

'So what'd you come here for?' Cherry pressed.

'I was created to serve the Thistlewood family, yet I was compelled to come directly to this cottage, though I knew not why.'

'This is Cherry Cerise; it's her cottage,' Verne said. 'This is Lil Wilson. And this is my dad's steampunk butler costume that the Nimius made real. Don't ask me how. He's called Jack Potts.'

'"Potts" will suffice,' Jack Potts told them. 'I am but a biddable domestic mechanism. I am, however, enchanted to make your acquaintance.'

'You sure it's safe?' Cherry asked Verne. 'I don't like hotshot appliances that answer back.'

The boy chewed his lip thoughtfully. 'He was controlled by Melchior Pyke before, so he must be free of that now. I wouldn't touch his toast though.'

Lil found Jack Potts fascinating. She had never seen any of the ludicrous inventions on that day of the town battle because she had been possessed herself.

'A real, actual, thinking, working robot?' she breathed in wonder. 'That's so galoptious.'

'Galoptious,' Jack Potts repeated. 'An archaic word, meaning splendid, delightful, delicious. Why, I am none of those things, but I thank you most humbly.'

Cherry shrugged, unimpressed. 'I skipped being excited about whizz-bang gimmicks back when they invented the pocket calculator. The world's gotten dumber since people stopped workin' things out for themselves.'

She stared at Jack Potts's soiled clothes and the kitchen utensils that formed his hands. They weren't just spattered with dirt, there were also dark splashes of blood.

'Do not be alarmed,' he explained. 'Walking the country roads last night, I encountered an unfortunate sheep that had been hit by a car. I carried it gently to the verge and remained with it until the poor animal's suffering was over. I am most anxious to divest myself of these grubby garments and shall attend to my attire as soon as I return to the home of Master Verne, where I trust there will be a quantity of ironing to do. A stack of neatly folded, crisply pressed linen cheers the soul.'

'How would you know?' Cherry muttered. 'You ain't got one.'

'You can't come home!' Verne said quickly. 'Mum'd have you up for sale in a flash.'

'Well, the creepy heap of yappy scrap ain't stayin' here,' Cherry said flatly. 'I don't want that contraption rifling through my frillies and looming over me at night.'

'Then where am I to go?' the automaton pleaded. 'I beg you, do not turn me away.'

'You can stay with us,' Lil offered brightly. 'Dad won't mind a bit, 'specially as he's been doing everything around the house lately. Mum might take a bit of convincing, but it'll probably be OK.'

The impassive mask turned to her and the torch eyes shone on her eager face.

'That is most generous of you, Mistress Wilson. I am overwhelmed with gratitude.'

'That still doesn't solve my problem,' Verne said, holding up the Nimius. 'What am I going to do about this?'

'There is some difficulty?' Jack Potts asked.

'It's why you ended up here,' Verne explained. 'I pressed a symbol for wealth and now I can't go anywhere without people chucking money at me.'

'And you do not wish for these riches? Yes, I can see that would be most distracting.'

'What if you could block that gadget's mojo somehow?' Cherry wondered. 'Hey, Lil, you've been searching for a project to test your gifts. How about knitting Verne a muffler for it?'

'I could try,' Lil said.

'Remember, you gotta focus on what you want the spell to achieve and recite the intention with every stitch. The simpler the chant, the better.'

'I do not comprehend,' Jack Potts began. 'You speak as if you are witches.'

'You got a problem with that, Butlerbot?' Cherry demanded.

'In no way. I am, after all, a consequence of the occult studies of a seventeenth-century magician and natural philosopher. But perhaps if I may examine the

Nimius? I might find a more straightforward solution to Master Verne's predicament.'

He held out his metal hands and, before Cherry could stop him, Verne passed across the most powerful object in the world.

'The Nimius,' Jack Potts's metallic voice sang softly. 'How splendid it is.'

'Do you know how to work it?' Verne asked.

'Like, is there an off button?' Cherry said bluntly.

Jack Potts held it close to his face and the left eye flickered once more. The reels in his chest began to turn.

'The glittering wonder-worker,' he whispered. 'After so many years . . .'

'Hey!' Cherry called. 'Walking toaster oven – we're speaking to you.'

The automaton twitched to attention.

'Forgive me,' he said. 'I was wondering why this symbol of the lantern remains proud. Should it not have been pressed in conjunction with the one for wealth?'

'What?' Verne asked. 'I could've sworn they all sank back down.'

'Evidently not, Master Verne. See, here it is. I would hazard that you erred in pressing just one motif. Your command was not specific and that is why the result has been less than satisfactory.'

'So pressing that as well would do what? People start giving me light bulbs?'

'I cannot be certain, but I believe that the lantern is symbolic of more than mere illumination. Perhaps if pressed in tandem with the wealth rune, it could bring to light treasures that are normally hidden.'

'Buried treasure?' Lil asked. 'Like pirate gold or a stash of Saxon coins?'

'There are many things in this world prized more highly than gold,' Jack Potts said.

'If that thingamajig could sniff out a pair of size four Mary Quant ankle boots in bubblegum pink,' Cherry put in, 'that would be awesomeness in a bun.'

'Do you think we should try it?' Verne asked.

Cherry wrinkled her nose. 'I wouldn't fiddle with that doodad any more than you already have. It's way too strong, way too unpredictable and I don't like the vibes it gives off.'

'But it might stop people shoving money at me,' Verne replied. 'I'll never be able to go outside again if that carries on.'

Cherry threw her hands in the air.

'OK, go ahead. Pull out the pin and blow yourself up – but don't let Junkyard Jeeves do it. He's had it in his chrome-plated paws too long already.'

Verne reached to take the Nimius from Jack Potts. Cherry watched closely. Did she detect a momentary hesitation? Was the automaton reluctant to part with it?

She couldn't be certain.

The boy traced his thumb around the lantern's raised image and glanced over to Lil, who nodded encouragement. He pressed the symbol down. There was a click and he felt a soft tremor within.

'Is that it?' Lil asked after a pause.

'It's four hundred years old,' Verne said. 'Give it a – Wait! Look!'

He held the Nimius up and they saw a circular design begin to rotate and rise. Beneath it, spiralling out on a slender octagonal rod, was a round jewel with a ruby fire blazing in its heart.

There was a dazzling burst of crimson light drenching everything in a vibrant glare. Like a magical X-ray it passed through everything. Verne could see the bones in his hands and Lil was a red skeleton sitting on a transparent chaise longue, next to an upright jumble of cogs, chains and wires. Behind them he could see through into the hall. Turning, he saw Cherry Cerise as another skeleton, albeit one in a wig and sunglasses, and at her wrist the ammonites on her bracelet were shining brightly. Then he noticed around the room that Lil's crocheted flowers were gleaming with a faint light of their own.

Another fierce pulse from the jewel and Verne could look through into the neighbouring cottage, where Mrs Gregson's elderly bones were clutching a photograph of her late husband. Raising his eyes, Verne gazed through the ceiling over his head and stared into the room above. Locked inside a cupboard, papers and books were glowing. He wondered what they were – magical secrets of the Whitby witch?

The Nimius shook in his grasp and his thumb slipped from the lantern symbol. There was one more brilliant explosion of ruby light. A picture fell from the wall and a pan crashed to the floor in the kitchen, causing Lil's skeleton to jump. Then the jewel retreated and the gold disc screwed back in place.

The glare faded and everyone, except Jack Potts, scrunched up their eyes.

'We should've taken it up to the abbey,' Verne said. 'Imagine what it might've found there!'

'I do not think its efforts here have been altogether fruitless,' Jack Potts replied. He pointed to the fireplace, and Cherry swore like a fishwife as she leaped from the wicker seat.

Scarlet flames were licking up between the tiles of the hearth.

'Get a bucket of water!' she yelled, stamping on the unnatural fires.

Verne and Lil sprang to their feet, but Jack Potts halted them.

'It is not a consuming fire,' he said. 'It is merely a marker. See how it forms a perfect rectangle. The Nimius has exposed the hiding place of an object most intriguing. We must investigate.'

'You wanna excavate my floor?' Cherry asked. 'What are you, Tindiana Jones?'

'Could be a small coffin,' Verne said ghoulishly.

'Or a little chest of valuables,' Lil argued, clinging to the romantic hope of treasure.

'It would be but the work of moments to dig out,' Jack Potts suggested. 'My hands are the perfect tools.'

Cherry opened her mouth to object, but before she could speak there was a rumble underneath the hearth. The flames doubled in height and the tiles began to bubble and crack.

'Didn't I say that gizmo was too darned strong,' the witch muttered. 'Stand back, guys!'

The whole fireplace was juddering. The lava lamps on the mantel shook and soot came drizzling down the chimney.

The hearth bulged and the flames roared and leaped to the ceiling. Tiles split apart and dirt and rubble went flying across the room as something punched its way free. There was a wild crackle and spitting of sparks. With a sizzling hiss, the crimson fires were quenched, leaving a mound of stones and chips of broken cement. Lying on top, covered in grime and dust, was a rectangular bundle wrapped tightly in waterproof cloth.

'Oh Lords!' Cherry murmured. 'What have we got here?'

'A most disagreeable mess,' Jack Potts observed.

'Forgive me, Miss Cerise, I did not anticipate so violent and chaotic a consequence. I will of course put it all in order and clean up thoroughly. Where do you keep your vacuum cleaner?'

'Chillax,' Cherry told him. 'Let's see what this thing is first.'

Carefully she reached out and passed her hand over the strange discovery. Smudges of pink light flickered across her palm as Cherry's pale blue eyes began to shine and the walls of the parlour moved through different shades of purple.

'Whatever it is has been in this house over a hundred years,' she murmured slowly. 'I can see old wrinkled hands, human and something other – aufwaders? There's friendship there, and trust. Yeah, but that's just the wrapping. I can't tune in to what's inside – it doesn't seem to have any vibes of its own. Nothing is ever that blank. Even a flowerpot has some sort of emanation. This is so clean it could squeak.'

'Like wiping the fingerprints off a murder weapon,' Verne said gruesomely and he felt the torch eyes of Jack Potts turn upon him.

'Wait,' Cherry said. 'There is . . . something. Oh, that's just too wacky.'

'What is?' asked Lil.

Cherry half closed her eyes and concentrated harder.

'Best way I can describe it is like lookin' into a

mirror. I keep gettin' my colours reflected back at me. Never had that before. So bizarre.'

'But no malevolence?' Jack Potts enquired.

'If there is, then it's buried way down deep and I can't probe so far. That in itself scares me. Detective Verne might be right.'

She leaned back and gave her hand a vigorous shake. At the same time the mysterious parcel slid on to the carpet. A corner of the cloth flapped open and an envelope slipped out.

Cherry seized it and her blue wig shifted as her eyebrows shot up.

There was no name, no address, just a simple drawing of three ammonites.

'Guess it must be for me,' she said.

Using her fingernail as a paperknife, she opened the envelope, adjusted her sunglasses and removed the letter it contained.

'Swanky,' she said, admiring the quality embossed notepaper. There was a stylish letterhead depicting a slender woman in an evening gown, with an Airedale dog at her side, a biplane in the sky, a yacht on the sea in the distance, and the words ***Scribbled from the desk, dashboard, cabin or cockpit of Sylvia de Lacy.***

'Cop a load of this,' Cherry began, and she read the letter aloud.

Whitby, 1932

Dear future darlings,

I've had to relocate this troublesome packet from a hidey-hole in the kitchen wall, where it looks like it had been stashed for simply yonks, and inter it under the hearth here. Some oikish bluenose has been making a pill of himself in regard to it, but Holly and I saw him off. I hope it'll be safe in the new sanctuary, until you find it – or it finds you!

Bags of affection,

SdL

'Who is Sylvia de Lacy?' Verne asked.

'Keep up, Columbo,' Cherry said, handing the letter across. 'She's one of my predecessors and this changes everything.'

'A Whitby witch?' Lil asked.

'You betcha, and quite a gal by all accounts. A genuine adventuress, the type they don't make no more – and hardly ever did back then. If she vouches for this, whatever it is, that's good enough for me.'

Verne gazed at the confident handwriting, which looked as fresh as the day it had flowed from an expensive fountain pen, and he wondered if the drawing was in any way a good representation of Sylvia de Lacy. If it was, then she was exceedingly glamorous.

'So who was the "bluenose"?' he asked. 'And Holly? Was that the dog in the letterhead?'

'No idea,' Cherry said, starting to unwrap the bundle that was now on her knee. 'Holly might have been her cook or parlourmaid. Sylvia was seriously loaded. This cottage was her idea of a beach hut. Apparently her Rolls Royce was always blocking Church Street. Only rich witch I ever heard of and that's because she was born into it. Now what's this?'

She had removed two layers and only one remained, but sandwiched between the second and third was another note. This was a folded scrap of torn paper and had been there long before Sylvia had written hers.

'It's like pass the parcel,' chuckled Lil.

Cherry gave the message her attention, which was written in thick black pencil.

'You better read it,' she said to Lil.

Puzzled, Lil took the tattered note and let out a cry of disbelief.

'What is it?' Verne demanded. 'What does it say?'

His friend passed it to him and, though his mouth opened and closed, he was too stunned to speak.

Lil Wilson, this is for you!

'Got to be a coincidence,' Lil said. 'It can't mean *me* me.'

'Don't be daft!' Verne said, giving it back. 'Course it's you. Check out the handwriting!'

Lil took another look and gasped even louder. 'It's not possible,' she breathed. 'But . . . but – it looks like mine.'

Cherry slumped back in the wicker chair and whistled through her teeth.

'Dip me in glitter and throw me to a mob of roller-skating pixies!' she declared. 'This is turning out to be one head-fry of a day and it's still not lunchtime. Here, Lil, this is undeniably yours, kiddo. A present out of the past to you, from you.'

Lil took the bundle almost fearfully, questions exploding in her head like fireworks. Carefully she unwrapped the last layer of protective cloth and gazed at the uncovered object.

It was a plain and shallow wooden box, with tarnished brass hinges and a simple clasp locking the two halves together.

'P'raps there's magic wands inside?' Verne suggested. 'You might've sent yourself a witch kit.'

'We've got enough of those in the shop already,' Lil reminded him. 'Besides, Cherry says real witches don't use them.'

'A set of magic knitting needles then?' he said. 'Hurry up and open it!'

'Yes,' Jack Potts joined in. 'I too am curious.'

'Curious, my eye!' Cherry cried. 'I'm so stoked, I'm gonna need fresh underwear! Put me and my gusset out of our misery, for crying out loud!'

Lil fumbled with the clasp. It was stiff and took several moments of fiddly struggle before she could lift the lid.

Gazing inside, she gave a delighted laugh and angled the box around for everyone to see.

'It's paints!' she exclaimed. 'An antique box of . . . watercolours, I think. No wonder you thought your colours were being reflected back at you.'

The lower half was divided into seven compartments for the blocks of pigment and a narrow channel for the brush.

Verne couldn't conceal his disappointment. He'd expected something far more dramatic and otherworldly.

'Maybe they paint the future or something?' he said.

'They've never been used,' Cherry observed. 'Not so much as a spot of spit ever touched them.'

Lil prised out an ochre-coloured brick and examined it closely. It was slightly larger than a piece of Lego. Stamped on to the surface was a relief of a camel and, on the reverse, the pigment's name – *Sahara Sand*.

'They've all got little images on them,' she said. 'The white one has a cup and saucer; the red has a beetle; the yellow is a bit weird, looks like a starved cow – you can see the ribs.'

'Might be Indian Yellow,' Cherry suggested. 'The way they used to make that was gross. They fed cattle nothing but mango leaves, which did them no good whatsoever, then they boiled down the urine to a stinky powder.'

'Says *Scourge Yellow*,' said Lil, reading the back.

'Never heard of that one.'

'What's there, in the middle?' Verne asked.

The brick in the centre space was wrapped in creamy linen, embroidered at the edges.

'Looks like a hanky,' Lil said, carefully peeling away the fabric.

'Perhaps that colour is Bogey Green,' Verne said, grinning.

'You're kidding me!' Lil blurted, but she wasn't talking to him. She was staring at the object that had been cocooned in the handkerchief. It wasn't paint at all. It was a badge, made of polymer clay, one of the handmade badges that she made for the shop and often wore herself.

'Wow,' was all Verne could say.

'That settles it then,' Cherry declared. 'Remember that old sepia photograph of Victorian Whitby I showed you, with a girl in it who looked like you? That's the very badge she was wearing.'

'So I do go back in time,' Lil whispered, trying to take it in and convince herself this was real. 'But how? And why? And why do I send myself this paintbox? Why didn't I write a proper note explaining it all? Am I supposed to do something special with it?'

Cherry gazed at the Whitby witch brooch and clicked her fingernails, lost in thought.

'When did you make that particular badge?' she asked abruptly. 'Was it recent?'

'I haven't made any for months,' the girl answered. 'And I'm sure I've never made one quite like this before.'

'You must have,' Verne said. 'It's absolutely one of yours – a green-faced, goofy witch.'

His friend shook her head. 'I've never made one holding a turnip lantern,' she said firmly.

'Could you make me one?' Cherry asked. 'Just the same as that? Exactly the same, in every detail?'

'You can have this if you want. I've got lots at home.'

'No, you have to keep that, it's been waitin' for you a long time. I just want a copy.'

Lil nodded vaguely. She was more concerned about what all this meant.

'What if,' she began. 'What if this is a warning? Do I get stuck there, back in the past? I might never be able to get come back here – to now. What happens to me? I might die decades before I'm even born.'

'Hey,' Cherry said sharply. 'Quit the hysteria. I told you being a witch came with a hat full of curve balls. So you go back in time, big deal; some witches are always skippin' in and out of the centuries, that's their job. It's gonna happen to you and there's nothing you can do to change that; it's part of established history now so get over it. Whatever you do has already been done. Start thinkin' too hard about this stuff and it'll melt your mind. You know what, I've had a bellyful of kooky dramatics for one morning. This old broad needs to clear this mess up and groove out to some Bolan and Bowie.'

'You want us to go?' Lil asked, taken aback by the sudden switch of mood. 'But I need to talk about this!'

'Later maybe,' Cherry said, and Lil was astonished at the coldness in her voice.

'Did I say something wrong?' she asked. 'If I did, I'm sorry. But this has knocked me sideways. I'm scared.'

'Welcome to my world,' was the terse answer. 'Goes with the territory. Now, you kids, scram and take Captain Clankaroo with you.'

'All right,' the girl muttered, feeling hurt. 'Verne, come back to ours – and you too, Mr Potts.'

'Just Potts,' the automaton reminded her as they rose and left the parlour.

Cherry saw them to the front door, arms folded. 'I'd leave off usin' them paints,' she cautioned sternly. 'They'll be packed with toxic gunk. The white's gonna be chock-a-block with lead for a start, and some of the others might contain arsenic.'

'I'll be careful,' Lil assured her, hugging the box tightly as she stepped outside.

'Thank you for a most interesting time,' Jack Potts said politely, his voice muffled by the parka he had zipped up to conceal his face once more.

Cherry ignored him.

'And don't you go pressin' no more buttons on that bauble of yours,' she told Verne.

Verne scowled in reply. It was unsettling – she had practically swept them out of the cottage. Walking away in thoughtful silence, he pushed Mrs Gregson's wedding ring and pension money through her letter box as they passed.

'Hey!' Cherry called after them. 'Lil, that badge – don't forget. I want it exactly the same.' And she slammed the door.

'Does anyone have a clue what just happened?' Lil asked. 'Why'd she go all weird?'

'She's always been weird,' Verne said.

'One cannot predict a witch's humour,' Jack Potts said. 'They are as sleeping tigers.'

'Nah,' Verne disagreed. 'That's just girls.' And he yelped when Lil punched him on the arm.

Inside the cottage, Cherry Cerise slid down against the front door. The colour of the hallway drained to an arctic blue.

'Curse you, Cherry,' she uttered in a cracked and anguished voice. 'You shoulda seen this comin'. That's what you're here for! This could be the biggest disaster this town has ever faced.'

And she buried her face in her hands.

4

On their way to the Wilsons' Verne was relieved that no one tried to force money on him. When they arrived Lil wasted no time and found Jack Potts some of her father's Victorian-style clothes. He was soon looking respectable in a burgundy velvet frock coat with fawn checked trousers and a pair of black brogues. Inspecting the gothic-themed home, the automaton claimed to be overjoyed at the quantity of dust and clutter and immediately set about dealing with it.

While he got acquainted with the Hoover attachments, Lil and Verne remained in the kitchen. The mysterious paintbox was placed on the table and they resumed their examination and discussion of the note that Lil had apparently written to herself a long time ago.

'Perhaps you were in a hurry and couldn't go into detail,' Verne suggested.

'Or maybe that's all I was able to write before something dire happened to me?'

'But then who wrapped it up with the paints and hid it?'

They inspected the box thoroughly once more, for anything that might offer a clue.

'Maybe it's staring me in the face, but I can't see it,' Lil said. 'I'm going to do a drawing of it, jot down every detail and see if that helps.'

Cherry had told her that every witch kept a book of shadows, into which she wrote everything that was important to her: spells, charms, poetry, rituals, words, newspaper clippings, pictures. It was something Lil had been doing for a long time, before she even realised she was a witch.

As she fetched her journal to begin, Verne lifted the brush from its place in the box and twirled it in his fingers. The handle was made from ebony with an inlaid line of gold spiralling up to the tip. He flicked a finger through the black bristles.

'This is miles softer than any of your others,' he said. 'They're sable, aren't they? So what's this?'

'Sable's the softest there is,' Lil replied. 'Maybe that one used conditioner.'

Verne gave it a cautious sniff. 'Or perhaps it's moggy,' he declared.

Lil smiled then gave her attention to a label that was glued to the underside of the lid. Parts of it were foxed, but the writing was still legible.

Verne read it out to her as she copied it down.

A colour a day to brighten our play.
But once begun can't be undone,
till all are gone and washed away.

'That doesn't really make sense, now there's only six colours,' Lil commented. 'There should be seven if it's one a day.'

'Don't artists have a day off?' Verne asked, picking up the small witch badge. 'Wonder which colour this replaced?'

'There's always a green and a brown,' Lil said. 'And usually a lot more in a box of paints than just seven anyway.'

'Where's the hanky? Did you leave it behind?'

'Must have, if it isn't there. Still can't get over how odd Cherry went.'

'You going to make her one of these badges? She was more bothered by that than the paints.'

'Might get me back in her good books if I do. And I'll knit you a Nimius cosy – see if it blocks the power, like she suggested.'

'Can't see that working.'

'You're just worried in case my witchcraft is stronger than your precious gadget!'

'Am not,' he lied unconvincingly.

Lil chuckled and started drawing the skeletal cow from the first block of pigment. Underneath, she wrote the words *Scourge Yellow*.

A glass of water was put down at her side. Startled, both children looked up. They had not heard Jack Potts return to the kitchen.

'I'm not thirsty,' Lil told him.

'It is for the paint, Mistress Lil,' the robot replied. 'Were you not about to add a sample of the colour to your fine rendition and documentation?'

'I hadn't thought about that. Do you like my drawing then?'

Jack Potts bowed to the picture. 'You have captured it exquisitely,' he said. 'A most promising talent.'

'I suppose I should put a record of the colours on it.'

'That would be most thorough.'

'Hang on,' Verne said as Lil reached for the brush. 'Cherry warned you about using the paints.'

'Only that they might be toxic. I'll try to fight the urge to lick them. Besides, after the way she behaved, Cherry had a nerve telling us what we can and can't do.'

'She's only trying to keep you safe,' Verne said.

'I've got powers of my own. You saw my aura.'

Disconcerted, Verne leaned back in his chair. He hoped his friend wasn't letting her newfound abilities go to her head.

Before taking up the paintbrush, Lil hesitated and turned her face towards the hallway.

'Is something amiss?' Jack Potts asked.

'I thought I heard Sal barking,' she explained. 'Sally was my dog. She died. Sometimes I still feel her nuzzling next to me at night. Never heard her bark since she's been gone though.'

'See,' Verne said. 'Even Sally's ghost doesn't want you messing with them paints. Or perhaps the brush really is made from cat hairs.'

Jack Potts stared at him.

Lil shook herself. 'There's nothing to be scared of. I can do this. I'm a witch of Whitby now, and Cherry said this wasn't malevolent.'

'She said she couldn't get a reading off it,' Verne reminded her. 'Not the same thing at all.'

'Such a fuss over an old box of ordinary watercolours,' Jack Potts said, with a shrug of his mechanical shoulders. Pulling a pair of rubber gloves over his metal hands, he busied himself at the sink. The children did not notice his sidelong glances at them.

Lil seized the brush with determination. She felt

it was almost too fancy to use, but she dipped it in the glass and swirled it in the clean water. Applying the wet brush to the pigment block, she sloshed the sopping hairs across the raised image of the starved cow.

The antique box shuddered violently and there was an immense explosion.

Cherry had spent the best part of an hour clearing away the rubble heaped on her hearth and was staring into the hole that was left behind. She felt just as hollow and empty.

She tried to push aside the feelings of despair that had overwhelmed her earlier. The contents of the box had shaken her, but perhaps what she was dreading might never come to pass. If the world was going to end, it wasn't going to happen today. She would have to handle the situation very carefully and not tell Lil of her suspicions. That could ruin everything.

Her veteran stereogram was playing a favourite album, the greatest hits of T. Rex. Cherry was singing along raucously to revive her spirits, and the room was pulsing with vibrant colours, when there was a brisk knock on the door.

'My front door sure is popular today. Who's bustin' their knuckles on it this time?'

Cherry opened the door and almost burst out laughing when she saw the group of five serious faces before her. Leaning casually against the wall, she regarded them through her sunglasses. She recognised all but one. She'd been expecting this confrontation and she was going to relish it.

Police inspector Brian Lucas stood stiffly in his uniform; next to him, much shorter, but no less sure of himself and wearing his chain of office, was Finley Harris, the mayor of Whitby. Behind them, long thin nose flared as if smelling something unpleasant, was Jennifer Pidd, one of the most uptight members of the town council. With her was Rory Morgan, a younger councillor who mistakenly believed himself to be 'cool'. The man she didn't know had a face like thunder and, Cherry observed with a sideways smile, the trousers of his suit were soaked up past the knee.

'Miss Cerise,' the inspector began. 'May we come in?'

'You like some "Hot Love" at lunchtime, Inspector?' Cherry asked in a throaty drawl. 'I know I do.'

'P– Pardon?'

Cherry laughed. 'It's the name of the song – don't flatter yourself. So what is this? A deputation?'

'If we could come in?' repeated the flustered inspector.

'I don't invite sourpusses into *mi casa*.' She shook her head. 'Just say whatever it is you're itching to get off your chests and let's all carry on with our day.

I've got wigs to wash.'

'Three hundred thousand pounds!' the man with the wet trousers shouted angrily. 'What are you going to do about that?'

'Who is this soggy bozo with the red face and what's he yakkin' about?' Cherry asked.

The inspector coughed and introduced Mr Jackson, branch manager of the bank, whose cashpoints had been mysteriously emptied earlier that morning.

'Do I look like a bank robber? Not exactly inconspicuous.'

'It wasn't a normal robbery!' Mr Jackson answered. 'It was witchcraft! Ask anyone who was there!'

'We do have many eyewitness accounts of the money behaving unusually,' the inspector added. 'And the CCTV footage will corroborate it.'

'I see,' Cherry said. 'So you come straight to my door because I'm a witch. You know what that is? That's profiling.'

The mayor took this opportunity to clear his throat and, with his hands clasped over his mayoral chain, said, 'Miss Cerise, be reasonable. By your own admission, you are the town's resident witch. Of course we would consult you when something of this nature occurs.'

'Most of the money ended up in the river!' the bank manager ranted. 'We'll never get the rest of it back. It's even trending on Twitter with its own hashtag, #whitbyfreecash. How am I going to explain this to senior management? They won't believe it if I tell them it was black magic!'

'Wash your dirty mouth out!' Cherry snapped at him. 'If you don't apologise, right this instant, I'll cast a spell to make you fart in five different colours every single time you shake hands with someone at the bank. I can do it, you know.'

Mr Jackson let out a strangled cry of panic.

'They'll call you Rainbow Jacksy,' Cherry added with a mischievous cackle.

'Why don't we all calm down?' Jennifer Pidd spoke up, her oval face wreathed in a fake, politician's smile. 'We haven't come here to antagonise you, Ms Cerise. It goes without saying that my fellow councillors and I completely understand we owe you a debt of gratitude for what you did back in the spring.'

'Too right you do. Ain't a single one of you would be here if I hadn't saved your asses.'

Mrs Pidd's smile widened, making her nostrils gape even further.

'We just think it would be in everyone's interest if this sort of event didn't occur again,' she said. 'Or if it did, perhaps you could give us prior warning? Keeping the earlier events a secret has been very trying for everyone in this community.'

'Oh, poor them,' Cherry said. 'We witches have been keeping schtum for several thousand years.

We managed somehow, all on our little lonesomes.'

'You don't have to shoulder this burden in secrecy and solitude any more. If there's anything Whitby can do to assist you, the council is listening. But we cannot sanction unexpected and illegal acts like today.'

'Gee,' Cherry said, returning the insincere smile with one of her own. 'That's mighty swell of you. When the next attack comes, from the deepest reaches of the sea, by beings so ancient not even a geologist could imagine them, I'll send for you in your kitten heels, and you can whack 'em about the tentacles with your knock-off Hermès handbag. That's real reassuring.'

Mrs Pidd lost no composure, but there was ice in her voice when she replied. 'Yes, well, *if* such a threat exists, and we have only your testimony after all, I'm sure this country's naval forces can deal with it. There's no need for amateur and homespun deterrents, however well intentioned.'

She paused. Cherry was looking at her strangely, with her head tilted to one side.

'What . . . what are you doing?' Mrs Pidd asked.

Cherry winked at her. 'I was just wonderin' what kinda underwear a zipped-up dame like you goes for. I'm guessin' big and sensible. See, the next time you're at any official function, I'll fix it so your knickers fly off and hit the most important person in the room right in the kisser. Would that be a first for you, sweetheart?'

Jennifer Pidd's smile crashed down into her chin and she spluttered with outrage and disgust.

'Miss Cerise, please!' the inspector said forcefully.

'Cherry!' Rory Morgan cut in with chuckling camaraderie. 'Love the music, by the way, big fan of David Bolan here, adore his stuff.'

'Oh brother,' Cherry muttered.

'Call me Rory, or just Roar, cos I'm a bit of a tiger. So I'm a mega supporter of yours, always speak up for you at council meetings. Definitely Team Cherry, that's me – huge fan. I've been wanting to reach out and touch base with you, invite you into the offices to have a crucial meeting for a while. What I would love, and I've sounded out the guys on the tourist board – they're big fans of yours too by the way – what I would love, love, love is to build on Whitby's robust reputation for all things spooky and take it forward, to the next level. When people round the world hear the word Whitby, I want them to immediately think "magic". Now *there's* a hashtag and poster slogan for you #WhitbyisMagic.'

'How're you going to manage that, Mr Morgan?' Cherry asked flatly.

'That's down to you. You bring the shazam factor to the table. It doesn't have to be much, a few tricks that can't be explained. Maybe three or four a month to get the ball rolling and people talking. Then you could pull back and start on the bigger stuff. It would be incredible for tourism, 'specially if you save the real spectaculars for the winter months. Obviously, you'd be in for a healthy slice of the pie.'

'You're asking me to perform some "tricks" to help sell more ice creams?'

'Now don't dismiss it straight off. If you'd prefer to do it anonymously, we'd totally respect that. We could really work up a blinding campaign with that.'

'Whitby is magic,' repeated the mayor. 'I like it.'

Cherry took a long breath then scratched her forehead.

'You know,' she began. 'Soon as I opened the door and saw y'all, I was expecting the usual rude and ignorant insults, which Jacksy and Jennifer supplied with predictable monotony and a generous dose of halitosis. But I wasn't anticipating an offer of crass hexploitation. I really gotta congratulate you, Mr Morgan, you made me realise I'm still shockable. That's a real achievement. Now I think you'd better leave before I have time to cook up something extra special for you, although how you could be made to appear even more of a grade A . . .'

Her words faltered and she had to catch her breath. A wave of dizziness swept over her and her legs weakened. She almost fell head first into the mayor.

'You all right, Miss Cerise?' the inspector asked in alarm as he reached out to steady her.

'Did you feel that?' she asked in a shocked gasp.

'Feel what?'

'Like a part of me was torn out. You didn't feel it? Something is real wrong.'

Cherry clutched her chest and stared past him and the others at the narrow entrance to the yard. There was a commotion in Church Street beyond. People were calling out in astonishment and wonder.

'I gotta see,' she said, lurching forward.

Out in the quaint, cobbled road, the crowds of holidaymakers were staring along the street. Shouts of disbelief were echoing around and some people were holding phones aloft, recording the scene.

Rushing from Henrietta Street was an impossible spectacle. Everything was changing colour. Walls of houses, window frames, roof tiles, flowers in hanging baskets, even the cobbles were all turning a vivid yellow. It was as if a giant, invisible paintbrush was speeding through the street. The rampaging colour reached a parked blue van. There was a jolt and suddenly even the tyres were yellow. At the foot of the church steps the inexplicable yellow tide went shooting up the cliff, turning each of the 199 steps and the handrail the same bright shade of daffodil.

Cherry stumbled into Church Street just in time to see the unnatural force come sluicing down it. Nothing escaped that magical flood of colour, not even people. It tore past them like a sunny storm, sending them spinning or snatching the breath from their mouths.

Cherry threw her hands before her face and yelled words of protection, but it was too late. The power pummelled into her and sent her teetering sideways. The unstoppable force raged on down the street.

'Yep, that . . . that will do it,' Rory Morgan uttered in an awestruck voice behind her. 'Whitby is magic all right.'

Gasping, and feeling faint, Cherry turned to look at him. He too was now dressed from head to toe in yellow, and so was she, even down to her lipstick.

So was Jennifer Pidd, who stared around her, aghast.

'How are we going to cover this up?' she cried. 'This isn't something the town can keep secret. There are thousands of outside witnesses! What have you done?'

Cherry didn't stay to argue. Pushing through the incredulous tourists, who weren't sure whether to be terrified or impressed, she hurried to the church steps and began climbing. When she was level with the town's chimneys, she gazed down upon Whitby and her face went pale.

The whole of the East Cliff was yellow, even the grass and the gravestones in the cemetery behind her. There wasn't a patch of any other colour anywhere. Every building was the same, including St Mary's Church and the abbey itself. And there was no sign of it stopping.

Shielding her eyes from the sun sparkling over the river, Cherry saw the swing bridge quickly change. Then, road by road, house by house, the whole of the West Cliff was engulfed. It took only minutes for the tsunami of yellow to reach the whalebone arch and the grand hotels behind.

The preposterous vista was at once startling and curiously beautiful. This strange, new, monochrome world looked as if it was made entirely from cheese, with rich apricot shadows. Overhead the gulls were shrieking louder than usual. They too had been transformed and were swooping and squabbling in their new plumage, like monstrous canaries.

'What a foul-up!' Cherry uttered. 'If I weren't wearing these platform boots, I'd kick myself. Why didn't I stop Lil taking that paintbox? I was too busy worrying about the wrong thing!'

Growing fearful, Cherry ran back down the steps. She had barely set foot in Henrietta Street when she noticed the intensity of the surrounding colour was fading. The yellow was dissipating, billowing over the surfaces in tattering streaks. By the time she reached the Wilsons' cottage it had almost completely disappeared and her own clothes and wig were back to their usual garish selves.

Lil and Verne were out in the street, looking across the harbour at the West Cliff.

'Wasn't it glorious?' Lil cried when she saw her. 'It was the most mirificus thing ever! Even the lighthouses went yellow. Did you see them? They looked like massive corn on the cobs!'

'I wanted the river and the sea to change too,' Verne said excitedly. 'And be like an ocean of custard. But it was still the best thing ever!'

'Shame it's vanishing now,' Lil lamented. 'I hoped it'd last longer. That's what I call cheering the place up. No amount of yarn bombing could ever match that!'

They watched as the last traces of the eerie yellow rippled away from the streets and houses, shredding and melting into nothing. The world appeared darker without it.

'Boring and grey and ordinary,' Lil said.

'Honey,' Cherry said. 'We need to talk about them paints of yours. That's some serious megaton magic. No wonder they was buried all that time. They ain't safe.'

'I just thought they were normal paints,' Lil said. 'All I did was put a bit of water on the yellow. Then the box started to shake and, before we could dive under the table, there was a sort of yellowness explosion. You should've seen our kitchen!'

'It didn't hurt you?'

'No, we were winded and felt like we'd blasted off in a rocket, but fine. Jack Potts made sure we were

OK and we ran out here, soon as we realised what was going on.'

'I need to take another look at that box,' Cherry said.

Presently they were back in the Wilsons' kitchen, gathered around the table. Jack Potts was cleaning the cupboards, throwing away the occasional tin at the back that was out of date.

The paintbox looked the same as before, except that now the compartment that had housed the yellow pigment was empty.

'It figures,' Cherry declared. 'I guess each colour is a one-time deal.'

She passed her hand over the box once more, but this time the probing light took longer to shine from her palms and was noticeably weaker than before.

'I'm bushed,' she said, dropping into a chair. 'Today has clobbered me. I'm only gettin' the same reading anyway: myself reflected back. What I want to know is who made it, why, and what power went into it? Must be something pretty major.'

'You sure I can't use them again, just once more?' Lil asked hopefully. 'I'd love to see the town turn bright red.'

'The worthies of Whitby would disagree with you. I just had a visit from them and I expect you two will get the same. You better make sure Potts is out of sight when they call.'

'I can insinuate myself into the most cramped cubbyhole,' the automaton volunteered helpfully. 'Perhaps a wardrobe or broom cupboard? And, whilst secreted there, organise the storage to its optimum efficiency.'

Verne was looking at his phone. 'I've got texts from Dad and Mum asking if I'm OK,' he said. 'I'd better get home. The arcade was in a right state when I left.'

Picking up his rucksack, he waved goodbye and let himself out.

Lil examined her mobile. 'Nothing from my parents,' she said, wondering why they hadn't tried to contact her. 'But #Whitbyisyellow is all over Twitter.'

'You can't keep a lid on something that mind-blowing,' Cherry said. 'I better mosey on home too. Haven't felt this beat in a long time.'

'You taking the paintbox with you?' Lil asked.

'What for? It came to you, it's all yours. Just keep it safe and don't be tempted to use it again.'

Lil promised. 'And I'll make that badge for you. If you still want it?'

'More than you can guess, babe. And the sooner the better. Hey, sorry about the way I shooed you guys out earlier. We still good?'

'Sisters in witchery,' the girl replied, grinning.

Cherry gave her a hug and soon Lil was left alone with Jack Potts.

'I simply won't be content until I scrub this floor,'

he said. 'Would you care for a cup of tea before I commence, Mistress Lil? I see you have many different varieties, most impressive. I believe I shall be very comfortable here.'

'Provided we can convince Mum,' Lil reminded him.

'I can be extremely persuasive,' he said, flexing his metal fingers inside the rubber gloves. 'I'm certain she can be made to see the advantages of the arrangement. I am looking forward to having extensive chats with your mother.'

Lil looked at him. 'Is there a loose connection in your eye? Every now and then it flickers.'

'Sometimes the ghost gets into the machinery,' he replied with a metallic chortle. 'Nothing to concern yourself over.'

'OK, I'll have that tea then, please.'

'Perpetually delighted to serve.'

As Cherry passed through Church Street on the way to her cottage, she saw a small crowd gathered round a young family. The father had collapsed and his wife was kneeling on the cobbles, tending to him. Beside them, a toddler in a buggy was crying.

'You're shivering, Joe!' the woman cried, wiping her hand over her husband's icy forehead. 'Better get you to a doctor.'

The onlookers muttered advice and one of them offered to call an ambulance.

'I'll . . . I'll be fine,' the man stuttered as he trembled. 'Just feel a bit . . . a bit achy and nauseous. Give me a minute. Might have been them prawns we had.'

A sudden spasm made him crunch up. Jerking his head to the side, he vomited a jet of bile across the street. Then he passed out.

'Joe!' his wife yelled. 'Joe!'

A woman hurriedly dialled the emergency services. Before she could give any details, she too began to shiver and the phone slid from her hand. It crashed to the ground and so did she.

Cherry's eyes followed the trail of virulent fluid the man had expelled as it trickled between the cobbles towards her feet. It was repulsive and unnatural, shot through with veins and branches of putrid phlegm. Further down the street a woman carrying shopping staggered against a wall and fell. A man close by dropped like a stone. Then another. They all began retching.

'*Scourge Yellow*,' Cherry breathed in horror. 'The yellow scourge . . . oh my Lords, don't let it be true! What has Lil unleashed?'

5

'You've been watching amateur YouTube footage of an inexplicable phenomenon that took place this lunchtime, here in Whitby on the North Yorkshire coast, when everything turned yellow. So far no one has been able to provide an adequate explanation, but it has been suggested that it was a sophisticated publicity stunt by a leading paint manufacturer. If so, did the chemicals used trigger the devastating illness that has since gripped the area? I'm standing in front of Whitby Hospital, which is unable to cope with the sheer number of cases.'

Local news reporter Nigel Hampton was almost unrecognisable in a protective suit and polythene helmet, which muffled his voice.

'In the six short hours since, over seven hundred people have been stricken, with that figure rising steadily. Emergency services are stretched to the limit. The hospital here is overflowing, with some patients having to be treated in the car park. With me is consultant Hillary Lonsdale.'

The camera pulled back to reveal a tall, thin man with a grave face, also wearing a protective suit, but without the headgear.

'Dr Lonsdale,' Nigel said, his face still turned to the lens, 'thank you for taking time out on this hectic day to speak to us. What is your assessment of this alarming situation?'

The consultant answered in a measured, authoritative tone.

'It is alarming,' he agreed. 'I have never seen anything like it in all my thirty-two years in the medical profession. You have to understand that this is still at a very early stage; we don't even know what we're dealing with yet.'

'Was it toxic chemicals?'

'Highly unlikely. This is extremely contagious. Eight of my staff have been taken ill, but we have patients who have contracted this in their own homes, having had no contact with any other cases. Perhaps an airborne pathogen? We just don't know at the present. We are running tests, but this is demonstrating the classic signs of being a virus.'

'Virus?' the reporter repeated, visibly cringing. 'What are the symptoms? Can you tell us that much?'

'There does seem to be a pattern. First, there is extreme fatigue and weakness of the limbs. Then fever and projectile vomiting, followed by loss of consciousness. After several hours, jaundice sets in. We have two critical cases that are giving us great cause for concern.'

'Is it life-threatening?'

'At the moment, I believe it could be, for vulnerable groups: the elderly, sick and very young.'

'Can you give the rest of us any advice?'

The doctor looked into the camera. 'Stay at home,' he said. 'Call your GP and report your symptoms, but do not move from your house. Right now there is nowhere that can take you.'

Behind them an ambulance pulled out of the hospital.

'That will be one of the critical cases,' Dr Lonsdale said. 'They are being transferred to an isolation unit in Scarborough.'

The camera focused on the ambulance as it drove down Spring Hill. The vehicle was still in shot when it began weaving across the road, out of control. It pulled sharply to the right, then accelerated, scraping against a wall, before careering round the bend and disappearing from view. There was a loud crash.

The consultant was already running down the hill, pursued by the camera operator, before Nigel Hampton realised what was happening. His mind filled with the prospect of TV journalism awards, he set off after them.

The ambulance had smashed into the corner of the Bagdale Hall Hotel at the bottom of the hill. The rear doors had popped open and the medical attendant inside was lying dazed across the patient.

Dr Lonsdale glanced at them, then dashed round to the front. The driver was lying unconscious across an inflated airbag and the windscreen was covered in yellow sick.

'This needs containing,' the consultant said grimly.

Nigel Hampton came huffing up. 'If this can strike so . . . so unexpectedly,' he began. 'So sudd–'

The inside of his helmet splattered with yellow and he keeled over. The picture went black and cut to the BBC news studio.

Cassandra Wilson turned off the television and looked at her daughter.

Lil was curled up on the sofa in their living room, clutching a cushion under her chin. Her parents had closed the shop early, after a customer had fallen ill. Lil had spent the past hour explaining everything that had happened that day. She had never seen her mother look so angry and she wished she'd never set eyes on the paintbox.

'Do you realise what you've done?' Cassandra asked. 'This is all your fault. What if they die? Have you thought about that? What possessed you to meddle with it?'

'I didn't think it would do any harm. I thought they were only paints.'

'That's just it!' her mother shouted. 'You didn't think. You've been messing about with magic for a full five minutes and you believe you know everything. I had a feeling something like this would happen. I blame that mad Cerise woman. You were a sensible girl before you met her.'

'It's not Cherry's fault,' Lil said loyally.

'Don't waste your breath. You're not to see her again. Do you hear me?'

'You can't forbid me.'

'Yes I can. It's not normal, a barmy old woman like that spending so much time with a child.'

Lil stared at her mother in disbelief. 'Why are you being horrible?' she cried. 'You never used to be so mean.'

'Go to your room,' Cassandra ordered. 'You don't speak to me like that! I'm your mother!'

Lil looked across at her father who had been listening in troubled silence, but he muttered his support for his wife and Lil gave a fierce grunt of frustration.

Jack Potts appeared in the doorway with a tray.

'Is this an appropriate moment for buns?' he asked.

'And that,' Mrs Wilson said, jabbing a pointing finger, 'isn't going to stay in this house. I'm not having the Thistlewoods' steampunk rubbish in here.'

'He doesn't have anywhere else to go!' Lil protested.

'It isn't a he. It is a creepy machine and not my problem. It can go jump off Tate Hill Pier for all I care.'

'The house has never looked so clean and tidy,' Mike Wilson ventured, before a thunderous glance from his wife subdued him.

'As you wish,' Jack Potts declared, bowing over the buns. 'I shall leave as soon as it is dark, if that is convenient for you? I prefer the anonymity of night. My own clothes will be dry by then. I thank you for the temporary loan of yours, Mr Wilson.'

'You can keep them, if you want,' Mike offered.

'That is not necessary, but I am appreciative nevertheless. To avoid further embarrassment, I shall go and stand in the rear garden until the light fails. Please enjoy the buns. I made them with cinnamon. Mistress Lil told me how fond of it you are.'

Putting the tray down, he left the room.

'How can you be so cruel?' Lil stormed out of the room. Her parents heard her stomp up the stairs and slam the door of her bedroom.

'This isn't like you, Cass,' Mike said gently. 'What's the matter? You'd tell me if you weren't well, wouldn't you?'

His wife glared. 'Today our daughter's selfish meddling with forces she doesn't have the first clue about has caused an epidemic. And you think there's something wrong with *me*? I'm going for a walk. I need fresh air.'

Up in her room, Lil got out her phone to text Verne and discovered some messages from him. His brother Clarke was gravely ill.

Lil flung herself on her bed and wept. Her mother was right: this *was* all her fault. If she hadn't been so stupid, so proud of her own fledgling abilities, none of this would have happened. After several minutes' sobbing into the pillow, she felt a wet nose push against her neck and a small tongue licked her ear.

Lil reached out. For an instant she ran her fingers through silky fur, then it was gone.

'Bless you, Sal,' she whispered.

Sitting up, she wiped her eyes, furious at her own self-pity.

'No one needs your tears, Lilith Wilson,' she scolded herself. 'This is your mess, so stop bawling and do something about it.'

Reaching for her knitting bag, she pulled out a crochet hook and balls of coloured wool, and set to work.

Wrapped in one of her black velvet cloaks, which looked out of place over her stretched jersey leisurewear and trainers, Mrs Wilson ascended the 199 steps. Even though it was only early evening, they were deserted. Here and there the stones were fouled with putrid rivers, where tourists had succumbed to the illness during the afternoon. She avoided the livid yellow blobs that were still wet and glistening.

At the summit, she wandered into the graveyard, before glancing back at the familiar view. The streets down there were empty too. In the distance she could see lines of flashing blue lights and a helicopter was hovering above the traffic on the A171, shining a searchlight on the cars below.

'Poor Whitby,' she murmured. 'And poor me.'

Casting her eyes downwards, Cassandra meandered between the headstones. She couldn't possibly tell Mike what was really the matter. He wouldn't understand. Even she was confused by it, but one thing was certain: she despised herself for it.

Walking along the exposed clifftop she stared out to sea. A coastguard boat was patrolling beyond the harbour mouth. Night clouds were already gathering, thick and mountainous. It would be dark early.

Leaning against a tomb, she watched the light gradually fail and was so wrapped in her own thoughts that she was startled when someone spoke behind her.

'Mrs Wilson?'

Cassandra turned to find Jack Potts standing there, his face hidden by the zipped-up parka.

'What do you want?' she asked. 'Aren't you worried someone might see you?'

'There is nobody about,' he answered. 'People are too afraid to leave their homes. We are quite alone and unobserved and night's candles are already burning.'

'Good time for you to go then,' she said.

'You left your phone behind, so Mr Wilson sent me to find you. A state of emergency has been declared. The town is now under quarantine. Every road out of Whitby is being barricaded, no one is permitted to leave. So you see, I am trapped here. I must find some bolthole until the crisis is over, perhaps a neglected shack or overturned rowing boat.'

'Quarantine?' she repeated, and realised what the blue flashing lights meant in the distance. 'How long for?'

'I do not know. I was constructed mainly for ironing shirts and getting the most from a crevice tool, not virology. Mr Wilson also wished me to tell you that Mistress Lil has gone missing.'

'There's only one place she'll be,' Cassandra said with a shrug. 'Round at that mad old bat's house. She just couldn't wait to disobey me.'

'Are you referring to Cherry Cerise? Forgive me, I am but a humble mechanical domestic and the delicate nuances of human interaction are foreign to me, but do I detect disapproval on your part towards her?'

'Can't stand her,' Cassandra answered sharply.

'Because of her friendship with your daughter?'

The woman reared her head to answer in stinging tones, then seemed to deflate and she stared off into the distance.

'Because of what she is,' she said after a pause. 'She's a witch, a proper one.'

'You are prejudiced against such people?'

A cool breeze was blowing in from the sea. Cassandra pulled the velvet cloak tightly about her, then continued, talking more to herself than Jack Potts.

'Ever since I remember, I've always been drawn to the gothic. Hardly surprising when you're born here, where history and legend brush against you every day. I felt it was in my blood. As a kid, I watched the old Hammer horrors on TV and when I was fifteen all I wanted for Christmas was Christopher Lee to bite me on the neck. I read every book about the occult I could find and decided being a witch was my true destiny. I dressed the part, married a lad who felt the same and we even started a business around it. Being a witch was my everything and I thought I had all I'd ever wanted.'

Frowning, she gave a slight shiver.

'Then that old curse possessed the town and the flower-power reject everyone used to laugh at, and who I used to pity, revealed she's some sort of official secret witch and can actually do proper, flashy magic. She's got it dripping from her fingers, like runny nail varnish. And I saw my life as it truly was for the very first time. *I* was the local nutter, living a massive lie, just one huge sad joke. Can you imagine how that felt? No, I don't suppose you could.'

'Why do you say that?'

'Robots don't have feelings.'

'You misunderstand. I ought to have been clearer. I meant, why were you fooling yourself? Why was your life a lie?'

'Because, as Lil says, I was only pretending. No natural talent, just . . . just a useless, deluded pudding in too much eyeshadow, spouting gibberish. And, as if to rub my nose in it, Lil ups and gets . . .' Her voice trailed off and she shook herself.

Jack Potts tilted his head at her. 'Surely you know that not even the greatest magicians of history were born with such gifts? They attained power by channelling energies from outside themselves. Even Sir Melchior Pyke relied on his instruments, arcane studies and the skills of his manservant. If you so desired, you too could be the conductor of paranormal forces.'

'You don't think I tried? I used to make myself faint calling on the Goddess. I've fasted, jumped over fires, swum naked under the full moon, drunk revolting potions . . .'

'I crave your pardon, but that does sound highly ineffectual. There are more direct methods of contact.'

Jack Potts unzipped the parka and pulled the hood down. 'If you wish, I could demonstrate and act as a transceiver, boosting the signals from one plane to another. Would you like to see things that are usually hidden from mortal eyes?'

Not really believing him, Mrs Wilson gave a weary nod.

Jack Potts reached into one of his pockets, drew out several ten-pence pieces and pushed them into the side of his tin head. Then he spread his arms wide and tilted his head back. The left eye began to flicker and flash. On his chest the bellows pumped faster, the reels spun around until three skulls stopped on the win line and the indicator lights blazed green.

From his tea-strainer mouth there came squeals and static as he tuned through wavelengths. The eerie noises went wailing across the churchyard and Cassandra began to grow uneasy. She shifted apprehensively and stared into the deepening gloom around them.

'Stop now,' she muttered. 'I don't like it.'

But the automaton stood as motionless as an iron scarecrow, and the unearthly din grew shriller until it hurt her ears. Clamping her hands over them, she backed away. Then the sounds were gone, soaring too high for human hearing, replaced by a silence that seemed to buzz inside her head.

Shapes began to crackle in the surrounding shadows, with figures, lit by a cold grey light, jumping in and out of view. Cassandra saw a woman in a crinoline and bonnet moving between the tombs, singing softly to herself. A boy in a cap, no more than six years old, ran by. An old couple holding hands and gazing lovingly at one another shuffled through the grass. A man in a frock coat was stooping before his own headstone, glowering at the eroded, unreadable surface. The clifftop thronged with the spirits of people long dead.

Cassandra spluttered and gulped great gasps of the night air. She couldn't believe it, but she wasn't afraid. She was thrilled.

The countless ghosts wandered over graves and passed through the walls of the church, taking no notice of her.

When a stout gentleman with well-groomed whiskers ambled by, she cleared her throat and tried to address him.

'Hello,' she said. 'Can you hear me? Can you see me?'

'I really wouldn't bother with that one,' an amused voice told her.

Cassandra spun around. Lounging against a headstone, with arms folded and long, booted legs casually crossed, was the spectre of a distinguished-looking man in Regency clothing, with glittering eyes and a self-assured grin.

'Why not?' she asked, marvelling that she was actually conversing with a spirit.

'Because he was deathly dull when he was alive, and now he's dead he's simply dull.' The ethereal

stranger let out a short laugh, then looked around.

'Why would you want to engage with any of them anyway?' he asked. 'They're such a stagnant and insipid herd. At least the three babies who haunt the far corner have a dash of vivacity in them. They like to lure people to the edge with their plaintive crying and trip them over the side. Mischievous rascals. But the rest, they have no interests beyond the mundane trifles that measured their humdrum lives. They're not in the least curious as to what happens beyond the boundaries of this moribund boneyard – oh and the endless, droning litanies of remembered ailments and what carried them off in the end . . . I could merrily strangle each and every one, if it would have any effect.'

'And you're curious, are you?' Cassandra asked. 'About the world outside?'

'Ravenously so!' he answered, flashing an attractive smile as he sauntered forward, hands clasped behind his back. 'I'm positively blunderbussing with questions. Why do so many of you breathers stroll around with cigarillo cases against your ears and why do you shout into them?'

Cassandra laughed. 'They're phones,' she said, then realised she had to explain what those were. 'Erm . . . devices we use to speak to people far away.'

'Dead people? Ah, I understand. That would account for the trance-like state you enter into when you stare at them.'

'Ha, no. Living family and friends mainly – and business contacts.'

'I was never any good at business, not the honest variety anyway. Dame Fortune was my living, especially cards. Unfortunately I was discovered harbouring one knave too many one evening and my reward was a blast of lead in my vitals. Ah, but where are my manners? As there is no one here to perform society's niceties and introduce us, necessity allows me to introduce myself. My name is . . . no – you shall call me Queller. That will meet both our requirements.'

Cassandra was fascinated by him. He must have been a handsome rake when he was alive. He looked no older than thirty, with a mane of thick dark curls, and was the perfect image of a Jane Austen romantic hero.

'And how would you know what a twenty-first-century woman requires?' she asked.

'Your species has not changed in the centuries that my disreputable bones have lain 'neath sod and soil. You want what every female has always wanted.'

'Oh really? What's that then?'

'Whatever you cannot have,' he answered with a lusty chuckle.

'Bet you were a smash at balls and parties,' she said dryly.

He looked her steadily in the eyes and she found his direct stare compelling.

'In life,' he admitted, 'I had a lion's portion of passionate liaisons. Those memories have kept my mouldering remains warm in the chill grave. What a calamity of Fate that you were not born in my time, for we should have had a most sprightly dalliance.'

'Is a ghost actually flirting with me?' she asked, amused yet flustered to feel her cheeks blushing. 'Watch it, Casanova, I'm a married woman, with a daughter and a self-cleaning oven, not to mention the cellulite.'

'Fear not, dear madam, I was but having a game with you. I know what it is you truly want. You wish to penetrate the spheres invisible and open the hearts of ancient mysteries. You would be a conjuror – a sorceress.'

Cassandra blinked at him. 'How did you know that?' she asked. 'Can spirits read minds?'

Queller laughed and clapped his hands. Then he put a finger to his lips, guiltily. 'I confess, before you could see me I was listening to everything that passed between you and your metal manservant earlier. I learned what it is you wish for by ear alone. I should deem it a privilege to offer my services to so gracious and discerning a lady. Might I know your name, you buxom enchantress?'

She snorted with laughter. 'Cassandra Wilson,' she replied. 'What service do you think I need, Mr Queller?'

'Why, a spirit guide of course. You want to pierce the veil, investigate the deeper questions of existence, do you not? I can be of inestimable value in that regard, dearest Cassandra Wilson. That would redress the balance.'

'Which balance is that?'

'The one between you and your daughter. That is the blade that truly cuts you deepest: the fact she has a natural aptitude for witchcraft. Is that not why you resent her so very much?'

Cassandra's expression froze. She struggled to deny it, but couldn't. Horrified that her innermost, secret feelings had been uttered aloud, she whirled about and stumbled away.

'This was a mistake!' she cried out. 'I can't do this. I don't want it.'

The phantom watched her flee the graveyard and go hurrying down the many steps. Around him the other spectres vanished. Jack Potts lowered his arms and raised his head.

'A bravura performance,' the automaton congratulated. 'I was most impressed.'

Queller rubbed his thumb and forefinger together and filaments of electricity sizzled between them. His grin changed into an ugly leer as the handsome face dissolved. A long scar sliced up from the chin to the right eye and his neck became crooked.

'Easier to bag than a stunned rabbit,' he gloated. 'What a stupid creature she is, so ripe, so desperate.'

'Should I go after her?'

'No need. She will return soon enough. Before this night is over, she'll bite the bait fully.'

Jack Potts bowed low. 'As you wish, Mister Dark,' he said.

6

Lil hadn't taken long to crochet a hand-sized heart shape out of blue wool. She knew from conversations with Cherry that it was the colour of tranquillity, bestowing calm and healing. With every stitch, she had chanted, 'Clarke be well, Clarke be well,' and tried to focus her power. Finally, she trimmed it with a white border for protection, then crept downstairs and slipped outside.

Lil hurried through the empty streets, which reeked of disinfectant. Running over the swing bridge, she was soon haring along Pier Road and, minutes later, banging on the Thistlewoods' door.

Verne's father let her in, looking fraught and dishevelled.

'You shouldn't be here,' he said sternly. 'They're telling everyone to remain indoors.'

'I want to see Clarke,' she insisted.

'You can't. He's . . . he's bad with it. Listen, on your

way over, did you see any ambulances or medical teams? They should have been here hours ago.'

Lil shook her head. 'I saw flashing lights, way off, but I think they were police cars.'

'What's keeping them?' he ranted. 'My boy needs treatment!'

'That's why I've got to see him!' Lil explained, brandishing the crocheted heart. 'I made this. It might help. Where's Verne? He'll tell you.'

Mrs Thistlewood appeared at the top of the stairs. She looked alarming, dressed in a cagoule with the hood pulled tightly about her face, rubber gloves and with a tea towel covering her mouth and nose.

'Have you witched it?' she asked bluntly.

Lil nodded.

'Then for heaven's sake, Dennis, let her up!' Noreen yelled.

Dennis relented, but first took Lil to the kitchen, where he gave her a pair of washing-up gloves and a tea towel that had been sprayed with antibacterial cleaner to breathe through.

Lil ascended the stairs and Noreen ushered her into Clarke's room.

Even though Mrs Thistlewood had tried to disinfect everything in the room, including the walls, Lil could still smell the sickness.

Clarke looked deathly. Lil had never seen anyone so ill. His skin had a yellow, waxy translucence and she could almost see his skull through it. A fever drenched his body in sweat, but his lips were cracked and dry. Beneath their half-closed, crusted lids, his sunken eyes were floating from side to side, but he was oblivious to his surroundings.

'Clarke?' Lil said. 'It's me, Lil, Verne's friend.'

There was no response.

'He was fine this afternoon, till about five,' his mother said, her voice wavering. 'Now look. What's going on? Verne's so upset he's locked himself in his room and won't come out.'

Lil took a step closer to the sickbed. Faced with the stark reality of the unnatural illness, her crocheted heart seemed absurd. How could anything she did possibly have an effect on this? It was cruel to raise Noreen's hopes even a little.

'Please, Lil.'

She glanced round. Mr Thistlewood was now standing behind his wife and his eyes were glistening.

The girl took a deep breath. She had to at least try.

'Clarke,' she said again. 'I've brought something for you. Something I made. It's special. I'm going to give it to you now. Keep tight hold and don't let go.'

Very gently she clasped his left hand. It was limp and clammy.

'Be well,' she whispered as she placed the charm in his fingers. Closing her eyes, she tried to summon any power she might have. And then, from some remote place, deep inside, she found her strength and uttered words that weren't her own.

'*By the secret flame within me, that burned before the Three beneath the sea, by moon and steering star, by the legacy of the long sisterhood of witches, I bid thee. Abjure the chains that bind thee close. Stray no longer upon that shadow shore. Heal and be hale. I cast my net and haul thee home. Return to those who love thee dear. So mote it be!*'

Clarke's parents watched anxiously. They saw pinpricks of silver light shine out from the crocheted stitches. Then a radiance welled up in Clarke's hand, glimmering through the veins and bones like moonlight behind winter branches. He heaved a rattling breath.

'Clarke!' Noreen cried, ripping the tea towel from her mouth and rushing forward to hold him.

Lil stepped away, feeling groggy.

'Look!' Mrs Thistlewood called to her husband. 'I'm not imagining it, am I? There's a bit of colour in his cheeks. Oh, Lil, bless you. Thank you!'

Dennis gave the girl a rejoicing hug. 'You're better than any medicine!' he shouted.

'Have you cured him?' asked a familiar voice.

They turned to see Verne, who had finally emerged from his room.

'Come see!' his mother said. 'There's a difference!'

Verne looked at his brother and agreed he appeared less ghastly than before.

'You going to knit a charm for everyone in Whitby then?' he asked Lil. 'Because we're all going to need one. So that'll be, what, over thirteen thousand of them? I know you're fast, but you'll never make that many in time.'

'Verne, what's the matter?' Dennis asked. 'Lil's worked a miracle for your brother.'

The boy stared at Lil and she saw grief and guilt in his eyes as he said, 'That's great for us, it really is, but they've just announced on the news that the two most serious cases have died. One miracle isn't enough.'

Lil choked and clutched his hand for support.

'Dead?' she uttered, aghast. 'Actually dead?'

'And there are other critical patients now,' he said. 'Probably a lot more they don't know about because they've not been able to get round many houses.

They're calling it a plague now.'

Leaving his parents to tend to Clarke, Verne led Lil into his room where she sat on his bed, numb with shock. His computer was streaming live news.

Images of the overcrowded hospital flashed up, then footage of the quarantine barricades on the roads, which were now being guarded by the army.

'We did this,' Verne said. 'We as good as murdered those two people and we're going to kill hundreds if not thousands more.'

'Do your mum and dad know about the paintbox?' Lil asked.

'You joking?'

'You're not to blame at all! You tried to stop me.'

'I could've tried harder. And we both jumped about like monkeys as we watched that yellow filth spread over the town. Can't believe how stupid we were.'

Verne reached into his top drawer and took out the Nimius.

'I shut myself in here because I was trying to see if this could help,' he said. 'Old Pyke must've included a healing function. But I can't work out what symbol it might be, or if you have to press two or more, like this afternoon. Do you think Jack Potts would have a clue?'

'He might.'

'I feel like a caveman trying to start the Hadron Collider.'

Running his fingers over the scrolling gold, Verne stared at the grim news footage on the computer monitor.

'I've been thinking,' he said slowly. 'This isn't a normal plague. I don't think it's something the doctors can cure. What if . . . what if the people who die . . .'

'Please tell me you're not going to mention the z word. This is serious; as serious as it gets.'

'That out there looks pretty apocalyptic to me,' he answered. 'This might be how it starts.'

Lil rose.

'I need to go,' she said. 'I have to talk to Cherry. Maybe there's something she can do, although if there is, she's probably already doing it.'

'Can I come?'

It was a testament to their friendship that Lil didn't hesitate to agree, even though she would have preferred to see Cherry on her own.

Verne hid the Nimius back among his socks and they looked in on Clarke to see how he was doing.

'The fever's going down,' Mrs Thistlewood said, with a relieved smile. 'I can't ever thank you enough, Lil. You saved him. You're an absolute angel.'

The girl lowered her eyes; she didn't deserve any praise.

'And tell your mum I'm sorry,' Noreen continued. 'Soon as I can leave Clarke, I'll go see her and make it up.'

'I'll tell her,' Lil promised. 'Mum's not been herself. She obviously misses you like mad too; you've been friends forever.'

'Be careful on your way home,' Mr Thistlewood cautioned. 'It's got dark early. Want me to drive you?'

'It's only over the river, Dad,' Verne told him. 'Besides, we're both going. We need to see Cherry.'

His parents began to protest, then Dennis caved in and surrendered.

'What's the point?' he said, holding up his hands. 'You two are a law unto yourselves and, one thing I've realised, you're stronger together.'

The children hurried down the stairs and were soon walking through the empty streets. Hearing nothing but the subdued chatter of TV news and the coughing of the sick in the huddled houses, the two friends headed for Cherry's cottage.

'OK, first of all,' Cherry Cerise ordered when she opened her door, 'smack them glum faces clean off, or you don't come in. I know what you're thinking, Lil, doing the whole guilt-trip thing, but forget it. This is not down to you.'

Lil and Verne followed her into the parlour. Papers and books were strewn everywhere and they had to clear a space before they could sit down.

'Of course it's down to me,' Lil disagreed. 'I should've left well alone.'

'Nuh-uh, sweetheart,' Cherry corrected. 'There's no way you could've stopped yourself using that paintbox. I been doing some research. This is one heck of an elaborate multi-hex. It's so complicated I melted my wig trying to get my brain round it. Soon as you touched that thing, you was snared. There was no way you wouldn't have put water on that paint. You was *made* to do it, just as you was made to think it was all your own idea.'

'Made? Why and by who?'

'The "why" is all over the news, honey. This is an attack. But the "who"? Well, that's even more obvious. *They* failed in the spring to destroy this town so now They're having another go. This plague is just the opening barrage to soften us up.'

'You mean the Lords of the Deep and Dark?' asked Lil. 'You're always talking about them, but you never explain who or what they are.'

Cherry eased herself into the hanging wicker chair and put her hands between her knees as she tried to describe the indescribable.

'OK,' she began. 'Forget everything science or religion ever told you about how the universe was made. At the start, all there was was a never-ending emptiness – and the First Mother, who crawled in from outside.'

'Outside?' asked Verne.

'You mean outside this dimension?' said Lil.

'Hun, I'm just repeating a way old tradition, and trying to keep it simple. Call it another dimension, reality, existence, beyond, whatever. Our clumsy words aren't up to the job. Just imagine a creature, galaxies wide. She's called the First Mother because She gave birth, but She impregnated herself, so go figure.'

'Wait, the Lords of the Deep were Her children?' asked Lil.

'Yep, or three of 'em anyways; She kinda splurged out a whole mess of bambinos. That's the cataclysmic event scientists call the Big Bang. The Big Push would be more accurate. Anyway, it killed Her and what the offspring didn't eat – yeah, gross – They formed the universe with.'

'They made the earth?' gasped Verne. 'The solar system?'

'Kick-started it, let it do its own thing, until it got interestin'. Then They moved in and ever since They've played around with it, like kids with plasticine. That's what we're up against: creatures so old, so powerful and terrible, we'd be out of our puny minds to even dream of getting mixed up with Them. We shouldn't even know They exist.'

She paused and raised her eyebrows.

'How we doin' so far?' she asked. 'Handling this OK? I know it's a mind bender.'

Verne shrugged. 'Actually, I think it makes a

funny sort of sense,' he said. 'Well, about as much as everything else around here.'

'So why *are* we mixed up with Them?' Lil asked. 'What is it about Whitby They hate so much?'

'You're looking at her, babe. And of course there's you too now. It's us witches. They really don't dig what They can't control and our sisterhood has been kneein' Them in the tentacles for a long, long time. No one else has ever stood up to Them and gotten away with it.'

'If They're so great and mighty, how has that been possible?' asked Verne.

'Because the feminine energies we call on are the residual echoes of the First Mother's mojo. It's still ricocheting round the cosmos, but for some reason it resonates real strong here in Whitby. The Three got no clout over that, so there's been a wary truce. But every now and then They try to subvert the ancient laws. That's what the paintbox is – the latest sneaky way to cheat the rules. I shoulda realised, but They was devious and played a long game with this one.'

'A Trojan horse,' Verne said.

'Is there anything we can do to stop the sickness?' Lil asked. 'I crocheted a spell of healing for Clarke, but I can't do that for everyone. Surely there's something else we can do?'

'Not till the rest of it plays out,' Cherry answered. 'Like I said, this is a multi-part assault. It won't end till each stage is gone through.'

'The label under the lid!' Verne blurted. 'Remember, it said there was a colour a day and it wouldn't be over till they were all washed away – or something like that.'

'We've got to use up every paint block?' Lil asked in dismay. 'But that's another five days! The sick can't wait that long. And what will the other colours do? The next one along is red. Is that going to be the Red Death? A bloodbath? And what about the black?'

Cherry shook her head. 'I got no answers,' she said. 'We're just gonna have to get through it, face each new threat best we can and hope it don't kill us.'

'If each colour is as bad as the yellow,' Lil murmured, 'it'll be horrific.'

'I know, babe,' Cherry said grimly. 'So we better brace ourselves. The paintbox was created for our humiliation and destruction, so chances ain't lookin' good for us.'

They sat in silence as this frightening prospect hit home. Then Verne stood up.

'We're going to need a good night's sleep if we start on the red paint tomorrow,' he said. 'I'll get on back. What time does it kick off?'

Cherry beamed at him. 'You might look like a stick insect, kid,' she said admiringly, 'but you gotta truckload of guts and you give me hope. I'd like to begin early. Can you be here at 7 a.m?'

He nodded and Lil said that wasn't a problem for her either.

Cherry showed them to the door.

'Almost forgot,' she said, as they were leaving. 'You left that hanky behind earlier. Did you see the initials embroidered on it?'

Taking it from her pocket, she showed it to Lil.

'*N B*,' the girl read. 'Who was that?'

Cherry had already popped back into the parlour and returned with a leather-bound book open at the back page. There was a list of names. Apart from the first three, they were written in different hands.

Batty Crow
Maudie Dodd
Nannie (Nellie) Burdon
Myrtle Warters
Elsie Knaggs
Sylvia de Lacy
Irma Swales
Adeline Weatherill
Alice Boston
Cherry Cerise

'A register of Whitby witches,' Lil guessed.

'Only goes back to the early nineteenth century,' Cherry said, 'but that kinda continuity is real comforting. All those game gals doing their witchin' thing, watching over this town. And that'll be Nannie Burdon's hanky. Some of the names have dates next to them. Hers says 1868–1892. That's her time as resident witch.'

'It's more than comforting,' Verne declared. 'It's proof Lil makes it through this. Those first three names are in her handwriting again.'

'I started this register,' Lil murmured. 'Or rather I'm going to. But what about you, Verne? And you, Cherry? What happens to you?'

'Let's see what this week dishes out to us,' Cherry told her. 'Now you two get that shut-eye and be here on the dot. Sooner we find out what form the next wave of the attack takes, the better.'

Lil parted from Verne in Church Street and they went in opposite directions to return to their homes. When she opened the door of the Wilsons' cottage she smelled the same fetid reek that had fouled Clarke's room and her heart pounded.

Fearfully, she ran into the living room and discovered her mother crouching at her father's side. He was lying on the settee, sweating, and his skin was yellow.

'Where've you been?' Cassandra demanded. 'I found him on the floor when I got back. He could've died here on his own. Where were you? As if I need to ask.'

'Dad!' Lil cried, kneeling beside him. 'Dad, it's OK. I'll witch something for you. I did it for Verne's brother and it's making him better. You'll be OK.'

Her father didn't hear her.

'He will be all right, Mum,' Lil assured her. 'It works, I promise.'

But the expression on Mrs Wilson's face unnerved her.

'What's the matter?' she asked. 'Why are you looking at me like that?'

'If you're going to whip up some magic, then hurry up about it!' Cassandra shouted.

'I need to fetch my knitting bag.'

Flustered, she raced into the hall, and was about to tear upstairs when a violent thumping thundered against the front door.

'Crisis control!' a strident voice shouted outside. 'Let us in or we'll force an entry.'

Bewildered, Lil opened the door and stepped back in alarm at the sight that greeted her.

A figure in an inflated plastic suit, connected to its own portable oxygen supply, filled the doorway. Behind it, taking up the width of the narrow street, was a long white windowless van. Beyond that were four more. Lil heard the neighbouring cottages being hammered upon and the same barking command rang out.

'You got the sickness here?' the unseen face behind a dark visor asked.

Mrs Wilson joined Lil in the hallway. 'My husband,' she said anxiously. 'He's here in the front room. Can

you give him something? Have they found a cure?'

'Anyone else?'

'No.'

The figure stepped away and another inflated suit barged inside, pushing past Lil and her mother to go into the kitchen.

'What are you doing?' Lil challenged. 'You don't need to go in there.'

'Emergency powers,' answered the first. 'We have

the right to search every property to make sure no contagion is being harboured.'

He waved at the nearest van and two more inflated suits appeared from the back, with a stretcher.

'What's that for?' Cassandra asked as they strode inside.

'Who are you?' Lil demanded. 'You're not from the hospital.'

'Name and age of subject?'

'Mike Wilson,' Cassandra answered, distracted by the second figure who had returned from the kitchen and was now going upstairs. 'He's . . . he's forty-one.'

The person in front of her tapped the details and the address into a hand-held device that printed them on to a wide cable tie.

'Leave him!' Lil cried, following the ones with the stretcher into the living room. 'I can make him better!'

They didn't reply and lifted her father off the settee.

'What are you doing?' the girl yelled as they carried him into the hall where the cable tie was fastened round his ankle. 'The hospital is full and no one can leave the town, so where are you taking him?'

'You'll be informed in due course,' the voice behind the visor said as Mr Wilson was removed from the cottage.

'You can't do this!' Lil yelled, forcing her way past the first suit and into the street. 'Those aren't even proper ambulances!'

She was about to go after the stretcher when two figures emerged from the van, bearing assault rifles.

'Remain in your home,' she was ordered.

Lil could tell they weren't bluffing. Along the rest of the street, other victims of the Yellow Scourge were being put inside the windowless vehicles.

'Mum, do something!' she shouted, but Cassandra was too shocked to respond.

When they had done, the vans began reversing and the armed figures retreated backwards, making sure no one followed. Moments later Lil was standing in her doorway, staring at a Henrietta Street that was empty except for bewildered and frightened neighbours.

Lil returned to the house. Her mother was on the settee, a hand on the sweat-stained cushion that had been under her father's head. There was a deadness about her expression that startled and frightened Lil.

'You all right?' the girl asked. 'What are we going to do?'

Mrs Wilson turned a blank face to her.

'I've watched you,' she said quietly, 'taking it all for granted, those amazing, incredible gifts you've been given, powers that you never even wanted, and yes, I can admit it now. I was jealous. More than that, I resented it, so very much. But it's got worse, and I know I'm a terrible, terrible person, because I'm your mum and I should love you whatever, but after what you've done today, I can't. I just can't any more and

I'll never be able to forgive you.'

Lil recoiled. Unable to believe what she was hearing, she sank to the floor.

'What you are,' Cassandra continued, choosing her words carefully and delivering them in a flat, considered monotone, 'it's everything I always wanted, absolutely everything I prayed for. I know I should have been proud of you and I think I truly was, at first. Since then, watching you and Cherry together, sharing that bond with her that I can't ever be a part of, I finally realised . . .'

'What?' Lil whispered, dreading the answer.

Mrs Wilson stared at her as if she was seeing her for the very first time. 'Believe me,' she said. 'I've tried, but I can't fight it any more. I simply can't. The deceit is destroying me.'

'Fight what?' Tears began to fall from Lil's eyes.

'I can't bear to be near you,' came the cold reply. 'Can't even look at you any more. There, I've said it. Such a relief. You being a witch has made me hate you. It's as simple as that.'

Mrs Wilson rose. 'I can't be around you right now,' she said. 'I left that robot up on the cliff so I'm going to fetch him down. We'll need all the help we can get.'

Feeling as though her soul had been torn out, Lil watched her mother go into the hall.

'You can't leave me! Mum!' she cried. 'Tell me you

don't mean any of that. Please! I'm sorry!'

Cassandra left the cottage and Lil doubled over in anguish.

When her phone rang, she fumbled to answer it. 'Mum?'

'It's me, Verne!' the caller replied in a voice as distressed as her own. 'That heart you made – it's turned yellow. Clarke's as bad as he was before.'

Lil closed her eyes.

'And there's a line of white vans pulled up outside,' Verne continued anxiously. 'Guys in creepy protection suits are knocking on all the doors. Some of them have got great big guns! What's happening? What have we done?'

Mrs Wilson made her way to the 199 steps and hurried up them, feeling strangely excited. As she neared the top, she saw the pale grey figure she knew as Queller posing, haughty and heroic, next to the Caedmon Cross.

'You were right!' she said, running up to him. 'I do resent my daughter. I do want you as a spirit guide. Can you help me? They've just taken my husband away. I don't know where. There must be a way to cure this and make everything right again.'

Queller smiled at her.

'If there is,' he promised with warmth in his deep, manly voice, 'then we shall discover it together. But it will be a grim journey and you must not baulk at any of the things we may need to do. You will need courage, lovely lady.'

Mrs Wilson smiled back. Her heart was beating fast, like when she was a teenager. Embarrassed, she looked away and gazed around the churchyard.

'Where are the other ghosts?' she asked.

'Your mechanical servant fell asleep and the link with the spectral plane was severed,' he lied.

'But you're still here.'

'I wanted to meet you again.'

Cassandra saw Jack Potts standing in the deep shadow of the church, some distance away. All his lights were off.

'Must have run out of money,' she said, glad of an excuse to move away from Queller's piercing gaze. 'I'll just go and fix that.'

Taking deep breaths, trying to calm her emotions, she walked the path between the graves until she reached the automaton. His pockets were empty, but she found one ten pence in her own and pushed it into the side of his skull.

The torch eyes flashed on.

'Mistress Wilson,' he greeted her. 'Can I be of assistance?'

'I changed my mind,' she told him. 'You can stay at our place.'

'That is most generous. I thank you.'

'Does the invitation extend to me?' Queller asked.

Mrs Wilson bit her lip. 'Of course,' she said, her heart pounding again.

'In that case, we must perform a small ritual of bonding that will cleave my spirit unto you. Otherwise I will not be able to leave the confines of this churchyard.'

'What sort of ritual?'

He beamed at her. 'To seal our pact with a drop of your sweet blood upon my phantom lips. It is the bridge that will allow me to follow you anywhere.'

'My blood on your lips?' she repeated, her skipping heart in her mouth.

'Just a thumb prick, no more. A taste only.'

'OK,' she agreed.

'Allow me to be of assistance,' Jack Potts offered. 'My forefinger is as sharp as a knife. One deft nick and it will be done.'

Cassandra offered her upturned hand to him. The automaton took it in his cold metal grasp. She held her breath and waited, turning to the entrancing features of Queller beside her.

'No, wait!' she said, slipping deeper into his power. 'Not there – not my thumb.'

She unfastened the collar of her cloak. With one hand, she pulled the neck of her top clear and with the other pressed the forefinger against her skin.

'There,' she said.

The torch eyes shone on her exposed throat. An instant later a dribble of bright red blood was trickling down to her shoulder.

Queller moved close.

'You have a pretty neck,' he said.

She tilted her head back and held her breath. His spectral arms wrapped round her and she felt his lips touch her flesh, like a whispering winter kiss.

'Blood is the bridge,' he said softly in her ear. 'Now I am yours to command, and you are mine.'

Lil slept badly. She had stayed up into the night, crocheting more hearts for Clarke and now her father. She made five for each, trying to pour as much power into them as she could. If only she knew where the two of them had been taken.

She was still awake at 3 a.m. when she heard her mother return. Lil pulled the covers over her head, too drained for another hideous confrontation. She didn't know how she could ever face her again. Lying in the dark, she wished Sally would visit and comfort her, but it was one of those nights when the furry blanket on the bed remained empty. Eventually Lil fell into an unpleasant sleep, in which she dreamed a shadowy stranger looked into her room, only to be called away by her mother.

At a quarter past six, the whirring din of a helicopter outside jolted her awake. Then an amplified voice rattled the window.

'Residents of Whitby, do not be alarmed.'

Lil sprang out of bed and dragged the curtains back, just in time to see a naval helicopter fly low over the roof.

'Emergency medical centres have been set up in public buildings where the sick have been taken. Everything possible is being done to help. Do not panic. Further bulletins will be broadcast throughout the day.'

The helicopter swept over the East Cliff, blaring the same recording, before swinging round and repeating it across the river. At the end of the stone piers, at the mouth of the harbour, two flagpoles had been erected, each flying the black and yellow quarantine flag known as the Yellow Jack.

Five minutes later Lil was downstairs, the paintbox tucked under her arm. Before she could slip out, Jack Potts stepped in front of the door.

'Good morning, Mistress Lil,' he said. 'Did the aircraft wake you? Such a quantity of decibels. Shall I prepare breakfast? It is important to commence the day with adequate nutrition.'

The torch eyes glanced at the object under her arm.

'Is that the box of watercolours? Where are you going with it?'

'Never you mind,' Lil said, looking up the stairs and wondering how her mother could have slept through the racket. 'If Mum asks, not that she will, say you haven't seen me.'

Jack Potts nodded.

'Hey, I'm glad you're back,' she told him, managing a weak smile as she left the cottage.

He watched her set off down the street, then closed the door.

'Good luck, Mistress Lil,' he said quietly.

Verne was already at Cherry's when she got there. He hadn't had much sleep either.

'Mum and Dad are driving around, trying to find Clarke,' he told her. 'They're going to all the schools and church halls that've been turned into emergency wards. Mum's out of her mind with worry.'

'Madness is what it is,' Cherry said, serving up three cups of steaming green tea. 'No need for all that brutality. Ain't the folks in this town frightened out of their wits already? They broke down Gregson's door last night and gave the moaning old bag the screaming abdabs. She walloped them with her stick, but they still took her away because of her age. One of them stormed in here too. I came real close to filling his protective suit with extra hot chilli sauce.'

Lil placed the paintbox on the coffee table.

'Before we do this,' she said, 'I need to find my dad. I made more hearts last night. Even though they don't last long, it would help him for a while. I've got some for Clarke too.'

'I know this is tough for you, Lil,' Cherry told her,

with a stern shake of the head, 'but we don't have time for that. We gotta get through this next stage, soon as we can. After that, you got all day. Now drink your tea. It'll keep you sharp.'

Agitated, Lil drained the cup. She wanted to tell them about what had happened with her mother, but decided that would have to wait too.

'Ready?' Cherry asked.

The children nodded.

Lil opened the paintbox. There was nothing to suggest it was anything other than an old set of watercolours, and that made it worse somehow. The bright, cheerful pigment blocks were deceiving, betraying no sign of the malevolence that had gone into their creation. She hesitated a moment, then removed the red pigment from its compartment. Turning it over, she read, '*Carmine Swarm.*'

'And the little image on the front is a beetle,' Cherry observed. 'Okey-dokey, then I think we know what to expect from this one. As far back as ancient Egypt, they got the best red dye from squishin' a certain type of insect. Still goes on today, and it's in just about everything – just ask my make-up bag.'

'So this one won't be another virus?' asked Verne.

'Who knows?' Cherry answered. 'Bound to be gross whatever it is. OK, Lil – paint the town red.'

Lil took up the paintbrush and stirred it in the tumbler of water Cherry had brought in with the tea.

'Wait a minute,' the witch said. 'Let me call up some protection for us first. Take my hands.'

She closed her eyes and the walls of her parlour became a velvety purple. The air smelled faintly of violets and the children felt their fingertips tingle and the hairs on their neck rise.

Cherry exhaled and sucked her teeth critically. 'That was kinda sluggish,' she declared, annoyed with herself. 'Must be getting rusty. Go ahead, Lil, let's boogie.'

Lil put the fancy paintbrush to the watercolour block and swirled it around. Verne flinched in anticipation and gripped hold of Cherry's hand.

'Here we go,' she said.

The paintbox began to vibrate, emitting a low hum. Then, out of the red pigment crawled a small, ladybird-like insect. It climbed over the lid and rested, as if the effort had been too much.

'Doesn't look too bad so far,' Verne said, watching the creature slowly hinge open its outer wings.

The hum grew louder, becoming a fierce buzzing.

Cherry slapped her forehead. 'I'm such a doofus!' she yelled above the angry noise. 'We shoulda done this in the yard!'

It was too late to take the paintbox outside. It rattled and jumped violently, cracking the smoked glass table top beneath it. The horrendous din peaked and the red paint block burst apart as millions of flying beetles erupted into the parlour.

A never-ending torrent of them gushed into the air. Within moments the room was in darkness, all light choked by countless insects. The noise of their tiny wings was deafening.

Lil let go of Cherry's hand and almost screamed, but she didn't want them to fly into her mouth. She pinched her nose while hundreds more buzzed into her ears. They clung to her lashes and infested her hair, dropping down her collar and flying up the legs of her jeans.

Verne *had* opened his mouth and was coughing and spitting out the dozens he hadn't accidentally swallowed, while slapping and scraping them off his face.

Cherry still had hold of his other hand. She pulled him towards the hall, groping blindly through the almost solid flying fog, squishing and crunching thousands underfoot as they went.

The zooming cloud wasn't as thick in the hallway yet, and a dim path of light could still be seen, filtering through the coloured glass in the front door. But that small window was quickly disappearing under a seething curtain. Cherry pushed Verne towards it, then stumbled back into the parlour for Lil.

It was pitch-dark in there. A torturous, droning hell, crammed from floor to ceiling with teeming life. Cherry could only feel her way forward. Every surface was buried beneath scuttling mountains and after a few steps she was completely lost and disorientated. But there was no trace of Lil.

Anxious, Cherry pressed on. She cracked her knee on the chaise longue, then almost tripped over a cushion. Halting, she crouched quickly. Reaching out, she realised it was no cushion. Lil was lying on the floor, completely covered.

Cherry grabbed her and dragged her into the hallway, praying she wasn't too late. Then she lifted the girl in her arms and ran to the now open front door.

Verne was kneeling on the ground outside, frantically smacking and brushing the beetles off himself. He was covered in red splotches and looked like he'd been in a terrible accident. Glancing up from his crimson hands, he saw Cherry come staggering from the cottage.

'Lil!' he bawled.

Cherry laid the girl on the ground and they urgently scooped the beetles off her face. She was motionless.

'Lil! Lil!' Cherry called, shaking the girl. 'Come

back to us, honey. Come on, you're not checkin' out yet.'

Just as Verne thought Lil was never going to recover, she suddenly spluttered and spat out a fist-sized clot of squirming beetles. Yelling in disgust, she leaped up and ran around the yard, thrashing her arms and legs.

Cherry kissed the ammonites on her bracelet in thanks and smiled at Verne, but the boy was staring over her shoulder. Cherry followed his dumbfounded gaze.

Issuing from her front door was a dark river. The mass of flying insects soared up like a column of thick smoke. When it was chimney high, it spread outwards, swelling like a menacing storm. A cold shadow reached across the narrow streets of the East Cliff as the buzzing cloud expanded, stretching towards the bridge. And still incalculable numbers surged from the cottage.

Lil raked her fingers through her hair and shivered in revulsion. She was drenched in vibrant red, as though she had been swimming in blood. Blinking up at the mounting threat above, she rejoined Verne and Cherry.

'I thought you put protection around us!' she barked.

Cherry was cleaning her sunglasses. She looked tired.

'Did either of you two get bit or stung?' she asked.

'No,' Lil said.

'Nor me,' added Verne.

'Then you were protected,' Cherry told them. 'The rest of the town won't be so lucky.'

Lil stared with fresh horror at the beetle-filled sky.

'They're going to attack?' she murmured.

'I'd bet my signed Hendrix shirt on it.'

'We have to warn everyone!' Lil cried.

Cherry looked at her front door: the raging flood was beginning to thin.

'Too late,' she said.

'We must do something!' said Lil. 'Think, Cherry! There must be a way.'

'I can't throw protection over the whole of Whitby!' Cherry answered testily. 'What we need is . . .'

'Is what?'

Cherry stared at her keenly.

'We need a wild, ragged witch,' she told her. 'Someone really plugged into Momma Nature, who can sing up a wind. Real old-school primitive. We need Scaur Annie.'

Lil edged back. 'What do you mean?' she asked nervously. 'Annie is gone. We laid her ghost to rest.'

'Yeah, but she gave you some of her gifts. There might be something we can use, locked up in that head of yours. If I could . . .'

'Not your party piece!' the girl protested.

'Sorry, hun,' Cherry said, her pale blue eyes blazing brightly. 'I weren't asking. This is my job. Now let me see what else that seventeenth-century gal left behind.

Don't struggle – you just make it worse for yourself.'

Cherry's eyes burned even more fiercely and Verne watched his best friend go limp. He had never seen Cherry do this before and it panicked and frightened him. Then, with a cold, sick feeling in his stomach, he realised the last of the insects had flown from her cottage. The massed cloud above was complete.

On the outskirts of Whitby, beyond the barricades, the assembled TV crews were setting up for the first report of the day. The mystery epidemic was still confounding experts. Inexplicably, even the emergency teams that had gone in wearing protection suits had suffered casualties, so none of the rest were allowed out again. Whitby was in strict lockdown and no more teams would be sent in.

Protest groups had started to gather, and makeshift camps were set up within sight of the tanks and armoured vehicles that now patrolled the boundary. Activists objected to the draconian treatment of those trapped within the town. But, until the pathogen had been identified, containment was the only defence. Whitby was a sealed no-go zone.

As the news crews prepared to go on air, they spotted a dark plume snaking up from the East Cliff. Was it a fire? Lenses rapidly zoomed in and someone yelled that it looked more like a colossal swarm of insects. The media watched in dumb fascination as a broad cloud formed above the town. When it had spread so far as to cast its shadow on the West Cliff, it hung menacingly in the morning air, as if waiting. A cable news channel launched a drone to get closer aerial footage.

Then, suddenly, the cloud burst, spilling down upon the streets like heavy, torrential rain.

Even far away, the screams could be heard.

Hovering over the rooftops, the camera drone captured the nightmarish scene in high definition. The Whitby residents that were out, visiting the emergency medical centres, were pursued down the narrow streets. Thick formations hunted them, surrounding their screeching heads, biting with sharp, tiny jaws. Panic and terror were everywhere. The drone flew lower, over the swing bridge, towards the West Cliff. The image became swamped with blurred shapes hurtling past, as its course cut through the path of a large swarm. In moments the drone was totally covered in a thick layer of insects. It faltered in the air. The four propellers scythed through hundreds of angry bodies and scarlet rain drizzled down, before the grotesque numbers clogged the blades and stopped them spinning. The drone toppled from the sky and splashed into the river.

From the safety of the barricades, the news teams watched with disbelief. Then they saw that the helicopter was approaching the town from the sea, to broadcast an updated bulletin.

'Call them back!' the reporters yelled. 'Get that thing out of there!'

The colonel in charge of the armed presence radioed the helicopter's ship that was anchored a mile out to sea, but it was no use.

As the aircraft flew over the harbour, the many separate swarms regrouped, forming an almost solid monstrous mass. With nauseating speed and hideous purpose, it rushed towards the helicopter and swallowed it whole.

Engulfed within that furious horde, the noise of the rotor blades changed. They chugged and juddered and the engine screeched and whined. A vivid red trail poured into the waters below as the helicopter lost control. Spinning free of the seething cloud, it plummeted down, crashing on to the rocks of the Scaur. A ball of searing flame erupted against the cliff.

The news crews turned back to the cameras, ashenfaced.

The hashtag #PrayforWhitby began to trend.

8

Stepping into Lil's mind, Cherry Cerise moved through a dreamlike, warped vision of Whitby. It was bathed in silver moonlight that sparkled over diamond-dusted cobbles. The streets were narrower here and the buildings leaned in overhead. All was crooked and oversized, and large knitted decorations festooned the eaves like bunting.

Strange creatures sat in shop windows, waving and pulling faces. Many were cartoonish caricatures of the owners; others were freaky distortions of what they sold. Gibbering clown masks crowded the joke shop, pressing rubbery noses against the glass.

The bookshop was filled with flocks of flying books, flapping their pages against the panes. In the jewellery and clothing shops, shadowy images of Lil were trying on outfits and necklaces, and admiring themselves in distorting mirrors. An obese and spotty Lil was guzzling the contents of the fudge shop.

Cherry chuckled as a teacup the size of a bath came clattering down the street, chased by a Whitby Lemon Bun as large as an armchair. Then she passed the opening that led to her own cottage. It pulsed with welcoming rosy light and she could hear her favourite 1970s music drifting on the air, combined with gales of laughter. A selection of her beloved kinky boots and platform shoes were grooving on down in the alleyway.

Touched and flattered by this mental image, the colour witch hurried on. Some of the other alleys contained watching, huddled figures that whispered the word 'freak' or sniggered when she went by, but they were just manifestations of everyday paranoia and Cherry ignored them.

When she came to the 199 steps, she smiled. In this mindscape they were an escalator that smoothly ascended a vastly enlarged cliffside, where giant gravestones jutted like wonky teeth and the abbey was a craggy crown, with pinnacles that ripped the moonlit clouds.

She passed into Henrietta Street. The change here was abrupt and startling. It felt cold. There were no more knitted decorations. Ugly faces and cruel names were scrawled on the walls and the shadows were impenetrable and intimidating. When Cherry saw the Wilsons' cottage she caught her breath. Lil's home was a forbidding castle, with turrets and battlements and dimly lit slits for windows. A shrill voice was yelling inside.

'You might have killed your father! You're nothing to me. I wish you'd never been born! I want nothing to do with you! Keep away from me! You're worthless! Are you listening? You ruined my life! I hate what you are! You're disgusting! Hate you . . . hate you!'

The front door swung open and a caricature of Mrs Wilson stormed out. She was dressed in a widow's gothic finery with her hair piled on top of her head, elaborately entwined with black roses and sable ribbons, and a veil covering her tearful eyes. She got into a waiting horse-drawn carriage and departed, her accusations echoing through the streets with the sound of the horses' hooves.

'What was that about?' Cherry murmured, taken aback. 'Land sakes, Lil, what's been goin' on with you at home?'

Inside the grim castle she could hear a girl sobbing, but there wasn't time to investigate this private wound. Cherry turned round and looked across the harbour. A glittering palace, ablaze with friendly light, towered over the quayside. It was the Thistlewoods' arcade, where a small figure holding something large and golden was flying overhead, squealing and whooping with joy.

Cherry lowered her gaze to where a fluffy white dog was scampering over Tate Hill Sands, chasing and playing with a much younger version of Lil.

'Come on,' Cherry urged herself. 'Annie's gotta be here someplace. There must be a bit of her left behind.'

It was then she heard the singing. There, down on the rocks, was the shadowy shape of a slim woman, with a tangle of hair, paddling through the shallows.

> '*Does I love a bonnie sailor, or shepherd?*
> *No sir.*
> *Did I kiss the brave young soldier lad I met at*
> *Scarborough Fair?*
> *And farm boys and fishermen, they all to me*
> *would woo,*
> *But I'll laugh and snap my fingers, a Lord*
> *alone will do.*'

'Gotcha!' said Cherry, and she ran over to her.

Annie stopped singing.

'You doesn't belong in this place,' she scolded, not bothering to look up. 'Poaching and trespass, that's what it is.'

'Right back atcha,' Cherry replied.

'Nay. This daughter of Whitby is gone; she's with her gentleman now and evermore. What you see is just a parcel of dusty old thoughts, remnants wrapped in her shape. Nothing more.'

'OK, so you're a walking scrapbook. Whatever you are, Whitby needs you.'

'You wear the snake stones now. The town is under your care, not mine.'

'Get real, Annie, you know it don't work like that. You can't split from your responsibilities so easy. As the incumbent witch, I'm ordering you to get your dirty cockle toes outta here and help us.'

Annie raised her eyes. Her stare was keen and piercing. 'You know the danger if I do,' she warned gravely. 'These lingering shreds were never meant to cloud the girl's waking thoughts. She might never be the same.'

'That's a risk I have to take.'

'The choice is not yours.'

'As long as Whitby is my business, it sure is. So put your ragged booty in gear, sister. We have to leave this minute.'

*

As the helicopter fuel blazed black and orange up the cliffside, and the horde of flying beetles swung back to torment the town, Verne stood before Cherry's cottage, waiting and watching anxiously.

The colour witch exhaled abruptly and she coughed and fought for breath. Exhausted, she put on her sunglasses with shaking hands.

'Hey, you in there,' she told the girl. 'Wake up. Come on, snap out of it.'

Very slowly, Lil lifted her face, her eyes lightly closed. She raked her fingers through her hair and tossed her head. Then she opened her eyes and Verne gasped as a cunning, feral sharpness animated her features.

'Who's that?' he cried in alarm. 'Where's Lil?'

The girl grinned at him, then jerked her head around, taking in her surroundings. The courtyard was heaving with zooming insects. They battered against windows and clustered around doorways, creeping through gaps to fly inside and attack. For every beetle swatted and squashed, five more buzzed in to take its place, their tiny razor mouths greedily slicing through human skin, or squirting acid that blistered and burned. Whitby was filled with screams of pain and fear.

'Can you do it, Annie?' Cherry asked urgently. 'Call up a wind to drive them into the sea?'

The girl shook her head. ''Tis no weather charm

you're wanting,' she said in a voice that was nothing like Lil's. 'Be an army you need – but I know where to find one.'

She leaped away, darting with animal swiftness through the alley and into Church Street.

Verne grabbed hold of Cherry's arm. 'Where's Lil?' he snapped.

'She's still in there!' Cherry assured him. 'Don't worry. She'll be back, soon as Annie's done.'

'She'd better be!' the boy answered angrily as he set off after her.

The cobbles of Whitby were stained a vibrant red where insects had been crushed by lurching feet, like the grisly aftermath of some mass slaughter.

Verne saw Lil's possessed figure ahead of him. She had thrown off her shoes and was jumping down on to Tate Hill Sands.

The boy hesitated when he saw the black smoke pouring into the sky in the distance. The buckled rotor blades of the helicopter made it look like a giant burning spider. He shuddered, wondering if the pilot had got out alive.

Dragging his eyes away from the wreckage, he gazed out across the town. The West Cliff was blanketed in a huge dark smear of tormenting insects.

On the beach below, Annie had taken up a stick of driftwood and was drawing shapes in the sand.

Verne stopped himself going down to her. The

shapes she traced weren't random squiggles, they were signs, painstakingly executed, and she sang strange-sounding words over each one. When the beach was completely inscribed, she hurled the stick into the water and twirled around, skipping between the images, humming and whistling, making dramatic and specific gestures with her arms.

'What's she doing?' he asked when Cherry caught up with him.

'It's a summoning. Those are witchmarks, a sort of nature alphabet used for conjuring. There's a few examples in my books, but I don't have a clue about the meaning. Be surprised if anyone today knows . . . Ow!' She slapped her arm. A beetle had bitten her.

'Your protection is wearing off,' Verne said. 'We should get inside.' He flinched as an insect flew into his face and another bit the back of his neck.

'Shouldn't wear off so soon,' Cherry declared. 'What's with me today?'

On the sand, Annie gave a great shout, threw herself round like a spinning top, then flung herself down, arms outstretched.

'Is it done?' Verne asked, smacking the side of his head and crunching several beetles at once. 'Is Lil coming back now?'

The colour witch didn't know, and the bites were becoming more frequent.

'We gotta get out of this!' she cried. 'We'll be eaten

alive. Go down and get her.'

But Annie had already picked herself up.

'Come, my loves!' she called. 'Come, dine.'

'Who's she talking to?' Verne asked.

Cherry brushed the bright hair of her wig away from her ears. Amid the vibrating drone of the insects there was a new sound, one that grew louder with each moment.

'Glory be,' she breathed, then spat out the seven beetles that flew into her mouth.

Tens of thousands of seabirds came squawking round the cliffs in a chaotic, clamorous riot. The tremendous draught of their wings scattered the oily smoke rising from the helicopter. Rushing down the valley was an even greater multitude of sparrows, finches, blackbirds, pigeons, crows and starlings. They were joined by a host of herons, geese and ducks, and a squadron of swans swooped down on to the river, their voices like hoarse bugles declaring war.

Verne had never seen so many birds.

They immediately set about gorging themselves, diving and darting with their beaks and bills wide open, scooping and guzzling great quantities of insects. He almost felt like cheering.

'That's what I call an army,' Cherry murmured with an admiring nod. 'You did good, Annie.'

The feast raged on. Windows and doors were flung open by overjoyed townsfolk and the feathered liberators were welcomed into every invaded home, where the rooms were swiftly cleared. It was a tumultuous, frenzied blowout.

A flock of chattering starlings circled Cherry and Verne, striking with expert accuracy at the beetles that clung to their clothes. The boy held very still. One of them squared up to his ear and glared inside, then scooted across his shoulders and did the same to the other. The next thing Verne knew it was on top of his head, searching through his hair. When he saw two more weaving in and out of Cherry's nylon tresses, he laughed and the one on his head flew off in annoyance.

Annie left the beach and clambered up to join them. All three stared at the glad, gluttonous uproar rampaging across Whitby. It was an incredible, exuberant display, but it lasted only as long as the birds were hungry. Yet there were still festering patches of beetles streaking through the air, encrusting the rigging of fishing boats and creeping out from the cover of pantiles.

A crease lined Cherry's brow, but at that moment unexpected reinforcements arrived to finish the task. Bats from every tunnel, cave, church roof, attic and barn around Whitby braved the daylight and flitted over the town, performing incredible feats of aerial agility as they caught and devoured the juicy banquet's leftovers. Annie rocked on her bare heels and grinned proudly.

'The ragged witch knowed a thing or two,' she boasted. 'None can gainsay that. And she had better friends than people, just see if she didn't.'

Verne turned his delighted face away from the bats and frowned at the girl.

'Time for Lil to come back to us now,' he told her.

'Annie won't be put in them shadows again,' she refused, with a defiant gleam in her eye. ''Tis grand to feel proper sand 'twixt the toes, smell the brine and have the sun on your neck. Annie won't give it up again.'

Cherry removed her sunglasses.

Annie tried to run, but Verne caught hold of her arms. She twisted, snatched at his hand and bit him. The boy yelled. Cherry grabbed her shoulders and held her firm.

'Whoa now, you ain't goin' no place. You're just shreds and scraps of Annie's memories, not the real deal. We're mighty grateful for what you just did, but don't try claim jumpin'.'

'I don't want to be scraps no more!' Annie answered. 'I want this! I want proper life!'

'What you'll get is me jumpin' in there again to kick your bony behind into touch and lock you in a memory dungeon so deep you won't never climb out. Don't think I wouldn't!'

Annie struggled, but Cherry's eyes began to shine fiercely.

'Do them tricks while you can!' Annie said

angrily. 'Soon you won't be able to do owt! What use is a colour witch with no colours left in her? Go on, have your little witch girl, but she won't never be the same. I'll stay by her closer than before, crouching and waiting and, when she's weakest, I'll take over!'

Cherry gripped her more tightly than ever, a confused and scared look on her face.

'What does she mean?' Verne cried, nursing his hand. 'Get rid of her. Bring Lil back!'

'No colours?' Cherry repeated. 'Make sense. What are you talking about?'

Annie laughed at her. ''Tis under your nose, yet you don't see it. But then you're blind to most matters. You haven't unpuzzled it yet, have you? Not a whisper of a guess who it is standing behind the pain and loss and dealing out your ruin.'

'Who is it?' Cherry demanded.

Annie grinned and closed her eyes. 'Oh,' she said, 'you'll know him right enough, when he unmasks himself. He's come back.'

'Who has?'

But Annie went limp and almost sank to the ground. Verne helped Cherry support her.

'Tell me!' Cherry shouted.

'She's gone,' Verne said, staring searchingly into the unconscious girl's face. The wild, primitive edge had softened into the features he recognised.

'Lil,' he called. 'Lil. Can you hear me? Lil? It's Verne. Come back. Wake up.'

'She'll be OK,' Cherry promised.

'You don't know that. You had no right to barge into her mind and let that Annie person loose. No right at all!'

'What else was I supposed to do, kid? It worked, didn't it? She just needs to rest awhile. Let's carry her home. Grab her legs.'

The Wilsons' cottage was nearby. Jack Potts opened the door to them and they laid Lil upon the sofa.

'This calls for a strong pot of tea,' the automaton said. 'It will refresh and revive Mistress Lil when she awakens.'

'Did none of those beetles get in here?' Verne asked, looking round at the living room. 'I can't see any red splats.'

'We were mercifully spared,' Jack Potts answered. 'Doubtless they would have reached us in due course.'

'Lil's mom not in?' Cherry asked, wondering why Mrs Wilson hadn't rushed to see her daughter.

'I believe she is attending to her attire. One moment – I think that is her tread on the stair now.'

Cherry's eyes narrowed. 'Well, pardon us for interrupting her titivating,' she muttered under her breath.

Heavy footsteps clumped down to the hall, and Cassandra Wilson swept into the living room.

Even Verne raised his eyebrows. All his life he had been used to seeing Lil's mother in her goth gear, but he had never seen her dolled up to this extent before.

Mrs Wilson's eye make-up was an elaborate work of art, with five separate colours spiralling out around the dramatic, thick black liner. Her lips were a deep, dark purple and her hair framed her face in rigidly lacquered waves. She was wearing one of her most expensive velvet bodices trimmed with ruffles of beaded black lace. A broad choker bearing a cameo made of jet was around her neck and a cloak that matched her lipstick, fastened with a silver moon brooch, draped from her shoulders.

'Holy Liberace!' Cherry declared. 'How come you're all trussed up like Frankenstein's Easter egg?'

Cassandra regarded her with barely concealed contempt.

'What's the matter with Lil?' she asked, casting a cursory glance at the sofa.

'Your daughter's had a shock; the whole of Whitby has. Or did you miss what went down out there just now?'

'I was otherwise engaged. Have you been causing more misery?'

'Are you for real? You're not tellin' me you were so engrossed tarting up your face, you didn't know what was goin' on?'

'In case you didn't know,' Cassandra replied acidly, 'because of you and my daughter messing about with things you don't understand and can't control, my husband is extremely sick and was taken away last night. I'm on my way to him now and I wanted to look my best. I don't suppose the likes of you would understand that.'

'The likes of me?'

'You have no family, do you? No one to care about, no one close.'

Cherry bit her tongue.

'Potts will see you to the door,' Cassandra said coldly. 'He can attend to Lil. You don't need to hang around. Verne can stay, if he wants.'

'You kickin' me out?'

'As I see it, you're directly responsible for the deaths of everyone who has died of this disgusting sickness. Why would I want you in my house? Leave now or I'll get Potts to eject you. I'm sure he's quite capable of using force if necessary.'

Cherry took a calming breath, sensing all was not as it appeared to be. Something had happened to Cassandra Wilson. She may have always been a silly and muddle-headed amateur, but now . . . there was a flinty confidence about her and Cherry couldn't work out where it came from. She stared hard at her for a moment then turned to leave.

'Look after Lil, kiddo,' she instructed Verne, who

was just as stunned by Mrs Wilson's behaviour. The boy nodded distractedly.

Cassandra stood aside as Cherry pushed by to go to the front door, where Jack Potts was already waiting to show her out.

Cherry paused before leaving and turned back.

'Whatever it is,' she said to Mrs Wilson, eyeing her up and down, 'I'd stop now, while you can – unless it's too late already.'

'Don't come back here,' Cassandra said, and the threat was unmistakable. 'It wouldn't be sensible.'

Cherry made her way back to her cottage. An ambulance and fire engine hurried through the narrow streets of the East Cliff, on their way to attend the downed helicopter. They were followed by a police car that stopped outside the alleyway leading to Cherry's cottage.

She had only just returned home when Inspector Lucas knocked on the open door and entered without waiting to be invited.

'Miss Cerise,' the inspector addressed her. His stern face was peppered with acid blisters and tiny bites and he could barely contain his anger.

'Walk right in, why don'tcha?' she said. 'Goin' to throw me in the slammer because you think this is all my fault?'

'Your tone is not appropriate, Miss Cerise. Twenty-seven people are now dead of the sickness, with a lot more expected to follow, and there were three crew on board that helicopter. Four of my officers are gravely ill and, without any backup from outside, I can predict the rule of law is going to break down pretty quickly here. So yes, I will formally ask you: is it your fault?'

'Sorry to disappoint, but no.'

'Then who is responsible? For pity's sake, this has got to stop! If you're withholding information . . .'

'Inspector, I wish I had nice easy answers for you, I truly do, but more people are gonna die and there's nothing anyone can do to stop that. And, you know, hasslin' me really ain't the smartest move, cos I'm the only hope you got. Besides, the bad guys behind this are way outside your league and jurisdiction. I think there's a human agent working with them, but I'm not a hundred per cent sure who that is yet.'

'If you even suspect someone . . .'

'I wouldn't tell you. This isn't some ordinary felony case. You got no idea what's involved and if you did you'd soil your uniform. You just gotta let me deal with it, cos that's what I'm here for. So thanks for the visit, but don't get in my way or more people are gonna get hurt than is necessary.'

'Actually, Miss Cerise,' the inspector said, not bothering to hide his animosity, 'the reason I came here was to warn you. Local feeling is running high and many people are already blaming you for this.

If things turn ugly, I don't have enough officers to protect you.'

'Then call a freakin' town meeting and get the mayor and councillor Jennifer Icypants Pidd to do their jobs and put people straight.'

'I'd like to do that very much, Miss Cerise. Unfortunately, both of them died last night. Good day.'

Cherry watched him leave. 'I hate a pithy, slap-in-the-face exit line,' she said. 'But I hate what is happening to this little town a whole lot more.'

She shook herself. The strain was beginning to wear her down, but there was so much to do.

Climbing the stairs, she went into her spare room. It contained two wardrobes and one wall was covered in hats. On top of a brightly painted dresser, with different coloured drawers, was a cage.

Cherry tapped the wire framework and something stirred in the straw.

'Hey, Ziggy,' she said, opening the small door. 'You up for a spot of snoopin'?'

A mouse's small furry face emerged and stared up at her. Cherry removed her sunglasses and her eyes shone brightly.

9

'Breakfast tea,' Jack Potts said, bowing to deliver a rather lovely cup on its saucer to Lil who had finally come round. 'An ideal reviver, with two sugars for shock.'

'This was my nan's special china,' she said, sitting up. 'No one uses this. It's too precious.'

'A fine example of Royal Worcester, with gold frilled edges and a most enchanting chime to the porcelain, like a sweet little bell. It should be used regularly, not hidden away in the corner of a cupboard.'

'Put it back after this, yeah? And carefully – my nan loved it.'

'How are you feeling?' Verne interrupted.

Lil blew across the steaming tea.

'Escoimus,' she answered.

'Nauseous, queasy,' Jack Potts translated.

'But I'll be OK. Did it work?'

'Don't you remember?'

'Only bits, like a fading dream. Did we get rid of all those insects?'

'If any got away, they'll be too few to worry about. You totally saved the town.'

'I didn't. Annie's memory did. Where's Cherry?'

'Your mum sent her packing.'

'What?'

'They had a bit of a barney. I don't want to sound horrible or rude or anything, but your mum was a bit . . . strange.'

Cassandra's callous words the previous night came into Lil's mind. The pain of them was still raw.

'Where is she now?' she asked quietly.

It was Jack Potts who answered.

'Mistress Wilson has gone to be with your father.'

'She knows where Dad is? Where?'

'In the ballroom of the Royal Hotel. Apparently the hotel has been commandeered as an overflow hospital.'

'I spoke to my mum half an hour ago,' Verne added. 'Clarke's there too.'

Lil put the cup down without finishing her tea and jumped up.

'Let's get there then!' she cried. 'I can help them!'

Once Lil had fetched her knitting bag, the two friends rushed out of the cottage. Jack Potts emitted a mechanical sigh, plumped up the squashed settee cushions and took the porcelain cup into the kitchen where he emptied, washed and dried it.

Opening a cupboard to return it and the saucer, he paused, held the cup close to the window and gazed at the sunlight glowing through the fine china. Then he tapped it with one of his metal fingers and his eyes dimmed as he listened to the pure ring.

'If I had a soul,' he said wistfully, 'this would be its eternal joy. A vessel fit to hold ambrosia, for goddesses to drink from. What everyday marvels and wonders humankind is capable of. Small perfections, that is where great happiness is found . . . do you not agree, Miss Cerise?'

He turned to the kitchen table where a mouse with pale blue eyes was watching him from the shelter of the fruit bowl. Caught in the glare of the robot's bright lenses, the mouse hesitated a moment, then darted away, scooting down the furthest leg and disappearing under a cupboard.

Jack Potts hummed to himself, set the cup down on the window ledge and admired it some more.

*

Lil and Verne made their way through the town, anxious to reach the Royal Hotel. The scarlet-stained streets were busy with people doing the same as them, trying to find their loved ones. Others were panic-buying food and essentials from the few shops that had opened and were lugging swollen bags back to their homes.

Even though Cherry had insisted it wasn't her fault, Lil couldn't help feeling that it was. All the deaths, the horror and misery were down to her; she had set the whole thing in motion. It made her mother's cruel rejection all the more terrible, because she was right.

Hurrying over the river, they cut across the snaking Khyber Pass, clambering up the steep banks. The winding road had been cut into the cliff in Victorian times by the intrepid George Hudson, 'The Railway King', so that the building materials for his splendid hotel and ambitious Royal Crescent could be transported more easily. The crescent was only half completed, because he ran out of money, but the Royal Hotel was still a grand and stately edifice, overlooking the harbour.

Several of the long white vans that had been so alarming last night were parked outside the main entrance and concerned visitors were hastening in and out of the hotel.

Lil and Verne made their way inside and covered their noses immediately. The stench of the sickness was almost unbearable.

The hotel's reception area had been turned into a triage room, with one fraught and exhausted looking junior doctor trying to assess as many people as possible, and either allocate them space in the makeshift wards or send them home if their condition wasn't too extreme or life-threatening. The fresh cases that morning were mainly bites and blisters, with one broken arm, which had occurred trying to escape the Carmine Swarm. The Yellow Scourge patients were already packed into the rooms beyond.

The children slipped through. The hotel bar and restaurant had been cleared of furniture and every guest room had been robbed of its mattress and chairs of their cushions. They now covered the floor, leaving narrow aisles between tightly crammed rows. Most of the hotel staff had been struck down with the sickness, so it was left to the frazzled manager and one chambermaid to try and keep the place disinfected, but it was an endless task. Three nuns from the local convent had volunteered their services and they ministered to those who had no relatives to care for them.

Verne and Lil were shocked to see how severely the sickness had progressed. The flesh of most patients was a deep sulphurous yellow and some had large swellings beneath the skin. Fever gripped them all and they muttered and groaned in their delirium.

The children picked their way through. There were many faces they recognised. Lil could feel unfriendly stares following their progress and she heard reproachful whispers. Ignoring them, she looked for her father, but neither he nor Clarke was here.

'Potts did say the ballroom,' Verne reminded her.

'This isn't an emergency medical centre,' she said with a shudder. 'It's a pest-house, like in the time of the Great Plague.'

'This is a plague,' Verne said.

Leaving the restaurant behind, they found the ballroom and almost choked. It was a much larger space, packed with four hundred patients, and the smell was terrible. It was stifling too and the stale air was filled with the sound of suffering, prayers and despairing phone calls to friends and family outside Whitby.

Shuffling forward, taking care not to tread on an outstretched hand or trip on bags or tangles of sodden linen, the two friends continued.

'I know you!' a small, tearful woman cried, lurching to her feet. 'You're friends with that mad old bag who says she's a witch! Aren't you supposed to be one yourself? Don't try and tell me any of this is normal. Just look at my Jim down there. He's as yellow as a banana and too weak to open his eyes. If you can help, what are you waiting for? Or did you bring this down on us?'

'I'm trying to find my dad,' the girl answered

apologetically. 'If I *can* do anything, I will, but I have to find him first.'

The woman sneered. 'Your daft mother's over there by the stage. She looks like Dracula's ugly sister and she's ponging out the place with her hippy stink – as if it didn't reek enough already. This used to be a decent, God-fearing town, then you goths and witches and Lord knows what else moved in and took over. Deviants of the devil is what you are. This is a judgement on us for letting you live here.'

'Come on, Lil,' Verne said, pulling his friend away. 'You don't need to listen to this.'

Lil could see that the people nearby shared the woman's views and she was grateful to Verne for getting her past them.

With her back resting against the raised platform of the stage, Cassandra Wilson sat next to her husband, stroking his head and singing softly under her breath. In those ghastly surroundings she looked more bizarre than ever. Four frankincense sticks were smouldering by his bed and the threads of their cloying smoke wound around her.

Lil rushed to her father and clutched his hand. He looked pale and was clammy to the touch, but he seemed to be sleeping peacefully. She noticed a herb pouch had been strung around his neck.

She eyed her mother nervously, afraid of the hurtful things she might say.

'How is he?' she asked.

'Better than when I got here. I've invoked protective and purification forces and given him a charm for healing. Don't wake him; let the herbs and incantation do their work.'

Lil knew that what her mother called magic was meaningless nonsense, but she said nothing and reached into her bag for the crocheted hearts she had made.

'Put them away!' Cassandra snapped harshly. 'I don't want you anywhere near him with your stupid wool. Haven't you done enough damage already?'

Her voice was so loud it carried halfway across the room. The praying ceased and people stared. One delirious patient began to scream.

'But this will work,' Lil insisted.

'I said, put it away.'

Reluctantly, Lil stuffed the hearts back into her bag.

'Can we talk about what you said last night?' she asked after a pause. 'We can't go on like this. You can't have meant it.'

'Course I did.'

'So . . . where does that leave us?'

Mrs Wilson shrugged. 'Don't you think there's more important stuff going on right now? Everything can't always be about you all the time.'

'I never said it was!'

'When this is over, we'll sort out a different living

arrangement. Until then we'll just have to put up with it. I won't be in the house much while Mike's here anyway.'

'Different living arrangement?' Lil uttered in disbelief. 'What, you want to get rid of me? Move me out?'

Mrs Wilson ignored her and turned to Verne to inform him that his family had been moved into the games room. The boy had been so astonished at her treatment of Lil he could barely reply with a stilted 'thank you'. He gave his friend's shoulder a reassuring squeeze and headed off to find them.

'You might as well go with him,' Cassandra told her. 'You're no use here. I don't want you hanging around, getting in the way, and your father certainly doesn't need you.'

Lil reeled.

'I'm your daughter! I love you! You're my mum! Why are you doing this?'

She stared into her mother's ornately made-up eyes and was distressed and horrified to see the bleak coldness there. There wasn't a trace of maternal love left.

'Get going,' Cassandra said. 'I've arranged a TV interview and they'll be Skyping any moment. I don't want your sulky face in my eyeline.'

'So that's why you're decked out like a gothic Christmas tree! It's because you're going to be on the telly. And you say it's all about me?'

Wiping her eyes, Lil could bear it no longer. She called to Verne and hurried after him.

Unruffled, Cassandra returned her attention to her husband.

'Lil?' the sick man murmured, stirring in his sleep. 'You there?'

'Hush,' his wife said, dabbing his forehead with a black lace handkerchief. 'We don't need her. I can make you well again. I've been promised.' Smiling, she touched her neck and ran her fingertips along the choker.

Her phone began to ring.

Since the outbreak of the Yellow Scourge, many of those trapped in Whitby had been speaking to the media. They shared their dramatic stories of how swiftly and radically their lives had changed and how they feared for the lives of their loved ones. The owner of Whitby Gothic was the first interviewee to defy the local conspiracy of silence and claim that these dire events were outside science and the natural order.

'I'm sorry?' the TV newsreader said in response to Mrs Wilson's assertion. 'You're saying that this unidentified illness is the result of black magic?'

'Absolutely! There is a malevolent force at work here and I know who's behind it.'

The newsreader shook his head at the large screen in the studio, where Cassandra's outlandishly made-up face stared back at him in deadly earnest.

'Since you contacted us earlier, Mrs Wilson,' he said, 'we've done some research and found that you're quite the publicity seeker. Don't you think exploiting this immensely serious emergency for your own ends is rather cheap and shabby?'

'You can sneer all you wish. That doesn't alter the facts. This town is under supernatural attack.'

'Medical experts are saying it's a new mutation of a rare virus; not one of them has mentioned witchcraft.'

'They're wrong. Closed minds like yours are the reason evil breeds. I could vanish in a cloud of glittery smoke right before your eyes and you still wouldn't believe in magic.'

'I wish you would.'

He turned away from her, the annoyance and disgust on his face plain to see. She was replaced on the screen by a graphic of the town as he gave an update of the situation.

In the Royal Hotel, Lil's mother put her phone away. Her confidence and composure weren't even slightly dented. Every resident here knew she was right. They would support her.

Lil spent the rest of the afternoon with the Thistlewoods. Clarke's condition had worsened and Verne broke down when he saw him. One side of his brother's face was covered in pustules and he was struggling for breath. The only doctor in the building hadn't examined him since they arrived in the middle of the night and the broad-spectrum antibiotic he had given Clarke had had no effect at all.

'Please, Lil!' Noreen implored. 'Help him. He can't fight it much longer.'

And so Lil repeated what she had done previously. When she pressed a crocheted heart into Clarke's hand he looked slightly better and his breathing sounded easier. But within half an hour the blue wool had turned yellow and he was as bad as ever. So she did it again, and then again.

In between her treatments, Lil started on a larger crochet work. Her fingers moved incredibly fast and she closed her eyes to concentrate. After three hours, when she had almost run out of wool, she had crafted a medium-sized blanket and, calling on the energies of the First Mother, covered Clarke with it.

The change was immediate and startling. The blanket sparkled and the hideous yellow retreated from his skin. The pustules withered and he opened his eyes and asked for a drink of water.

His family were overjoyed. They held and kissed him and praised Lil. Verne hugged her tightly.

'I think that will last longer than the hearts,' she said.

The other people present begged her to do the same for their loved ones, but there wasn't much yarn left. It was a horrible position to find herself in, deciding who to help. Eventually she chose a six-year-old girl called Paula, whose forehead was a mass of yellow fluid and whose arms were covered in boils. Lil managed to crochet a square that was only a quarter of the size of the one she had made for Clarke, but she put just as much effort and focused thought into its creation.

Placing it across the little girl's chest, Lil called on the same forces and the wool sparkled as before. The ugly swelling on Paula's forehead deflated and her arms began to clear.

Her parents couldn't thank Lil enough, but she felt it was the very least she could do and wished she had more wool to help the others.

The day's exertions had left her drained and dead on her feet and she remembered she hadn't eaten a thing. Dennis Thistlewood offered to do a food run, but his wife could see Lil needed to go home and rest properly.

'I saw your mother today,' Noreen added. 'Only at a distance, across the other side of the ballroom. I've not seen her so tarted up since she first started going out with your dad when she was a lovesick teenager. I really must make it up with her.'

Lil didn't know what to say. She was so exhausted, she knew she would collapse in tears if she explained how things stood with her mother. Verne came to her rescue.

'I'll see you out,' he said briskly. 'I'll stop here tonight with my folks, but call me if you want anything and I'll dash right over.'

'I feel so useless,' Lil confessed as they made their way through the hotel. 'I should be doing a lot more for everyone here.'

'You're worn out. You'll be no good to anyone if you faint. You need a solid night's sleep. Remember, there's another colour to get through first thing in the morning.'

'I don't need reminding of that. What's going to happen this time? Hard to imagine it getting any worse than it already is, but obviously it will.'

'No point worrying until tomorrow. Just go eat something and put your head down.'

'I'd better collect the paintbox from Cherry on the way back. I don't think she likes having it in her cottage.'

They had reached the reception where the doctor was sprawled across a sofa, taking advantage of a quiet moment before the next case was brought in.

Lil pushed open the main door and stared out across the harbour. In the evening light Whitby looked the same as ever, tranquil and cosy, the inspiration of countless artists. She said goodnight to Verne, but before she went he tugged on her hand.

'Thank you,' he said. 'What you're doing for Clarke and that little girl – it's awesome. I know your mum is being horrible. If it gets too much, you're more than welcome to stay at ours. You can even bring Sally's ghost with you. Mum and Dad won't mind.'

A tear ran down Lil's cheek. She brushed it away hastily. Taking a breath, she managed a smile and nodded.

'And what I'm trying to say,' he continued, his eyes looking past her, at the darkening sky, 'and making a right Klumsythumbs pig's ear of it as usual, is that I'm dead proud to be your friend. You're amazing – don't you listen to anyone who says otherwise.'

Lil didn't know what to say, but when she hurried away she found herself feeling better than before.

Hours later, when the town was quiet, and the hands on the clock of St Mary's Church moved beyond twelve, two figures walked past the graveyard, towards the entrance of the abbey.

In full funereal splendour, with a damask cloak lined with purple satin and dripping with jet jewellery, Cassandra Wilson strode across the car park, followed by Jack Potts in his parka.

The craggy ruins of Whitby Abbey were surrounded by a high stone wall. Access to the grounds was through the visitor centre. The door was locked and all the lights were off.

'How do we get in?' she said impatiently. 'Where is Queller?'

'A moment, if you please,' Jack Potts said.

The robot jolted and stood rigid. A stream of pale grey-green vapour poured from his hood. It spilled to the ground and formed a column of smoke that took on the ghostly shape of the man Cassandra knew as Queller.

Mrs Wilson grinned to see his dashing face again.

'I've missed you,' she greeted him breathlessly. 'I thought we were meeting in the abbey grounds? It's more romantic there. The perfect setting for an assignation.'

'It is not prudent to enter there yet, my dear,' his rich voice answered.

'Why?'

'I have kennelled my pets therein. They must be very hungry by now. I would not wish for any harm to come to you, sweet Venus-bosomed lady.'

Cassandra was so deep in his power, she would have done anything he asked. Jack Potts took her left hand and cut across it with his finger. The woman winced. Then, from his pocket, he took a paintbrush with a gold and black handle.

'Isn't that the one from my daughter's paintbox?'

'The very same.' Jack Potts replied. 'I took the liberty of abstracting it before we left. I shall return it as soon as we go back. She will never know.'

'But what's it for?'

'To summon an old friend of mine,' Queller told her, with an enigmatic smile.

The robot brought the paintbrush to her hand and dabbled it in the pool of blood that had welled in her palm.

Cassandra flinched. The brush hairs felt stiff and sharp as they poked and dragged along the fresh wound. She wanted to pull away, but didn't like to appear weak. She looked up at Queller's face; his eyes were closed and he was whispering words she couldn't understand.

Then the sensation changed. It felt as if a small, rough tongue had taken the place of the brush and was lapping up her blood.

Jack Potts withdrew the brush, but the licking sensation persisted. With blood dripping from the hairs, the automaton traced an outline in the air and an ethereal form shimmered into view. It was a large cat, with ridged scars on his head clamped together by metal staples. Grafted to his shoulders was a pair of great bat wings.

'Catesby!' Queller welcomed. 'It is agreeable to see you again, you wicked old sheep killer.'

The feline apparition continued drinking Cassandra's blood.

'Catesby!' Queller said more forcefully. 'She is not for you. You've supped enough to summon you. Don't be greedy.'

The cat's ears flattened against the scarred skull and he hissed. Baring a set of savage fangs, he lunged at Mrs Wilson's exposed wrist.

'No!' Queller commanded, lashing out and sending the creature spinning with the back of his hand.

Catesby spread his wings and reared up, slashing the air with vicious claws.

'Know who is master!' Queller thundered. 'It was I who made you, I who razored and sawed you open, spliced morsels of ape brain into your cloven skull and stitched flight to your back. I can unmake you just as easily and deny your patchwork body the life that is promised. Obey me.'

His wings thrashed and yellow eyes gleamed with resentment, but the ghostly cat flew down and alighted on Queller's shoulder. The man stroked the scarred head and rubbed his fingers together. Blue sparks sizzled and Catesby pressed his metal staples into them, purring like an engine.

'Yes, you had forgotten that blissful joy, had you not? But I have need of you. Fly to the abbey yonder. There you shall find two ravenous beasts. They are yours to tame and command.'

The cat nuzzled against him once more then soared up, over the high wall.

Cassandra stared after it in fear and shock.

'Bind your hand, dear lady,' Queller told her. 'You must not squander your delicious scarlet juices.'

'That . . . that thing!' she exclaimed. 'What was it?'

'A cosseted darling from my former life. He is most useful. If the abbey is to be our meeting ground, it must be guarded and Catesby is such a diligent watch cat.'

'I've heard the name before. Lil spoke of it . . . didn't she?'

'Do not overtax yourself, my love and why speak of the daughter you hate?'

'I . . . don't know. It seemed important – something I should remember.'

At that moment, hideous yowls and terrified animal screeches broke out behind the abbey wall.

'Ah,' Queller said with a chuckle, 'Catesby has found my pets and is instructing them in the ways of the new order.'

'Excuse me, Master,' Jack Potts interjected, tilting his head on one side. 'We are not alone. Someone is approaching from the south-east.'

'Interesting,' Queller said. 'What curious, midnight creature roams abroad in this stricken town? What secretive work are they about?'

'They shall round the corner of Abbey Lane in approximately fifty-seven seconds,' Jack Potts informed him.

'Pull your hood low,' Queller instructed. 'I shall melt into the shadows. Cassandra, my love, go meet this unexpected interloper.'

The woman nodded and began walking across the car park. The moon was wrapped in thin clouds, so the abbey plain was smothered in a dim gloom. Soon she heard furtive steps running on the footpath beside the high wall that surrounded the abbey and a figure dashed into view. It halted when it saw Cassandra and jerked its head around like a hunted animal.

'Who's there?' Mrs Wilson called out.

'You live here?' answered a female voice. 'You live in Whitby? Yeah? Not with the military or special forces or some crap like that?'

'I live in Henrietta Street.'

The stranger jogged over, but it was so dark Cassandra couldn't see her properly until she was close.

She was a girl in her early twenties, dressed in a baggy, badge-covered camouflage jacket, with a rucksack and a cycling helmet with a camera attached.

'Really thought I'd be challenged coming along here,' she declared. 'Was sure there'd be an inner security fence to breach.'

'Who are you?'

'Sure, yeah, of course – they call me Orkid,' she said, holding her hand up for a high five that Cassandra didn't acknowledge. 'Me and my group have set up camp, close as we could get. We're part of the anti-capitalist, anti-globalisation, anti-big-pharma alliance, the Living Planet Conscience Coalition. You heard of us, yeah? Leaves in Tears?'

'No. Aren't you afraid of the virus?'

'Come on, there's no virus. That's a DA Notice cover-up ordered by the government. It's no coincidence Fylingdales is only a spit and a cough down the road here. There's been a leak or some accident with the emissions from their cell-frying radar. I've got a Geiger counter and I'm going to prove all you poor sods here have suffered a massive dose of radiation and blow this dirty lie wide apart.'

'You're mistaken. You can't scientifically measure what's happening here.'

Orkid ignored her and removed her rucksack, taking out a small yellow and black device.

'Sensitive to really low levels of microsieverts so it'll tell me in seconds how bad it is.'

It was too dark to see the liquid crystal display so she used the torch app on her phone and held it near, waving the counter towards the town.

'Just over point one seven,' she said, in bewildered disappointment. 'That's barely average. Can't be . . . was sure it was radiation. Maybe Cloggy was right and it *was* a chemical spill, or a new bioweapon that escaped the lab. Yeah, must be that.'

Her torchlight swept across Cassandra's face and Orkid saw her properly for the first time.

'Wait,' she said. 'I know you. You're the crank with the witchcraft shop who was on the news today. Ha – chances of you being the first person I run into!

I've got to get a selfie with you to send to Jasmin and Mank; they'll think it's hilarious.'

She pressed herself closer to Cassandra, pulling a spooked expression as she took a photograph.

'Hang on – might want another for Instagram . . . Hold up, who's that over there?'

She had seen a figure standing in the background and peered across the car park as it walked towards her. Jack Potts removed the hood from his head.

'What. Is. That?' Orkid demanded. 'This *is* some secret military operation, isn't it. Is that some new type of weapon, yeah? Like a Terminator?'

'A teamaker, if you please,' Jack Potts corrected her.

Orkid began backing away and pointed to the camera mounted on her helmet. 'Right, I've got enough evidence on my GoPro – night vision! The cat's well out of the bag now and all hell will break loose.'

'To be more precise,' the resonant voice of Queller declared by the door of visitor centre, which unlocked and swung open by itself, 'the cat is out of the gift shop – and he's brought along a couple of friends. You're more or less correct about the latter part of your statement however.'

Orkid shone the light around and saw a large cat-like shape with wings fly out of the building. Then four eyes reflected the light back at her as two great Rottweilers followed.

The dogs bared their teeth. Orkid let out a terrified

yell. Dropping her phone and Geiger counter, she fled down the lane.

Catesby rushed between the Rottweilers and they bounded after obediently.

'Come, my dear,' Queller called to Cassandra. 'Let us admire the nocturnal serenity of this desolate ruin, undisturbed.'

He took her hand in his wraith fingers and led her through the darkened visitor centre to the abbey beyond. Mrs Wilson barely heard the moment when the dogs caught the young activist. The screams beyond the high encircling wall were nothing compared to the charming presence of Queller.

He danced her round the truncated remains of stout carved pillars, ranged along the neatly mown lawn, and into the three enclosing walls of the north transept, his devastating smile captivating her utterly.

'Did I not promise you your husband would be spared the worst ravages of the sickness?' he asked. 'And did I not keep the Carmine Swarm from your threshold?'

'My husband? Oh yes . . . he . . . he was much better today. Not like the rest.'

'Tomorrow you shall be seen to heal others and that will win you followers. Bring them here. Together we shall call on powers to bring an end to the terrors afflicting this town.'

Round and around he waltzed her. In a fog of

dazed pleasure she felt her feet leave the ground and the abbey walls drifted by as the pair of them rose into the air. The floating sensation was exhilarating, but Queller's smiling face was even more wonderful. Presently Cassandra found herself standing upon the stone apex of the abbey, directly above the rose window, a staggering height. An intoxicated grin lit her face and she tore the choker from her neck.

Queller made her wait for his kiss. From that high vantage point, he could look down on to Abbey Lane where Orkid lay in the road. He watched Catesby land on the activist's back and claw at the camouflage jacket.

'Now feed well, my pet,' he murmured. 'Cross the blood bridge and be living flesh once more. Be as you were, a breathing, blood-filled horror.'

Catesby fed and soon let out a mewling cry of triumph as he stretched his new muscles and flexed his leathery wings – no more a ghost. Taking to the air, he soared over the cliff, wheeling in exuberant circles.

Watching with pride, Queller returned his attention to Cassandra and pressed his deathly lips to her neck.

'OK,' Cherry said, with a nervous laugh, 'so the next colour is called *Despairing Black* – how bad can it be, right?'

It was seven o'clock the next morning and she and the two children were in the courtyard outside her cottage. The paintbox was on a stool in the middle of them and Lil had just read out the name on today's colour. The image on the front was a crescent moon surrounded by clouds.

'An eclipse?' Verne suggested.

'Anything is possible,' Cherry answered. 'Don't think it'll be that literal though.'

'Whitby jet, that's black – and local. And it was a mourning, funeral thing, so that's the despair part.'

'Somehow I can't see it rainin' Victorian jewellery on us,' Cherry said.

'Ready?' Lil asked, reaching for the paintbrush.

'The answer's never gonna be yes, hun, but you gotta do it.'

Lil dipped the brush into a jar of water and steeled herself. Carefully, she washed it across the watercolour. Holding their breath, they waited.

The paintbox juddered.

There was a bone-rattling blast and a gigantic spike of black lightning ripped into the sky where it forked and crackled throughout the town, jagging from aerial to letter box to car. Every street lamp shattered as the bulbs exploded and sparks spat from electrical sockets.

'Oww!' yelled Verne, scrambling to wrench a smoking watch from his wrist while Lil pulled her fizzing mobile from her jeans.

All across the beleaguered town it was the same – everything that used electricity sparked and fused. In the hopelessly overrun hospital the medical machines failed and the electrics in every car were fried.

A circle of black mist flowed out from the box. Moving slowly, like treacle, it rolled to the ground, pushing out to form a sea of inky vapour in the yard. It swirled about Cherry and round the children's legs, and their skin crawled at the touch. Then it spread through the alleyway and out into the streets, with sluggish, deliberate purpose.

Cherry clutched her chest and lumbered to her front door. Tripping on the step, she fell into the dense mist.

'Daddy?' she bawled in her mind as she sank deep into painful memories. 'Daddy, I'm sorry. Don't go, don't leave us. I didn't mean to turn the malt pink. I didn't know I could do that! I won't do it again! I promise. Please, Daddy. Please!'

The six-year-old girl had screamed herself hoarse the day her father left home. The pain and guilt of it unfurled afresh like a dark flower in Cherry's psyche. She had driven her father away, destroyed the family, brought shame. Years of isolation and self-loathing followed. And then one day, at her lowest, when she was propping up a bar in a cheap club in the Old Town part of Chicago, she saw him again. He was older, thinner, more beaten down by life, but he still wore pomade in his steel-grey hair and took care of his out-of-date suit.

Her first instinct was to shout out to him, run over and throw her arms round his neck. A glance in the mirror behind the bar slapped that down. She had changed so much and looked bad. He'd never recognise her.

'Hey, Pete,' she called to the bartender. 'The guy at the end there, what's he want?'

'Cheap liquor, same as everyone else. He's just some dude. Salesman, I guess. Why?'

'Didn't say his name?'

'Who does in this joint?'

'Get me black coffee, will ya? A gallon – with added backbone.'

'Aw come on, Cherry, you drunk already? You're on in a half-hour.'

'Java, mucho strongo, now-o.'

Cherry scalded her mouth on the coffee that Pete set in front of her. Forcing it down, she motioned for him to fetch another. Then, sliding it along the bar, she sidled up to her father, with a friendly smile.

'Hey,' she said. 'Haven't seen you round before. I'm not hustlin' ya. I work here and I like to get to know the Joes who come in; makes it more bearable for me. I'm a people person.'

'Lady, I'm sure you're real nice, but I just want to be left alone. I only come in to get out the rain.'

It had been a long time since anyone had called her a lady. Cherry almost buckled right there, but she took another slug of coffee instead.

'The Windy City can be mighty lonely if'n you don't know nobody. Oops, that came out sounding a bit like Doris Day in *Calamity Jane*, but you know what I mean. I know what it's like being a stranger in town – I'm a Canuck.'

He looked up slowly. 'You're from Canada? Whereabouts?'

'Ontario.'

A flicker of life kindled in his eyes.

'Ever been to a place called Whitby there?'

Cherry drained the coffee and called for a third to give herself time to think.

'No,' she lied. 'We was Ottawa. Don't recall we ever went to Whitby. That where you're from? What's it like? Is it pretty?'

The man returned his gaze to the glass.

'Parts were very pretty.'

A sorrowful smile appeared on his lined face. 'You know,' he continued, 'it's named after a place in Yorkshire, England. Always wanted to go see that one day, sounds beautiful. Was gonna take someone with me too; she'd have gotten a real kick out of it.'

'Never too late, mister. Say, what's your name? Can't keep callin' you "mister".'

She had pushed too far too soon and he clammed up again.

'What you wanna know for? You some kind of undercover cop or something? What's with the third degree?'

'Cherry a cop?' the bartender laughed as he poured the coffee. 'That's a real laugh riot! You think the CPD are that desperate?'

'Pour the coffee and go, Pete,' Cherry told him.

'Hey, buddy,' Cherry's father said sternly. 'Watch your lip. You don't get to bad-mouth no lady in front of me, you got that?'

Pete sauntered round the bar, still snickering.

'Never thought a gallant white knight would come into this joint,' she said, greatly moved.

'I'm no white knight.'

'You are to me, mister. Hey, see that wall over there? The one with all the photos? That's our rogues' gallery where we put all our best and favourite customers. Would you mind if I took your picture and pinned it on there?'

There was an unusual desperation at the back of her request. The man couldn't understand why.

'Just one lousy picture, mister, please?'

'I won't be coming back here.'

'Even more reason. How else am I gonna remember what my white knight looked like?'

He could see tears brimming in her eyes and her voice was unsteady, but he thought it was just the booze.

'Sure,' he said.

Cherry leaned across the bar and took the management's instant camera from a shelf above the clean glasses.

'Say cheese.'

'Wait, what'd he say your name was?'

'Cherry, Cherry Cerise.'

'OK, I'll say "Cherry" instead of cheese. Never did like cheese.'

Cherry smiled in sudden remembrance. That was a detail she had forgotten about her father.

'Ready?' she asked, holding the bulky camera to her eye.

'*Cherrrryyyy*,' he said.

The cube flash went off and he blinked, temporarily blinded.

'So,' he said, rubbing his eyes, 'who gives their daughter such a cockamamie name?'

'Nobody,' she answered, pulling the undeveloped photograph out of the camera and placing it under her arm. 'It's a stage name. I'm a dancer here.'

The man looked at the small platform by the band, hung with silver streamers and he regarded her with disgust.

'I had me a daughter,' he said. 'By the looks of you, I reckon she's about ten years younger. If I ever found out she worked in a place like this, I'd die of shame. Now there's the laugh riot, cos I'm dying anyway. Got me just days left. Well, I'm getting out of here, don't want to spend my last gasps in the company of lowlifes. Be spending all the time in the world with roaches and worms soon enough.'

Reaching into his pocket he put a few crumpled dollars on the bar and left.

Cherry stared after him, quivering as though he had struck her. She dug her nails into the bar and they splintered and broke.

'Daddy,' she whispered.

Ripping up the photograph into tiny fragments, she

grabbed the ice bucket and snatched up the ice pick.

'Cherry!'

'CHERRY!'

Lil and Verne's frightened shrieks cut through the agony.

Jolted out of the bitter memory, Cherry jerked her head back. The bar was gone and she was in her small kitchen again. She had pulled open a drawer and was holding a knife to her own stomach.

'Put it down!' Lil shouted. 'Drop it!'

Cherry stared at the blade for a moment then gave a cry of horror. She threw the knife back in the drawer and slammed it shut.

'Oh, kids!' she wept, pulling the children towards her and hugging them tightly. 'Thank you. Bless you!'

'What happened?' Verne asked when the colour witch had calmed down.

'Hold on a minute,' Cherry said, running to the parlour where she delved into her Mary Quant bag and took out her purse. She fumbled with the clasp, then produced a flat leather wallet. It was well worn and most of the stitching had come away, but inside it contained a treasure. With jittery hands, Cherry opened it.

There was the faded Polaroid of her father with her name on his lips.

'It's not ripped. It didn't happen that way. No, course it didn't.'

'You OK?' Lil asked.

'Gimme a moment, babes. I need to relive what really went on then. Let me just remember . . .'

She closed her eyes and concentrated, fighting through the false memory that the black mist had tormented her with, cutting through it to the truth, to what had actually happened that night so long ago.

The idle dirge of the out-of-tune band swelled around her again. She was back in that crummy Chicago club.

'A dancer?' her father repeated. 'As long as it makes you happy, Cherry.'

'It doesn't.'

'Then find something that does. Look at me, learn from my huge mistake. I spent a lifetime running away from what really made me happy.'

'Why'd you do that?'

'Because I was scared – or dumb. Or both. Didn't think I could hack having a daughter who was different; didn't realise till it was too late that she weren't different. What she was was special – an honest-to-God miracle.'

'Why didn't you go back and tell her that?'

'Cos I was ashamed, and by the time I stopped feeling sorry for myself I'd left it too long. My little girl had run away and there was no way of tracing her. She never writes her mom, so she's lost to me now. I tried three detective agencies, but they turned up squat.'

'Don't give up, she might be real close.'

'Nah, she's better off without knowing me now. You see, I got me this ulcer, real nasty. Nothing they can do about it, only a matter of time, and some days it hurts like I swallowed a grenade. But when I think about my beautiful daughter, living her happy life, it's like a lion tamer gets that ulcer to jump on a chair and sit up and beg. Reckon I'd have caved in to it weeks ago if I didn't have that to focus on. Even though I know it's just the fantasy of a stupid old man, it keeps me strong. I need to hold on to that perfect image I got.'

Cherry peeled the film backing off the Polaroid and propped the picture against his glass.

'Well, any gal would be proud to have that smiling guy as their daddy,' she said warmly. 'Hey, this might sound a lil strange, but would you dance with me? We're two Canucks in a strange city. Let's pretend for five minutes we're family. Say I'm five years old, and it's Christmas morning and the radio is playing something by, oh, I dunno . . . Nat King Cole, and we're dancing in the wrapping paper we just ripped off our gifts.'

'Hey, Nat was always my favourite.'

She held out her hand and he let himself be led to a small cleared space between the tables.

'Shut your eyes,' she said. 'Imagine I'm your little girl.'

Feeling foolish, he complied and she threw a look at the amused band to quiet down.

Then a small, shy voice began to sing an old song, 'Take Me Back to Toyland'. It was her father.

Cherry rested her head against his lapel and they danced with the reserved awkwardness of strangers.

She clutched the precious moment to her heart, but it was over all too soon.

Her father squeezed her hand and returned to his bar stool.

'Well, I'll be getting along,' he said, putting on his overcoat. 'Think the rain's eased off some. Thank you, Miss Cerise. Felt a mite silly, but you know something, my ulcer's quiet as a lamb right now.'

'You be careful out there,' she managed to say.

He headed for the door then turned. 'Hey,' he said, 'you know what I'd tell my daughter if I did meet her one last time?'

'What?'

'I'd say, princess, you have been blessed with astounding gifts. Don't waste a single one. Learn how to use them, for the good of this world. Make your daddy even more proud than he already is. Yeah, that's what I'd say.'

With a smile that wiped away the care of years, he left the club.

Cherry sobbed beside the bar and reached for the Polaroid.

'C'mon, Cherry,' Pete said. 'You're on in five; it's funky time.'

'Pete,' she answered, staring lovingly at the photograph, 'you go funk. I quit. I got me a whole bunch of catch-up learning to do.'

The memory faded, melting into a golden mist.

Back in her cottage, Cherry kissed the Polaroid.

'He knew,' she said. 'He knew.'

Verne and Lil waited while she composed herself.

'The electric's off in here,' Verne said eventually. 'I think the whole town has gone *fzzzst*.'

Cherry put the wallet away.

'That's just a part of it,' she said, dabbing at her eyes. 'But neither of you felt nothin'? No bad and twisted memory that made you wanna die?'

'No,' the children said together.

'Guess it don't work on everyone, just like the sickness didn't. But *Despairing Black* will find its victims. Not everyone is lucky enough to have a Verne and Lil to save them.'

As she spoke they heard a bitter cry from one of the nearby cottages.

'So it starts,' Cherry said. 'And with no power, this town really is cut off. We're totally on our own now.'

11

Within just a few metres of the barricade, nothing electrical was working. Even landlines were dead.

Cherry, Lil and Verne hurried through the East Cliff. The oily mist was still curdling into doorways and creeping over the cobbles. Wails of anguish followed in its oozing wake.

'What can we do?' Lil cried. 'We can't save people from their own despair!'

'Get to the bridge,' Cherry urged. 'This old broad ain't quittin' yet.'

The swing bridge was thickly carpeted with the black mist. Two women had climbed on to the safety rail and were contemplating the deep river flowing beneath.

'Good mornin', ladies,' Cherry called, in as sunny a voice as she could muster. 'Why don't y'all get down from there? I got somethin' real neat to show you. You'll love it.'

The women turned ashen faces to her. It was as if they bore the burdens of the world on their shoulders. Cherry knew she had to be quick.

Holding up her hands, she put her thumbs and forefingers together and two bright points of pink light flared up. She blew on them and they floated like glowing thistledown towards the despairing women. Glimmering through the air, the magical lights flew to their foreheads where they radiated out, forming shining stars on their brows.

'I know you're deep in the pit of pain right now,' Cherry said coaxingly. 'And can't see a way out. You think the walls are too high to climb, but that just ain't the truth. This light is the promise of a better day. Push the darkness behind you and concentrate on the pretty pink star. When night closes over your dreams and you're flounderin' in the dark, remember there are stars out there, and inside yourself, to guide you and keep you safe.'

The women clambered down from the rail. Cherry touched their foreheads lightly.

'Go home,' she suggested. 'And sleep.'

The insidious mist had reached the West Cliff, winding up the Khyber Pass and climbing the steep, narrow ways behind Flowergate.

'Up there!' Lil cried, pointing at the Royal Hotel where a figure in a white coat was standing on a fourth-floor window ledge.

'It's that doctor,' Verne said. 'He's going to jump!'

'There's more on the quayside!' Lil shouted. 'Cherry! Do something!'

'Quick, Verne,' the witch said. 'Go fetch your dad. Hurry.'

The boy raced off and she turned to Lil.

'I got me just one card left to play. Don't be scared and don't say nothin' till it's done.'

Cherry closed her eyes and inhaled sharply. Lil held on to the iron latticework of the bridge rail and watched.

'I call upon the warmth and protection of the First Mother!' Cherry announced in a firm ceremonial voice as she folded her arms across her chest. 'I rouse her strength and compassion. For mercy's sake, may I be a conduit for her nurturing energies. By daylight's eye I summon thee; with the moon's tears I charge thee. Pierce every shadow; banish the titans of hopelessness that seek to crush our fragile spirits. Let a flame of hope burn in every downcast heart. This is the supplication of the Whitby witch! I beseech thee, use up the colours that are left unto me.'

Cherry's head slumped forward and she started speaking in a weird guttural language. A shimmering radiance welled up in the witch's flesh and the ends of her nylon wig began to lift. Letting out a tremendous yell that made Lil jump, she threw out her hands and flung her head back. A dazzling globe of light blasted from her, like the detonation of an enormous firework. Millions of scintillating particles went shooting over the town, punching through walls and rocketing down narrow streets. On top of the Royal Hotel, a fiery pink spark exploded against the doctor's shoulder and sent him crashing back through the window he had climbed out of. All over Whitby that most desolate, forsaken moment was punctured by a spark of hope. The black mist retreated, pouring into drains and cascading over the harbour wall to sink into the river.

'You did it!' Lil cried, scanning the town. 'Cherry! You did it!'

The witch said nothing. Lil glanced at her and sprang forward.

Cherry's face and hands were grey and she wilted into Lil's arms. The girl sat on the pavement with Cherry's head on her lap. She felt for a pulse and was frightened by how parched and shrivelled the witch's skin had become. It was if all the goodness had been siphoned off. The pulse, when she found it, was incredibly faint, but at least she was alive.

Lil stroked Cherry's face and carefully straightened her wig.

'Hang in there. You can't leave us yet. There's still so much we're going to do: you, me and Verne. You don't get to ditch this mad disco early, before they play the best tunes, Cherry Cerise. You're the Whitby witch – you're going nowhere. I won't let you.'

Presently, Verne returned with his father and Lil asked him to carry Cherry home.

Dennis took Cherry in his arms. She was lighter than Verne and her emaciated arms and legs dangled like sticks. It was no labour at all to bear her down Church Street and soon he was carrying her up the stairs of her cottage where he laid her gently on her bed.

'She looks like a wizened zombie,' Verne observed with unhappy bluntness.

'She sacrificed her colours,' Lil said. 'Her whole spectrum, every bit of magic she had in her, to save everyone.'

'What the heck happened?' Mr Thistlewood asked. 'It was crazy at the hotel, with people bawling and threatening to do themselves in. I had to stop a nun from chucking herself out the window. Then coloured stars were whizzing about everywhere and the wailing stopped.'

'When I got there the nun was kissing him,' Verne said.

Staring down at Cherry's withered face, he added, 'Is she going to die?'

'Not if I've got anything to do with it,' Lil answered with fierce determination. 'But I'm going to need one hell of a lot of wool.'

'There's tons in the hotel,' Dennis told her.

'After what you did for Clarke and that little girl yesterday, all the families brought every ball they could find, but . . .'

'But?'

'They might not let you have any if they know who it's for. There's nasty talk going round. Noreen and me have both heard it. People are saying all this, the sickness, the insects, is Cherry's doing.'

'That's a lie!'

'I know! And I've tried to put them right, but they won't have it. And I'm sorry, Lil, but I think they're getting all this from your mother.'

'What?'

'Cassandra's been doing her herbs and spells for anyone who asks and it seems to work a bit. Nothing like what you can do, but it's enough to impress most people in there. Anyway, that's where the rumours about Cherry are coming from.'

'Your mum's lost it,' Verne said flatly.

'I know,' Lil agreed. 'I don't know what's got into her. I'll try and talk to her later. I must do what I can for Cherry first. Verne, will you stay and look after her while I dash home and get my knitting gear?'

'Course I will.'

Mr Thistlewood left and Verne gazed around Cherry's bedroom. It reflected her 1970s taste, with garish orange and pink woodwork, tasselled lampshades and framed posters of David Bowie,

Steve McQueen and Roberta Flack. But the walls and ceiling were grey, the same ghastly shade as her skin.

'It's weird being in her cottage and not having the walls change colour all the time,' he said.

'They've been getting paler ever since I first used the paintbox,' Lil said. 'I think it's been robbing her power right from the start, leeching the colours out of her. She knew, but she never said anything. She's been having trouble with even simple magic, like her party trick.'

'She looks old. I never thought of her as old,' Verne said. 'She was always so full of life. Poor Cherry.'

'Don't leave her on her own while I'm gone.'

'As if!'

'Sorry. I won't be long.'

Verne pulled the padded stool from the dressing table and placed it by the bed. Sitting down, he looked into Cherry's face and took hold of her hand.

'Lil will be back before you know it,' he said. 'She's unbelievable with her knitting thing. She'll get you back to normal in no time. Chocolate milkshake for me, remember.'

Cherry's hand was cold.

Lil burst into the Wilsons' cottage and flung herself up the stairs to her room where she dragged every item of clothing she had ever knitted from her wardrobe and stuffed it into bags.

'Bright colours only,' she told herself. 'Verne can

unpick and I'll knit it up. But that's going to take time. What I need is a machine to do the unpicking . . .'

She slapped her forehead and, with the bulging bags in her hands, ran back down the stairs to the kitchen.

Jack Potts was seated at the table, motionless, his head bent over scattered tea bags. Every caddy and box of flavoured tea in the house was arranged before him.

'I forgot,' she groaned. 'You're electric and kaput like everything else.'

The robot raised his head and looked at her.

'I was immersed in deliberation,' he said. 'Forgive me, Mistress Lil. Can I be of service?'

'The paintbox didn't zap you?'

'Ah, is that why the vacuum cleaner no longer functions? I did wonder if I had offended it in some way. Appliances can be so touchy. I must also apologise to the freezer: earlier I unjustly called it an incontinent vulgarian.'

'I need you to come with me.'

'But I am engaged in important research.'

'What, with tea bags?'

'Decidedly so! I have devised a radical new method of brewing the cups that cheer but do not inebriate. It will revolutionise the beverage industry. Consider these many different varieties, so much wasteful packaging.'

'I don't have time for this. Get your parka on.'

'I should prefer to remain here. I was just preparing to snip open . . .'

'Why are you arguing? I need you at Cherry's.'

'Oh, if you insist.'

A short while later they were in Cherry's bedroom and Jack Potts was unravelling jumpers and scarves faster than any human could, and winding the individual colours into separate balls.

'I notice there are a great number of deaths occurring at the moment in Whitby,' he said. 'Is that usual in this resort, for this time of year?'

'It's not usual at any time of year!' said Lil. 'What's the matter with you?'

'Ah. My small talk is not all it should be. I was constructed to be a butler. I can draw the perfect bath, boil the perfect egg, iron a garment with complicated pleats, but there are gaps in my basic general knowledge.'

'You're telling me. Anyway, Cherry isn't going to die.'

'You speak with such passion and negativity about human death.'

'Course she does!' said Verne.

'Even though you know it is merely the end of one form of existence and the beginning of another?'

'You don't get it, do you?' Lil said. 'I keep forgetting you're only a machine.'

'If death is so bad, then to cause a death is also bad?'

'That's murder,' Verne told him. 'It's the worst crime there is.'

'It is not like opening a door for someone? That is considered good manners.'

'No!' both children said.

'Then it is a difficult concept for me to understand. When I can no longer function or be repaired, that will be a final end to Jack Potts. Your flesh and bone frame is but a prison for your spirit.'

'It's more than that,' Verne said. 'Life is precious and wonderful!'

The automaton's left eye started to flicker.

'One completed ball of lemon-coloured wool,' he declared, changing the subject.

Lil began to crochet.

By the end of the evening, Lil's young fingers ached.

She had completed a multicoloured blanket, with an emphasis on pink. But, when she had placed it on Cherry, nothing happened. The wool did not sparkle and there was no change in the witch's condition. Lil's hopes and confidence in her own abilities were dashed. Yet there were other people who needed her help.

Arranging a care rota with the Thistlewoods, so that Cherry was never on her own, as she felt uneasy about leaving her with Jack Potts, Lil spent the rest of the day at the hotel making blankets for patients in the games room. At least there she was relieved to see that her magic still worked.

Without electricity, the spacious hotel rooms grew

dark quickly when the sun began to set. Torches were no use, so candles were in great demand. Lil's mother had fetched a haul from Whitby Gothic and their flickering flames made the ballroom look like a church or temple. Lil had tried to speak to her about Cherry, but Cassandra declared she was too busy caring for the sick, and her followers made it plain that Lil wasn't welcome in the ballroom. She wasn't even permitted to visit her father.

Food was becoming a problem across the town. Without daily deliveries, supplies were running low. There was nothing fresh left and all the frozen produce had defrosted. The only solution was to cook everything before it spoiled and share it out. Luckily the big hotels and many houses had gas cookers, but other inhabitants had to devise different means of boiling water or warming tins of beans.

Lil spent the night on Cherry's bedroom floor. There was still no change. As the girl curled herself up and tried to go to sleep, she wondered how she and Verne would deal with whatever new terror the paintbox would hurl at them. Without Cherry to help it was a daunting and fearful prospect.

'Three watercolour blocks left,' she said. 'So that's three more days and then it's over. Oh, please be over.'

She fell into a disturbed slumber in which she dreamed something was scuttling across the roof and scratching at the window frame. Then she thought she heard Sally barking and jumping up at the window. There was a hasty, scrabbling retreat outside. After a time, a wet nose and silky fur nuzzled next to her.

That night the abbey ruins were aglow with flame and giant shadows cavorted across the stones. Within the grounds a celebration was taking place. Cassandra was crowned High Priestess of Whitby by her followers, and half a pig, stolen from a butcher's cold store, was roasted on a large fire. A makeshift throne had been put on one of the broken pillars and, from that exalted position, Cassandra commanded the music to commence.

The revellers were drunk on looted alcohol and they tore off their clothes to dance naked round the flames. Some held pig's heads in front of their faces.

Standing at the edge of the firelight, Jack Potts observed the worst of human nature then turned away and faced the abbey wall.

High overhead a winged shape circled over Whitby, mewling a gloating cry.

12

Lil woke early. The first thing she did was check on Cherry. The woman was still unconscious, but Lil was delighted when she saw that the strong bright colours of the blanket had turned pale.

'Must be doing something then,' she told herself, greatly encouraged.

While she waited for Verne to arrive, she set about using up what was left over of yesterday's wool. If she had looked out of the window, she would have noticed that much of the sill had been nibbled and eaten away in the night.

At roughly seven o'clock, because neither of them knew exactly what the time was, she and Verne were in the courtyard with the paintbox.

'*Sahara Sand*,' she read aloud. 'And there's a picture of a camel.'

'Are we going to be invaded by savage dromedaries?' he asked, only half joking. 'Or what

if it's sphinxes? What do we do if sphinxes come galloping at us?'

'I wouldn't be surprised if pyramids burst out of the ground,' said Lil. 'Let's just get it started.'

Taking up the paintbrush, she dipped it in the water jar. Before she applied it to the pigment, Verne took hold of her other hand.

Lil wet the paint, then they stood well back.

'Good luck,' Verne whispered to her as the paintbox began to quake.

The box revolved on the stool, slowly at first. Then it spun faster and faster. The pigment block rippled and spat. There was a deep rumble that shook the courtyard and one of Cherry's window boxes fell off the ledge. A hot wind came gusting over the rooftops and tore round the cottages, swinging the hanging baskets and howling in the alleyway. The children were thrown back, their clasped hands dragged apart. Lil's hair lashed her face and the breath was ripped from her lungs. Verne was flung off his feet and went flying backwards into a corner.

Squinting against the baking gale they saw a column of gritty, ochre-coloured smoke rise from the box. Unaffected by the desert squall it climbed steadily upwards, like a genie from a bottle. Higher and higher it ascended until it towered over the town, forming a dense, muddy mantle, which spread across both sides of the river. The sunlight that filtered through was brown and bathed Whitby in sepia tones, like the Victorian photographs of Frank Meadow Sutcliffe.

The roasting wind ceased as abruptly as it began.

Verne picked himself off the ground and walked back to Lil. His shoes crunched over the flagstones and he saw that a fine layer of sand lay over everything. 'Was that it?' he asked when he rejoined her.

The girl shrugged. 'I don't trust it,' she said, staring at the paintbox, which had stopped spinning.

She swept a hand through her hair and shook out a quantity of sand. Then she noticed Verne's shoulders were covered in it and, when she looked again at the paintbox, the open lid and empty pigment compartments were filling up with it.

Gazing round, she realised sand was drizzling out of the sky. Verne's shoes were already covered and the flagstones were completely hidden.

Lil snatched up the paintbox and they ran into the cottage.

'It's snowing a desert out there!' the boy exclaimed.

Watching from the window they saw the courtyard disappear. In half an hour the sand was up to the letter box and Lil had to tape it up.

'How are we going to get to the hotel?' Verne

asked. 'If this keeps up, we won't be able to open the front door!'

'I should try and get over there while I still can,' Lil said. 'There's no telling how deep this is going to get. It could last all day.'

'Yes,' Verne agreed. 'You have to go. They need you there. I'll stop with Cherry. *Ungh*, it's so maddening not having a phone! How will I know if you got there safely or when you're coming back? How did people manage before they were invented? We haven't even got any carrier pigeons! We need magicians' coats with one tucked up each sleeve and three more in the pockets.'

That made Lil smile. She went up to Cherry's room to fetch her knitting bag and took a long look at her. Was she imagining it or was there a bloom of colour in her cheeks? She reached for her hand. It wasn't as cold as it had been.

'I promise I'll be back,' she said, leaning down to kiss Cherry's forehead.

Returning to the parlour, she found Verne had opened the window.

'Easier to get out this way,' he said. 'Though you might not be able to go far; you might just sink into it like quicksand.'

Lil clambered on to the sill. The sand was almost level with it. Swinging her legs out, she pushed in her heels to test how firm it was.

'Seems OK,' she said.

'Take care.'

The girl grinned bravely and put her full weight on the sand. She sank to her calves.

'It's not bad,' she told Verne, after taking a few experimental steps. 'I'll be fine. Just like walking on a deep drift. It's soft but won't swallow me up, don't worry.'

'Wait,' the boy called, vanishing from the window and reappearing moments later. 'Put this on; it'll keep the sand out of your hair.'

Lil laughed. He was holding one of Cherry's flamboyant plastic sun hats. It was fuchsia pink, with fake orange and green flowers. He threw it out to her like a frisbee. She caught it, put it on her head and curtseyed. With a final wave, she turned and traipsed to the alleyway.

The sand had already filled the narrow passage up to waist height and Lil was compelled to crouch to go through it. Soon the entrance would be submerged completely. Then how would she get back to Cherry's cottage?

Emerging into Church Street, she marvelled at how strange and alien it looked. The sand was up to the shop windows and was already forming undulating dunes. Instead of heading towards the bridge, Lil trudged the other way.

Jack Potts was in the Wilsons' kitchen staring out at the garden when she made it home. The front door was thrust inwards and a metre of sand spilled inside, followed by Lil.

'Good morning, Mistress Lil,' he greeted. 'I was concerned when you did not return home last night. I regret I am unable to offer you something to eat.'

'There's still a few apples,' she said, emptying the fruit bowl into her bag. 'You don't need to worry about me.'

'But I do worry about you. You and your friend Verne are battling a force that is determined to destroy you. It has nearly destroyed Miss Cerise.'

'We don't have a choice.'

'That is true. You do not.'

'Get the spade from the shed. I want you to go to Cherry's and keep the alley clear. I think there's a snow shovel in there as well – take that too.'

'As you wish,' the robot butler answered.

'What are you doing with that?' the girl asked when she saw he was holding her nan's porcelain teacup. 'I told you not to mess with it.'

'It is a pure and beautiful thing,' he replied. 'This morning I am sorely in need of both. There is much ugliness in the world.'

'Put it away and look through one of our art books if you want to see pretty things, but not now.'

'May I tell you my innovation for making tea? I believe it is something you would wish to know.'

'Are you serious? We're in the middle of all this

madness and you want to talk tea bags?'

'Trust me,' he insisted. 'You must listen!'

He had waved his arms for emphasis, but in doing so the precious cup smacked the counter. There was an audible crack.

'What have I done?' his metallic voice gasped.

'You've broken it,' said Lil. 'My nan's favourite cup.'

'No, no. It is not smashed – see. It is still in one piece.'

He tapped it with a metal finger. Instead of a clear ringing chime there was a dull clack. Then he saw a line running round the middle.

'It is damaged,' he said, filled with remorse. 'It is no longer a perfect creation. My carelessness has removed a thing of beauty from the world. It is therefore a more ugly place because of me.'

Lil couldn't wait around.

'OK, it's done. There's a lot worse stuff happening in Whitby right now. People are still sick and dying. We can't cry over an old cup.'

'Finally I understand why you humans fear death. There is loss, and pain, and emptiness. The voices of those you cherish are not heard again. I am devastated by my actions.'

'Just get yourself over to Cherry's.'

'I shall do my utmost to assist you. But first you must know this. Your enemy is . . .'

His voice faltered and his left eye flickered. He seemed to be struggling to speak. The bellows on his chest pumped rapidly and the reels spun around.

'My enemy is who?' Lil asked. 'What are you talking about?'

The automaton straightened his back and, in a more controlled, less distraught tone, said briskly, 'Your enemy is cheap tea bags. Never purchase the economy sort. Always choose the finest quality.'

'I think you did get zapped yesterday,' Lil muttered. 'I'm going to the hotel. Get busy digging.'

When she had left the house, Jack Potts hung his head.

'You have made me do dreadful things, Mister Dark. I wish you had left me in the scrapyard. It would have been better for all if I had been broken up for parts.'

Cruel laughter echoed within his tin skull.

The sand continued to settle over Whitby. By the time Lil reached the bridge it had formed great mounds in the streets, and buried cars. Walking was an effort that tested the muscles. The bridge itself was sagging in the middle from the immense weight of the drifts that covered it. Ominous creaks followed her as she crossed and she was afraid it would buckle and crash into the river. She glanced down at the water. It was thick and cloudy and both shores were creeping towards the centre. Soon there would be no river at all.

She was relieved when she made it to the other side. Looking back she saw that the East Cliff was disappearing under the relentless sandfall. Roofs were caked in it and the ground floors were almost gone. The cliff was a steep, biscuit-coloured ridge, the 199 steps had become a smooth and perilous slope and the church of St Mary and the abbey looked like colossal sandcastles. The West Cliff was faring no better.

She wondered how much more this little seaside town could take.

Adjusting the plastic sun hat, she headed for the Royal Hotel. Throughout the day, the sand fell steadily. Everyone remained indoors.

Lil spent another long day in the games room, renewing her previous work. She was immensely pleased to see how effective her magic had been. Six-year-old Paula had made an almost complete recovery and Clarke was well on the mend. The doctor wanted her to try her methods in the ballroom, but Cassandra ruled that place with a will of iron and she banned the doctor from ever entering again when he suggested it. Her magic alone reigned in there, she had shrieked at him.

Lil hardly recognised her mother any more. Her make-up and backcombed hair weren't just gothic –

there was something startlingly ritualistic and warlike about her appearance.

By early evening, the windows of the ground floor were totally blocked by rising sand. Lil could do no more. Her fingers throbbed and she was desperate to know how Cherry was doing. There was no possibility of leaving via the main entrance, so she climbed the stairs to the hotel's first floor. Noreen accompanied her; she was anxious about Verne.

'I'm sure he'll be all right,' Lil assured her.

'I never worry about him when he's with you. He was never strong – you always looked after him, even when you were little.'

They had come to the first floor, but the only windows looking eastward were in the guest rooms. Lil tried the nearest door. It was unlocked.

Inside, the curtains were drawn, but there was light behind them and by it they made a grisly discovery. This was where those who had died of the sickness in the hotel had been brought. Eleven bodies, wrapped in sheets, were sardined on the bed and the floor.

Noreen jumped in shock and clasped her hands to her mouth.

'I might have been able to save them,' Lil reproached herself.

'Not your fault, luv,' Mrs Thistlewood told her, rubbing the girl's arm. 'Let's try the next room. Leave these poor souls in peace.'

The curtains of the neighbouring suite were open and they ran to the window to drive away that last awful image.

The scene before them took their breath away. They barely recognised the view as being Whitby. The Esk Valley was filled with sand. There was no river any more, just a desert that stretched between chimney pots and rooftops. The sea had retreated from the harbour, forming a new beach between the two stone piers.

'It looks so clean,' Noreen said, marvelling at the stark, blank sand unmarked by any footprint. 'Like a crisp, new, golden tablecloth. It'd be beautiful if it wasn't horrifying.'

'There are houses you can't even see any more,' Lil said. 'They're completely buried. What if there were people still inside?'

'Entombed, like a lost city of pharaohs.'

Noreen slid up the bottom sash of the window. The sand had piled against the hotel walls and formed a bank below that wasn't too steep.

'We can slide down there easy,' she said.

'You coming too?' asked Lil in surprise.

'I don't want Verne walking home on his own across that Martian wasteland. It'll be dark soon.'

And so they slithered down the slope and set off through an arid terrain of dunes and hollows. There was no point heading for the bridge; it had collapsed hours ago. It was quicker to cut across the sandy gulf where the river had once been.

Down by the area of sand that covered the railway station, three figures were methodically visiting as many buildings that were still accessible. One was Inspector Brian Lucas, another was Constable Reg Gibson and the third was Wayne Hunter, a personal trainer.

'We're never going to get round the whole town with just us three,' Reg complained as he consulted the detailed list he had been given. 'It's a mad idea. We should've got a bigger team together.'

'Keep your negative attitude to yourself, Gibson,' the inspector warned. 'And make sure you keep those records accurate. No one else *was* available: they're either too busy hacking their livers up or nursing those that are. Look around you – there's not one footprint in this sand except ours. We're all there is and what we're doing might just save a life.'

'Can't see the point,' Reg continued, removing his spectacles and wiping the lenses. 'We've got no authority, no backup, nothing. Don't see why we have to pretend to be rescue rangers as well.'

'Does he never stop whining?' Wayne asked. 'Just keep score there, man. Not as if you'll be doing any of the physical stuff. I'm the guy with the ropes, spade and muscles.'

'Wait, did you hear that?'

'No.'

'Ssshh!'

The inspector led them into a cramped alley between two buildings. A large clump of sand had just slid off the roof.

'Big heap of nothing,' Reg said. 'We're just chasing noises. I've had enough. My legs are killing me walking through this. I'm going back to the church hall.'

Handing the file to his superior, he plodded away, grumbling to himself.

Retracing their outward tracks, he scowled as he began to see other markings in the sand beside them. They looked to have been made by scurrying twigs. Reg knelt to examine them, peering over his spectacles. It was peculiar the way the marks disappeared every few metres, where the sand was kicked into piles.

'Too big for moles,' he murmured. 'Funny.'

A movement in the corner of his eye made him turn sharply. Something was travelling fast just beneath the surface. It stopped suddenly and two waving, segmented antennae poked through the sand.

'What the . . .?'

The area around him thrashed into violent life. Sand flew everywhere as several tortoise-sized creatures buzzed and broke out of hiding.

Reg covered his face and tried to run, but they rushed at him.

The inspector and Wayne heard his screams, but

by the time they reached that spot, he was gone. The sand was churned up and there were unmistakable signs he had been dragged towards one of the dunes. But the tracks ended there. He had either been plucked into the sky, or pulled into the ground.

'Are all those dark spots and splashes what I think they are?' Wayne asked in a scared voice.

Inspector Lucas stooped to pick up a pair of broken spectacles that were sticking out of the sand. They were dripping with blood.

'Yes,' he said.

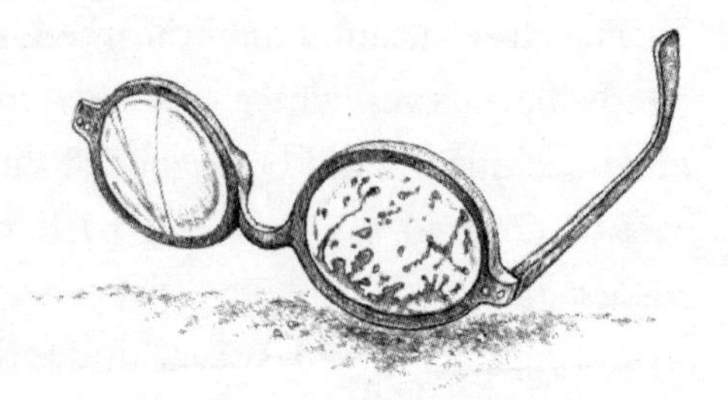

13

Church Street was just a long dip between two ranges of sand-covered roofs. The altered topography was disorientating. The only landmark from which Lil and Noreen could get their bearings was the clock tower of Market Place. With that behind them, they followed the trench, wondering how they would tell where the entrance to Cherry's yard lay.

The upended blade of a shovel sticking out of the sand solved that problem, but the opening was unreachable.

'There's no way we can tunnel our way down there,' Noreen said. 'We'll have to go over the roof.'

'Wait a minute,' Lil said, scooping handfuls of sand away to reveal the shovel's handle. 'Help me, will you?'

Mrs Thistlewood joined her in scrabbling the sand away, digging like dogs searching for a buried bone.

Presently they unearthed a metal fist clutching the handle. Lil let out a cry of triumph and redoubled her efforts. The pit grew larger until finally the top of a parka hood emerged under their fingers.

'That's not Verne, is it?' Noreen asked fearfully.

Lil tugged the hood clear and Noreen recognised the tin head immediately.

'Jack Potts!' she cried. 'But how? We thought he was junked with everything else in the spring.'

'He came back this week. He's been staying at ours.'

'Is he working OK? Hello, Jack, can you hear me?'

There was no response.

'Maybe the sand got in his gears and stuff?' Lil said sorrowfully. 'He must've been trying to keep the passage clear and seized up.'

'Why didn't Verne tell me he'd come back? Why was he at your place?'

Lil looked uncomfortable. 'Verne thought you'd put him on eBay. He knew how bad you needed the money.'

Noreen was crestfallen. 'I'd never have done that. Times are tough, yes, but that robot was fantastic. Verne should have trusted me. He must have been so miserable, poor luv.'

'I think we've all been making some big mistakes. If I hadn't shut my mum out, she might not have had this mad breakdown. She said some awful stuff to me, but it hurt most because I knew it was true.

I let the whole magic thing go to my head.'

'So you're a rubbish daughter and I'm a lousy mother. And there we were thinking we were perfect. You got any of your funny old words to cover this?'

Lil managed a smile. 'I suppose we've been fopdoodles and lubberworts.'

'Yep, sounds about right. Pull that spade out of Jack's hand and let's dig this metal wonder out. I've missed his polishing and shirt-folding . . . Wait a minute, wait a minute!'

She reached into her pockets and pulled out a ten pence which she inserted into Jack Potts's head. The indicator light flashed on.

'Not such a fopdoodle after all,' she said smugly.

'Mistress Lil,' the mechanical greeted. 'You found me! I hoped you would. That is why I held up the spade when I felt my last coin running out. Even if it had not, the sand was descending too fast. I could not do as you requested and keep the alley clear. I do apologise.'

Then he noticed Noreen.

'Mistress Thistlewood. How . . . pleasant to see you again. Does this mean I am to be auctioned?'

'I don't sell family members,' she told him. 'Now get yourself out of there.'

The butler's torch eyes brightened and he pulled himself free.

'What's with the parka?' Noreen asked.

'So he doesn't get seen,' Lil answered.

The woman laughed. 'After everything that's happened, you're still worried what the neighbours will think? I thought I was the uptight one. Take it off, Jack. Be yourself.'

Jack Potts removed the bulky coat and Verne's mother regarded him fondly. 'Much better. More honest, don't you think? Now, give me and Lil a leg-up getting over this roof.'

With his assistance it was hardly any obstacle at all and they were soon sliding into the courtyard beyond.

The bedroom windows of the cottages there were not wholly submerged. They hurried to the one with pink and yellow frames and knocked on the glass. The upper sash was yanked down and a familiar face leaned out.

'Where've you been, Rustbreath? Get your tin tushy in here. I'm gaggin' for a steamin' cup of green tea.'

'Cherry!' Lil cried.

Cherry Cerise was huddled in the blankets Lil had made for her. Both were now bleached of colour. She looked tired and frail, but the indomitable fire was burning inside her once again.

'When you knit, sister,' she said, with pride in her voice and a sparkle in her eyes, 'you really knock it outta the park.'

A little while later they were all in her parlour, which was illuminated by paraffin lamps. Jack Potts was heating a kettle between his hands and everyone was talking across one another. Cherry had only regained consciousness half an hour ago and Verne hadn't had a chance to fill her in on everything that had happened since she collapsed. It was then that Noreen found out about the paintbox.

'And you've been dealing with this on your own?' she asked her son, appalled. 'You're only eleven!'

'There was Cherry and Lil too! And I'm almost twelve.'

'Why didn't you tell me and your father? We could have helped and supported you. That's what families are for. We don't understand the whole magic thing, but we're always here for you. You have to trust us. Please, no more secrets.'

'That's what I told the kid,' Cherry put in.

Verne chewed his lip. Should he mention the Nimius or would that be one revelation too many?

'And you think all this will be over when the last watercolour is used up, the day after tomorrow?' Noreen asked.

'That's what we're hoping,' Lil said. 'We've got no real proof though, just the rhyme under the lid.'

'And what are the other colours? What is this . . . this devil's paintbox going to inflict on us next?'

Lil passed it over.

Noreen stared at it in sheer disbelief. That something so ordinary could be responsible for so much death and horror was outside the reach of her comprehension.

She ran her fingers along the empty compartments. Lifting out the last two pigment blocks, she read what was inscribed on their backs.

'*China White* and *Warrior Blue*. I don't like the sound of the last one.'

'Yeah, that kinda freaks me out as well,' Cherry said.

'What do you think it means?'

'Hot water is ready,' Jack Potts interrupted.

'Those are not my tea bags,' Cherry observed as he poured the boiling water.

'I took the liberty of using some of my own. I have been experimenting in the Wilsons' kitchen. I trust you find the flavours to your liking.'

'Is this that radical idea you've been raving on about?' Lil asked, rolling her eyes.

'It is indeed. These are only the fruit teas; the others would require milk, but we have none.'

'Mmm . . . orange and cinnamon?' asked Noreen. 'This is delicious.'

'I've got apple and blackberry,' said Verne.

'*Baked* apple and blackberry,' Jack Potts corrected.

'Raspberry and ginger here,' said Lil.

'Pear and honey,' said Cherry, cupping the mug in her hands and sinking back into the chaise longue. 'This reaches so many places I thought had raisined up years ago! Who needs witchcraft when you've got a wizard in the kitchen?'

'You really blended these different teas with what you found at our place?' Lil asked, impressed.

'I blended no tea leaves. This is just the ordinary *Camellia sinensis* variety.'

'I don't understand.'

'It's the bags!' Verne said. 'You put all the flavour in the bags themselves! Clever!'

'So you only ever have to keep one lot of bog-standard tea and a packet of fancy-flavoured empty bags,' said Noreen. 'I like that. It'd free up a lot of cupboard space.'

'You crazy Brits,' Cherry chuckled. 'Here we are on the brink of what could be the end of everything and you take time out to gab about tea. I love it.'

'Do you think my innovation is a good idea, Mistress Lil?' Jack Potts asked.

'It's nice, but it's not really important, is it?'

'I disagree. It is so much more. You see, the specially prepared bags . . .'

He twitched and his left eye flashed erratically.

'You OK, Jack?' Noreen asked.

'May I sponge down your walls, Miss Cerise?' he asked abruptly. 'Those beetles left such a mess.'

'Me and Verne had better get going,' Noreen declared. 'It must be dark outside by now and Dennis will be wondering where we are.'

'Allow me to accompany you,' Jack Potts offered.

'Hey, Lil,' Cherry said, 'you go home to your own bed. I'll be OK. I'm just gonna snore the night away. We need clear heads and every ounce of strength we can muster tomorrow. We might nearly be at the end, but I don't think the danger's goin' to ease off – just the opposite.'

Giving everyone a lamp, she saw them upstairs and watched them leave out of the window. Then she sat on her bed and put her head in her hands.

'Boy, I feel old as Noah's great-grandma,' she told herself. 'I hope I got enough zing in me to last this out.'

Lil and the others reached Henrietta Street without incident. Outside the upstairs windows of the Wilsons' cottage, Jack Potts forced the lock and she climbed inside.

'See you tomorrow, as close to seven as I can guess at,' Verne said.

'No need to guess,' Noreen told him. 'There's wind-up watches at the hotel. You'll be here at seven sharp and so shall I. You can't keep doing all this on your own.'

Waving them off, Lil saw them cut across the wide stretch of sand that had replaced the harbour, then closed the window.

This room was where her parents slept. Holding the lamp high, she smiled when she saw one of her father's waistcoats on a hanger. She missed him deeply and wished her mother would let her see him.

Thinking of Cassandra, Lil gazed at the gowns and bodices that had been pulled from the wardrobes. She was never usually this messy. Then she noticed something in the lamplight that made her grimace. The bottom edge of her mother's pillow was streaked with blood.

Backing away from the empty bed, Lil carried the lamp out on to the landing and into her own room. She had brought the paintbox with her and she placed it on the dresser. A reckless idea had come to her while at Cherry's. The colour witch had looked so delicate and weak that Lil knew there was no way she'd be able to face whatever perils the next paint block had in store for them. So she determined that, tomorrow, she would go it alone.

In the comfort of her own bed sleep came to her swiftly. She did not hear the noises of the night that scratched over the roof and outside her window, nor sense the long insect limbs that felt their way round the frame, seeking entry.

At the end of the bed, an invisible presence sat on the furry blanket that Sally had once slept on and a low growl sounded from the loyal dog's phantom throat.

The creature outside the window retreated back into the sand.

Up in the abbey grounds, the number of revellers had doubled since the previous night. The frenzied music was louder and Cassandra told them that tomorrow they would appease the gods and beg deliverance from the catastrophes that blighted Whitby. The cheering could be heard all the way to the barricade and the soldiers on duty wondered what on earth was going on.

An hour before dawn, Lil awoke. The night was turning pale and the sand outside her window almost looked like snow. When she had washed and dressed, she sat with the paintbox on her lap, trying to find the courage to carry out her intention.

'Got to do this,' she urged herself. 'Cherry isn't up to it and Verne is safer where he is.'

Her mind made up, she took the box downstairs to the kitchen and filled a glass with water.

She was disappointed that Jack Potts was not around. She would have liked his company.

Lil wondered if the sand outside would act as insulation against the box's power. Might it contain whatever frightening magic burst out of it today?

Taking deep breaths and keeping one set of fingers crossed, she dipped the brush in the water.

'*China White*,' she said, staring at the pigment which had an image of a teapot stamped on it. 'Let's see what you're made of. Pity Potts isn't here, sounds right up his street.'

She splashed the water over the paint block and waited.

The box began to tremble.

14

In the Royal Hotel, the candles that had burned through the night were almost spent. The only ventilation on the ground floor was via the wedged-open doors leading to the stairwell. It had become a sweltering underground bunker. Cassandra Wilson had extended her control to the bar and restaurant area, and no one from the games room was permitted to enter. Cassandra had also decreed that Lil must not be allowed back into the hotel. If her daughter was healing the sick, it could only be through evil means.

The patients slept fitfully, but their coughs and diseased murmurings did not disturb Verne. He was dreaming of the joyous time the Nimius had flown him over the town and he smiled in his slumber.

Lying next to him, his mother was wide awake. She was going over everything she had learned at Cherry's. He and Lil were as close as any brother and sister and that girl's life was never going to be safe and ordinary. Where she went, he would follow.

Gazing at him in the guttering candlelight she felt a tremendous surge of pride for everything he had done. She knew that at school some of the kids called him 'Flimsy'. His slight frame and introspective, nervy nature had caused her anxiety in the past and yet he had shown more courage than anyone she had ever known.

She put her hand out to sweep the fringe from his eyes, but her fingertips never reached him.

Outside, the dying night was ruptured by a searing flash of white light from the direction of Henrietta Street. It was so intense it shone through the deep sand, radiating out in a dazzling pulse. When it hit the hotel the submerged windows dazzled like arc lights and the panes exploded inward.

Blasted awake, people screamed as the sand flooded in and the candles blew out, but their voices were drowned by the sound wave that chased the energy burst.

It was like the noise of a finger rubbing the rim of a wine glass amplified to an ear-blistering level.

'Mum?' Verne yelled, when it was over and someone had relit the candles. 'Where are you?'

'Noreen?' Dennis called frantically.

She was nowhere to be found. Then they realised that others were missing. With sickening dread they looked at the tons of sand that had gushed through the shattered window. Noreen and the rest had to be buried under there.

Verne and his father rushed to begin a hectic rescue, digging through the sand with bare hands. After many frantic minutes they gave up in consternation. There was no one under it.

'Where'd she go?' Verne asked, holding on to his father desperately.

'Dad!' Clarke's panicked voice called from his place on the floor. 'Over here!'

Dennis and Verne approached and gasped with disbelief when they saw what he was holding.

'It was just lying here!' Clarke cried. 'I almost broke it when I turned over. My God – I almost smashed her!'

Dennis knelt down and took the delicate piece of porcelain from him. It was a finely modelled figurine, beautifully glazed with pale colours – a perfect likeness of his wife.

'What does it mean?' he spluttered. 'Verne, what's happened?'

The boy gazed at it with rising horror, feeling as though he had plunged into ice water. Around them, others were discovering that their loved ones had also been exchanged for statuettes.

A woman screeched. She was holding up the fragments of a figure that looked like her husband, which she had accidentally crunched underfoot.

The damaged pieces were hollow and miniature ceramic replicas of bones and internal organs tumbled out.

'Oh, Lil,' Verne breathed. 'You didn't wait. What have you done?'

'Tell me this isn't actually your mother!' his father implored.

The expression on Verne's face was all the answer he needed.

'Is she dead? Or is she still in there? Is she aware?'

'I don't know,' Verne said.

There was uproar in the other parts of the hotel. A number of the figurines had been destroyed by accident and their relatives were overcome with grief and fury.

The Thistlewoods could hear Cassandra Wilson's raised voice.

'More black magic!' she yelled. 'This supernatural terrorism has to stop. We must end this bedevilment! Burn it out from our midst!'

'We have to get out of here,' Dennis told his sons. 'I don't trust that mob. She's preaching hate and violence and it's going to erupt any time now. Clarke, are you up to walking?'

'I think so.'

'How about running?'

To leave the hotel, they had to cut through one corner of the ballroom. The crowd in there was braying for vengeance and justice and their High Priestess was promising both.

Keeping their heads down, the Thistlewoods squeezed round the back of Cassandra's followers. Dennis cradled the porcelain effigy of his wife in his arms, shielding it from jostling elbows. His boys followed him closely. They were almost at the door to the stairs when a man caught Dennis by the shoulder. It was Rory Morgan, the councillor. There was a manic intensity in his eyes.

'The Lady Cassandra has not finished speaking,' he said. 'We must all listen. Where are you going?'

'There's no air in here,' Mr Thistlewood said, attempting to bluff his way out. 'My lads are going to faint. We'll be back in a few minutes.'

'Hold on,' Rory snarled, recognising Verne. 'I've seen that kid with our Lady's daughter. She betrayed us all to that filthy Cherry woman. I was there when that foul witch made the town turn yellow and called this plague on us. You lot aren't going nowhere.'

There was a scuffle as Dennis shoved Rory in the chest to get free. More hands seized him and Rory snatched the figurine from his arms.

'Give her back!' Dennis bawled. 'Give my wife back!'

'Ask nicely!' came the answering taunt as he passed it from one hand to the other. 'Or I might drop her.'

'Don't! Please don't!'

The man laughed in his face then doubled over in pain as Clarke ripped a fire extinguisher from the wall and rammed it into his groin. Noreen went flying from his grasp and somersaulted high over Dennis's head. She spun towards the floor and her husband yelled in fear. Clarke leaped to catch her, but a fist punched him in the stomach and he was knocked further into the crowd. Dennis heaved against his captors, but they held him firm. He was about to let out an anguished howl when he saw Verne sprawled on the carpet, right arm raised, the figurine in his hand.

'Run!' his father shouted. 'Get out of here!'

There was nothing Verne could do for his father or brother. They were already being dragged through the hostile mob towards Cassandra. Hands came lunging for him too, but he dodged, kicked three shins and somehow wove his way out, with his mother tucked securely under his arm. Moments later he was pelting up the stairs to the first floor guest room.

Out of breath, he scrambled through the window and half rolled, half skidded down the scree of sand outside. Reaching the bottom, he examined the statuette and was beside himself with relief to find it undamaged. Lurching to his feet, he raced over the dunes.

The trampling of the previous night's drunken excursion to the abbey by Cassandra and her followers had marred the smooth expanse of desert between the two halves of the town. As Verne traversed that wide, churned-up route, he saw a motionless figure in the distance. The sunlight was glinting off its tin head.

When Verne reached Jack Potts he found that the mechanical had run out of coins again. He was annoyed to see that Jack's hockey-mask face had been vandalised with lipstick scribbles, and odd socks were hanging off his brass ears. The boy wiped the worst off with his sleeve, then searched his own pockets and those of the leather tailcoat, but couldn't find any ten pences.

'Lil will have coins,' he said. 'I'll be back in a bit.'

Hurrying to the Wilsons', he climbed through the upstairs window and called for Lil.

The house was deathly quiet.

Verne went in every room, finishing in the kitchen,

but there was no sign of her. The downstairs was encased in darkness and he had to fumble blindly to find the gas lighter that was kept near the stove. Lighting some of the candles that were everywhere in the Wilsons' house, he saw the paintbox lying open on the table. The white pigment block had been used up and he found the paintbrush on the floor by a glint of the gold around the handle. The windows were all shattered and the sand had engulfed the sink and the back door.

Thinking Lil must have gone to Cherry's, he was soon outside again and running in the long hollow beneath which Church Street lay buried.

Cherry Cerise was tying ribbons and tinsel to the gutters of her cottage and had spread a colourful rag rug on the sand in front of it. That morning her wig was a rainbow Afro, complemented by a jazzy pink and purple poncho.

'White's a tricky one,' she said, hearing Verne slide down a rooftop to drop into the courtyard. 'Personally, I never cared for it. But it's the colour of blossom and all that hey nonny May stuff. Denotes purity, grace and chastity – I guess that's why I'm not a fan. It's also a very acceptable colour for sacrifice, white bulls being a classic favourite, and is of course the colour of the moon and the Goddess.'

Attaching the final ribbon, she stood back to admire her handiwork.

'Couldn't stand being cooped up inside any longer,' she said. 'So thought I'd brighten up my new front yard a bit. Hmmm, looks kinda like Santa's grotto, if he was a bum. Anyhoo, thought you'd have brought the paintbox here today to do the biz. I may not be firin' on all Crayolas, but I'm better than I was. So what did this one do, apart from crack all my windows?'

'It turned people into china figures!' Verne blurted. 'Small statues of themselves. It did it to my mum!'

'Seriously? Total, instant transformation? That's smack-me-in-the-face-with-a-rubber-fish remarkable. I never figured on the china aspect. Whoever devised this has one real sick sense of humour.'

'My mum!' Verne repeated angrily. 'Is there something we can do to change her back?'

'You got her with you?'

'No, I was so scared of dropping and breaking her on the way I stashed her somewhere safe.'

'I'm real sorry, Verne, but we're dealing with hugely powerful forces. That stuff is outta my ballpark, even if I was my old razzle-dazzle self.'

'I thought maybe Lil could try something. Where is she?'

'She's not with you?'

'No, she did the paintbox on her own. I was still at the hotel. Really narked with her about that.'

'You been to hers?'

'Yes, she wasn't there.'

'You sure?'

'I looked everywhere and called. Where would she have gone?'

'I think today,' Cherry said in a voice filled with concern, 'the paintbox just might have bit the artist.'

'You mean Lil was changed too? I didn't check. It was dark in there and I wasn't looking for that.'

'We'd best find out.' Cherry closed her window. 'Been hearin' some strange things runnin' over the roofs lately. And they've been chewin' up the woodwork. Don't want them to get in.'

'What things?'

'Not sure yet. But sounds like they're gettin' bigger each night. Are the windows of Lil's place still intact?'

'The ones upstairs are,' said Verne.

'Say, you did remember to shut them when you left, yeah?'

'I . . . I don't know.'

'Then we better get there pronto! Anything could crawl inside.'

A near silent footfall sounded on the landing of the Wilsons' home. Four sable feet came padding noiselessly down the stairs and golden eyes pierced the dark. The candles in the kitchen were still burning and the intruder prowled in.

Catesby flapped his wings and flew on to the table.

He circled the paintbox and flicked his tail impatiently as he glared around the room.

The Wilsons' orange and black kitchen was filled with clutter; witchcraft-themed mugs and pots lined the shelves of the Welsh dresser and hung on hooks under cupboards. There were cauldron-shaped storage jars and dark green teapots with goblin faces. Witchy ornaments were dotted around on every surface, but Catesby was searching for one in particular.

There at the end of a shelf was the porcelain figure of a girl with her hands raised before her frightened face. It was Lil.

A low, menacing purr reverberated in Catesby's throat. He rose off the table and alighted further along the same shelf. Furling his leathery wings, he stalked forward, knocking off the obstacles that were in his way.

The figurine was almost in swiping reach and the mutant cat's claws slid from their sheaths. Closer and closer he came, head low, eyes shining with malignant intent.

Before he could lash out, the kitchen was filled with frantic barking. Catesby whirled around and hissed, the hackles rising on his back. The broken crockery covering the floor scattered as small paws rampaged and skidded in.

Sally's ghost bounded on to a chair and from there to the dresser. She had never manifested visibly before, but now the Westie's sturdy and compact form was revealed in the candle glow. She charged along the dresser counter, leaping up at the shelf, where Catesby was spitting and jabbing with his talons.

The dog barked even louder and clamped her jaws round the cat's outstretched leg. Catesby screeched and took to the air – with Sally attached.

The winged cat flew around the kitchen, trying to shake off the phantom Westie, but Sally held firm. Catesby wheeled about in rage, then tore into the hall and up the stairs, colliding with Verne and Cherry who were descending. There was a tangle of fur, wings and disco wig. Sharp claws snagged in the nylon frizz and Catesby shrieked in aggravated fury. Sally finally let go and was caught by a boggling Verne. The barking recommenced and Cherry hollered as she struggled to keep the wig on her head.

And then Catesby was free. He rushed over the landing and into the front bedroom where he shot out of the window, yowling like a scalded demon.

'What was that?' Verne spluttered, open-mouthed.

Cherry tugged the Afro back in place and pulled out a torn claw.

'I've been a senile old jelly brain,' she uttered, staring at it in fearful recognition. 'That Frankenpuss, kiddo, was, or is, the particularly nasty familiar of the worst devil I ever met . . . Mister Dark.'

'But he's dead!' Verne cried. 'He was blown up, you told me!'

'He was an agent of the Lords of the Deep. If they thought he could still be of service, a little thing like death wouldn't stand in the way. I really have been blind. No wonder this has been so personal.'

Verne wanted to ask her more, but Sally wriggled and jumped from his arms. She ran down the stairs, parping little ghost farts all the way, a habit of her earthly life.

Verne remembered why they were here.

'Lil!' he yelled.

They hurried after the Westie and found her

pawing at the dresser in the kitchen.

'Good girl, Sal,' Verne said. 'Good girl.'

Sally's tail swept to and fro on the floor like a windscreen wiper.

Verne reached up and took the figurine down gently. Both he and Cherry gazed at it in dismay.

'Why did you have to use the paintbox on your own this time?' the boy berated it.

'I don't think she can hear you,' Cherry told him. 'Her consciousness will be in a limbo someplace. She won't hear or feel a thing, unless that figure is broken – she'd feel that. Be the last thing she ever did feel.'

'What can we do?'

'She can't stay here. This house isn't safe.'

'You think that cat monster will come back?'

'For sure, but he won't be on his lonesome next time. 'Cept Catesby ain't what I've been hearing gnawin' at the window and clattering over the roof at night.'

'What was it then?'

Sally began to growl and turned to face the mountain of sand that covered the sink. A clicking sound was coming from within. There was movement. Rivulets of sand dribbled down the side, then two questing antennae came spiking out, followed by a stick-like leg.

'Yep. Pretty certain it was that!' Cherry exclaimed.

Sally barked fearfully. She lunged at the sand, then backed away as another segmented limb flicked out.

'Run,' Cherry told Verne.

'Get the paintbox!' he urged.

As Cherry reached for it the sand erupted and a creature almost as large as the sink itself slid on to the tiles.

Verne yelled in horror. It was an insect, just like one of the Carmine Swarm, but hugely magnified. The rough, ridged shell was blood red, bearing three black spiral markings. A pair of clustered eyes bulged and twisted in the boy's direction and repulsive mandibles fidgeted and frothed in greedy anticipation.

'I said run!' Cherry shouted, grabbing Verne's arm and pulling him into the hall. Sally remained to hold it off. The antennae flailed the air, then the enlarged beetle scuttled sideways, spraying a noxious fluid that made the floor tiles foam and burned holes in the cupboards.

Sally shrank back, shaking her head in alarm, before turning tail and chasing after the others. The beetle spun around and scuttled in pursuit, ripping the carpet in the hall with the knife-like pretarsi at the end of its legs. Hinging open its outer wings it took to the air.

Cherry and Verne were at the top of the stairs when it came buzzing. With Sally at their heels, they fled into the front bedroom and slammed the door behind them. There was a thud as the insect crashed into the upper panel and they heard it drop to the floor. Then a spindly leg came stabbing under the gap with the sound of chewing and splintering.

'Looks like Annie's bird buddies missed some,' Cherry said.

'But it's massive!' Verne cried.

'They never were ordinary bugs. Every day they've gotten bigger. By tomorrow they could be big as Volkswagens.'

'They? How many are there?'

'All I know is I've heard more than one of those nasty critters.'

'But where've they been hiding? Why haven't we seen them?'

Cherry looked out of the window at the dunes.

'No prizes for guessing.'

Verne followed her gaze.

'In the sand? You mean the stuff we have to walk on when we get out of here? The stuff that Whitby has been buried in?'

The attack on the door was becoming more frenzied. A jagged rip had been bitten out and they could see vicious mouthparts rending the wood.

'Time we shifted our cabooses,' Cherry said.

Verne looked down at Sally. She was beginning to fade.

'What about Sal?' he asked.

'Sounds crazy worryin' about a ghost dog,' Cherry said. 'But she's earned that and more. She saved Lil's life down there. Poor pooch just wants to stay close to her – how's that for devotion? From the looks of it she's used all her strength and can't maintain the physical form. Till she disappears completely we'll keep her with us. Lift her through the window.'

'Can't she float or fly?'

'You serious? She was a dog and remembers being a dog; when she's here she likes to do dog-type things.'

'She's my first ghost,' Verne muttered, picking Sally up, which prompted her to break wind. 'I didn't know there was rules.'

They climbed out and closed the window firmly behind them.

'With any luck,' Cherry said, 'Herbie in there won't go bananas when it finds the room empty and will lose interest.'

'Wait!' Verne said, before they set off. 'Jack Potts is only a little further on. If you've got some change we can bring him.'

Cherry looked up and down the sand-covered street.

'We shouldn't spend too long outside,' she said cautiously. 'But yeah, I want a word with the guy who puts the con in contraption.'

Jack Potts was where Verne had left him. Cherry cast a critical glance over the robot then shoved in a coin. The eyes lit up and Jack Potts thanked her.

'It is so aggravating not being financially independent. How long have I been immobile?'

'Depends what time Cassandra and her cronies left you behind last night,' Cherry answered sternly. 'Don't spin your chest barrels at me and come up with three haloes and act all singing-nun innocent. You've been playin' Lil and Verne all along. You've been workin' for Mister Dark this whole time, haven't you?'

Jack Potts took a step back and put a metal hand on his bellows.

'I assure you, madam,' he began to protest.

'Save it!' she snapped. 'People can lie real swell already; we don't need machines to join in. What's Dark gonna do next? What's he getting out of all this?'

Jack Potts flinched but made no answer. Inside his head small components began to rattle.

'I . . . I am conflicted,' he eventually uttered.

'Too darn right you am,' she said angrily. 'And I'll conflict your bionic butt right into next week if you don't level with me.'

'I don't understand,' Verne said. 'It's not true, is it? Jack, my dad made you. Why would you betray us?'

'The Nimius made me!' came the tormented reply. 'I must serve its true master and no other.'

'You think Mister Dark is the master of the Nimius?' Cherry cried in derision. 'What made you believe that baloney?'

'His hand helped craft Melchior Pyke's great

wonder. He wishes to continue Pyke's work and rid this town of witches, begging your pardon, Miss Cerise.'

'You got it all wrong!' she told him. 'I saw what happened when Melchior Pyke died. That was Mister Dark's doing. He wanted the Nimius for himself back then and I guess he still does. He's lied to you. Pyke loved Scaur Annie and they're at peace now. The feud is over. Pyke wouldn't want this town to lose their witches. You've been helpin' the very fiend who killed him.'

'Is . . . is this the truth?'

'Yes!' Verne insisted.

'If anyone's the master of the Nimius, it's Verne,' Cherry added. 'For cryin' out loud, the kid was possessed by Melchior Pyke!'

Jack Potts staggered backwards and held his head in his hands.

'Where is Mister Dark now?' she demanded.

'In the ruins of the abbey,' he said wretchedly. 'His unclean spirit has taken up residence there and no longer has need of me. He . . . he made me commit atrocious crimes! I knew no better, I swear it! His foulness has been polluting my poor wits. I must be dismantled at once and my *disjecta membra* strewn into the sea, to be corroded and consumed by brine.'

'You don't get to rust your way out of it that easy!' Cherry said curtly. 'I need you to fess up the whole diabolic kit and caboodle!'

'Whatever you wish. I am yours to command.'

'How can we possibly trust or believe him?' Verne asked, feeling hurt and foolish for having been taken in.

'You are the true master of the Nimius. I shall serve you faithfully until the instant of my dissolution. Mister Dark does want it, yes, but he can only attain the great prize once the final watercolour is used up and he is granted life once more. That is the pact he has made with the Lords of the Deep.'

'They're bringin' him back to life and lettin' him keep the Nimius?' Cherry cried. 'Have they gone nuts? He won't just destroy this town; he'll keep on going.'

'But how can the last watercolour be used?' asked Verne. 'Lil can't do it.'

Jack Potts looked at the porcelain figurine in the boy's hand and his eyes dimmed.

'Poor Mistress Lil,' he said sorrowfully. 'I tried my best to warn her, but Mister Dark would not permit me. The remaining pigment will be utilised by her mother. She is completely in his thrall.'

'So what is *Warrior Blue* going to do?' Cherry asked. 'What's the final humiliation?'

'Barbarism,' he answered bluntly. 'Everyone who is left, those who have not been stricken with the Yellow Scourge, or transformed into china figures, will become blue-painted savages and slay each other. That is the last revenge of the Lords of the Deep, for the proud little town that defied them.'

Cherry stared past him. Across the desert, there was activity on the West Pier. People were carrying furniture out towards the lighthouse.

'So we got until daybreak tomorrow to come up with something,' she said hopelessly.

'Much less time than that. The final pigment is to be triggered just after midnight tonight. Mister Dark is most impatient to be a living man once more.'

Over on the pier they were carrying what appeared to be a throne.

'So, while her friends and neighbours kill each other,' Cherry said, narrowing her eyes, 'Cassandra Wilson sits and watches.'

'On the contrary,' Jack Potts corrected. 'It is you who will be compelled to watch. By then Madam Wilson will be dead. You see, that is how Mister Dark will obtain his new life. Her blood is to be the bridge between two spheres of existence. He intends to eat her.'

15

There was a stunned silence. Cherry and Verne looked at one another, sickened.

'That's . . . it's disgusting!' Verne said. 'It's animal!'

'Don't expect anything less of Mister Dark,' Cherry agreed. 'Does Cassandra know? Or has her brain been completely Persilled?'

'There is little of Madam Wilson's true self left,' Jack Potts told her. 'Mister Dark, or Queller, as he is known to her, dominates her will utterly.'

'Queller? Yeah, sounds about right. Queller was another name for executioners, or killers. That would appeal to his sick ego.'

'His is a most compelling, overwhelming personality, as I know to my shame. When the time comes, she will submit to him not only readily but with enthusiasm.'

'If we could only get through to the walking Happy Meal, we might be able to prevent that.'

'Not even Lil was able to get through to her,' Verne said. 'We'd have no chance. She's never liked you anyway.'

'Could Mistress Lil not try again?' the mechanical asked.

Verne held up the small statue of his best friend. 'How'd you think she'd manage that?' he asked crossly. 'You've seen how she is now.'

'But surely the Nimius can assist us there? It is filled with miracles.'

'Forget it. I might be the master of the Nimius, but I don't know how to work it, remember. I can't even wind the thing up.'

Jack Potts straightened himself and the bellows puffed out.

'I am versed in all its functions,' he said.

'What? Why didn't you say?'

'Mister Dark forbade me. Until he takes possession, the Nimius is the greatest threat to his ambition.'

'And you think it could restore Lil to normal? And my mum?'

'There is but one way of finding out.'

'Let's go then!'

The shortest route to the Thistlewoods' apartment was across the harbour desert, but Cherry warned against going that way.

'We'd never make it,' she said. 'Look at all them busy bees on the pier over there. If we can see them,

then they sure have spotted us. We wouldn't get near your place.'

Verne agreed. The West Pier was crowded with Cassandra's followers and he suddenly realised what they were doing. The furniture from the hotel had been smashed up and stacked round the flagpole, where the Yellow Jack quarantine flag was hanging limply in the still air. They were constructing a huge bonfire.

'What's that for?' he asked slowly.

'You and I both know the answer to that, Kojak,' Cherry answered grimly. 'It's gonna be a beacon to tell the Lords of the Deep that Mister Dark has fulfilled his side of the deal. And I reckon yours truly has got a ringside seat.'

'How do you mean?'

'Tell him.'

Jack Potts nodded. 'The final requirement is the sacrifice of Miss Cerise,' he said. 'To achieve his goals, Mister Dark must burn the last of the Whitby witches.'

'Then you've got to get away!' the boy urged her. 'You could get past the barricade easily if you wanted to. Don't stay here! They'll get you!'

Cherry smiled. He had given no thought to his own safety.

'My place is here,' she said. 'This town is under my watch. I can't abandon it and betray all those sisters who went before me. Besides, those finks and flakes won't find it so easy to cart me over there. I still got a few tricks up my polyester blouse.'

She led them out of sight of the bustling pier and they set off to reach the Thistlewoods' home by a longer way round. Sally had almost completely disappeared: only a faint and broken outline of her little form and the indistinct impressions left in the sand by her paws remained.

The phantom Westie halted and began to growl. A bark followed, but it dwindled on the air as the manifestation finally melted away.

'Good girl, Sal,' Verne murmured in farewell.

Cherry looked around them. What had Sally sensed? Then she glanced up at the cliff.

At the top of the 199 steps, now swept clean of sand, two Rottweilers were beginning to descend side by side, with Catesby flying above their heads.

'Change of plan,' she told Verne. 'You and Mr Meccano go see if you can get the Nimius to do its thang. Here, take the paintbox – it should stick with Lil.'

'What are you going to do?' the boy asked.

Cherry grinned at him. 'Just call me Minnie. I got me a date with a mouse.'

Passing the automaton the watercolours, she pulled Verne close, as if hugging him, but it was so she could whisper.

'Be careful of Potts. He's up to something.'

With that, she hurried in the direction of her own cottage.

'Shall we proceed at pace?' the butler said. 'I know just how vicious those hounds are and I do not believe my unappetising, meat-free appearance would prevent them from tearing my limbs off.'

Verne agreed and they ran through the dunes.

They reached the West Cliff without meeting another soul and Verne was relieved that there was no sign of the Carmine Swarm. He wondered how the other emergency centres in Whitby were faring. How many people were still left alive in this tormented town?

At the high sandbank that was heaped against the buildings of Pier Road, he and Jack Potts crept along stealthily. They were uncomfortably close to where Cassandra's followers trailed down from the Royal

Hotel, with yet more wood for the beacon.

They waited until there was a gap, when no one was approaching or heading to the pier, then hastened up the bank and clambered through Verne's bedroom window.

The boy placed Lil's statue on his chest of drawers and flopped on to the bed, worn out by stress and exertion. Jack Potts deposited the paintbox next to it.

'Do you still keep the Nimius in the same place, Master Verne?' he enquired.

'Yes, be careful!'

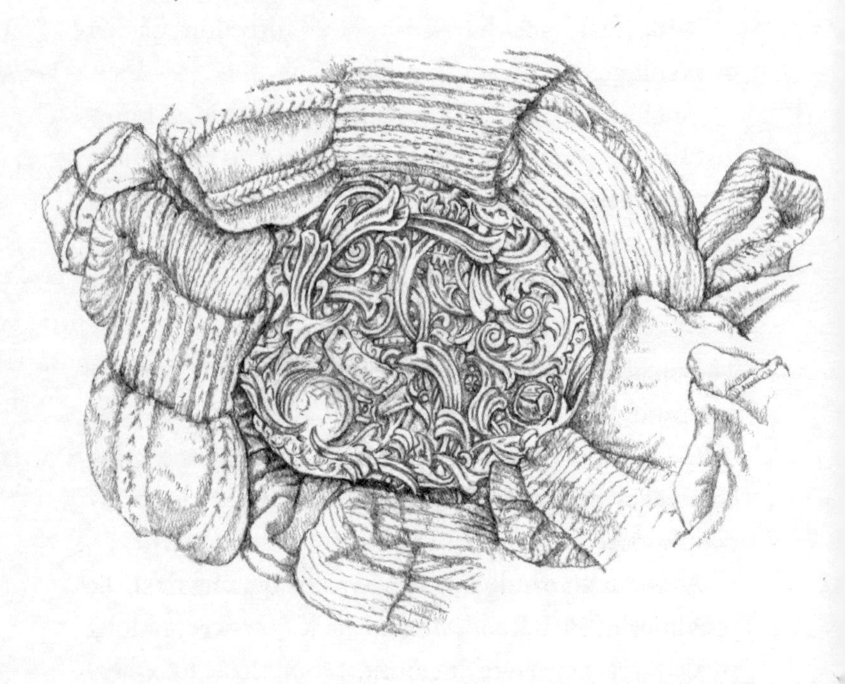

The robot had slid the top drawer open. The gold of the Nimius shone up into his hockey-mask face. Next to it was another figurine.

'I see you keep your mother in amongst your socks also,' he observed. 'I hope they are clean.'

'Don't touch her,' the boy said, jumping up to lift Noreen out and place her alongside Lil. 'It was the safest place I could think of earlier.'

'Most sensible.'

Verne removed the Nimius. He always caught his breath when he saw it.

'You really know how to work this?' he asked. 'And it'll get them back?'

'No.'

'What?'

'Or rather, yes. I do know the intricacies of its operation, but no, we cannot restore both Lil *and* Madam Thistlewood. The transformation will take many hours for just one of them. If you attempt to change both, it might not succeed at all. We are attempting to reverse the power of the Lords of the Deep and Dark, a Herculean challenge even for the Nimius. So you must choose.'

'Choose?'

'Who will you try to bring back? Mistress Lil, or your mother?'

Verne sat on the bed, aghast.

'I can't do that,' he uttered. 'It's not fair!'

'Fairness has nothing to do with it. You must be rational. The decision might have devastating consequences.'

Verne gazed at the porcelain features of his mother and screwed his face up. He knew what he had to do, but it felt like a terrible betrayal.

'Lil,' he said, hating himself. 'Bring Lil back. If there's the slightest chance of getting through to Cassandra . . .'

'So be it. If you would kindly return Madam Thistlewood to the drawer and position Mistress Lil in the centre there.'

Verne did as he instructed.

'I'm sorry, Mum,' he said, tucking her back into his socks.

'Very good,' the butler said. 'Now, may I operate the Nimius?'

'I thought you were going to show me how to use it?'

'And so I shall, once I have set the metamorphosis in motion. There is little time. It is a lengthy process.'

He held out a metal hand.

Remembering Cherry's warning, Verne hesitated.

'Can I really trust you?' he asked.

The torch eyes shone upon him.

'The ruler of the Nimius should not falter or doubt, Master Verne. I have sworn to serve and obey and protect you. The time of greatest peril is not yet upon us. We must have faith in one another or all hope is lost. Please?'

The boy took a deep breath and passed the Nimius over.

'Thank you.'

Jack Potts's dexterous fingers pressed one symbol then another and he tipped the Nimius on its end. Then he pushed one of the ornate, curling fronds aside and quarter-turned the small wheel that lay beneath.

The Nimius shuddered in his metal hands and a gold-rimmed emerald lens hinged out. Jack Potts held it in front of Lil's figurine and the jewel began to shine. Slender green rays went flickering over the porcelain, glimmering over every curve. The room burst with splashes of light that spun around until the walls curved inwards and streaked into formless, dazzling blurs.

Verne squinted in the glare. Only Jack Potts and the Nimius, the chest of drawers and the figurine seemed real and solid.

Then he heard a voice, distorted and warped by distance and time. One moment it was remote and faint, then it seemed to rush close by.

'That's Lil!' he yelled. 'She's crying!'

'Call her!' Jack Potts commanded.

'Lil! Lil, where are you? I'm here, it's Verne! Lil!'

'Call her name!'

'Lil Wilson!'

'Her full name! Or she shall be lost to you forever!'

'You never said that might happen!'

'Her full name!'

'All of it?'

'Do you want her to dissolve in the bleak isolation of non-existence?'

'Lilith Morgana Hawthorn Blossom Minerva Tempestra Wilhelmina Wilson!'

A terrified scream cut through the whirling lights. There was a flash and the room stopped spinning.

Verne lurched forward as if brakes had been applied to the bed.

'She screamed!' he shouted accusingly. 'I heard her!'

Jack Potts waited until the emerald lens slid back inside the Nimius, then sat beside him.

'What you heard was the moment earlier today when the paintbox transformed her,' he reassured him. 'The reverse transmutation has commenced; she is in no pain, but it will take time.'

Verne stared at the figurine. It looked the same as before.

'Are you sure?'

'Let me instruct you in the peerless functions of this most marvellous instrument, then you shall not need to ask.'

'There's got to be something it can do to sort out this nightmare. Show me.'

The automaton handed the golden treasure back to him.

'You see the image of the sun, just above the centre? Apply your thumb lightly, whilst simultaneously touching the skull inscribed with the spirals of Fate, just to the left there, with your middle finger.'

'OK.'

'Now tip it twice towards you.'

'Something moved inside! I felt it! The scroll with *Nimius* written on it has risen up!'

'Press it, Master Verne.'

The boy was so excited he obeyed without thinking.

The Nimius trembled in his grasp. The topmost dial twisted round and rose on a telescopic spindle, disclosing a blue jewel.

'What's it doing?' he asked. 'What did I just do?'

'The sun is the giver of life and power. The skull is death, naturally.'

'Whose death?'

'Yours, Master Verne.'

The blue jewel flared and sapphire lightning crackled from its heart. Verne shrieked in pain as jagged forces zigzagged round his body and discharged into his head.

The agonised cry died in his throat and he slumped on to the pillows.

The jewel retreated back inside the Nimius and Jack Potts took it from the boy's hands.

His eyes shone around the room. Finding Verne's rucksack, he put the Nimius inside. Then he opened the box of watercolours and removed the final pigment to examine the image stamped on the surface. It showed primitive spears and a shield.

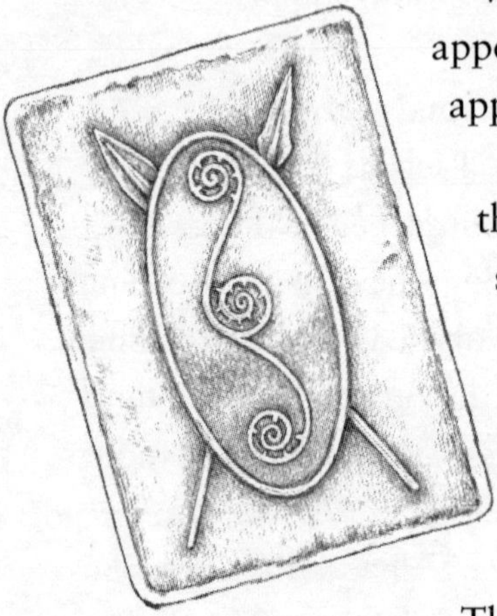

'*Warrior Blue*,' he said. 'Most apposite. The time of slaughter approaches.'

Closing the lid, he added the paintbox to the bag and stared out of the window.

'Now Jack Potts must wait,' he said quietly, 'for his appointment with Mister Dark.'

The day progressed. Many of the pier's old iron railings had been ripped out and, as evening fell, were replaced by an avenue of flaming torches. A small altar had been made from a section of the hotel bar. Tall candles were positioned at either end and incense was burning in a brass bowl. Cassandra Wilson swaggered down the pier in a gown of soft oxblood leather with a scarlet and gold cloak. Her hair was sculpted into a severe Mohican coxcomb and tribal slashes of black and red make-up sliced across her face. She placed a tumbler of water on the altar, and a ritual dagger, then smiled unpleasantly.

Three smaller bonfires had been built along that wide causeway, but the towering beacon at the far end was most impressive. It was almost as tall as the lighthouse. When lit, the flames would be seen for many miles.

Following her, in ceremonial procession, were eleven privileged followers she had chosen to be in her coven. They were also draped in long velvet cloaks, with hoods concealing their faces. Keeping a respectful distance, the rest of the crowd from the hotel watched and admired their High Priestess.

As she circled the great beacon, Cassandra swept the cloak around her melodramatically. The throne had been built into the bonfire, facing out to sea. Soon the last self-proclaimed witch of Whitby would be seated there. Cassandra smiled to think of the flames consuming Cherry Cerise.

Trawling her coven behind her, she returned to the crowd.

'This night!' she proclaimed. 'I shall bring an end to our suffering. These torments have been visited upon this town because of one who lives amongst us. Her evil must be ripped out. We shall appease the ancient gods and purify our land by a great burning. She and her wickedness shall be banished with fire – as will those who have helped her.'

The crowd parted and two bound figures were led roughly on to the pier.

Dennis and Clarke Thistlewood were bruised and limping. They were dragged to one of the smaller pyres, hoisted on to the top and tied to the central stake.

Clarke was almost unconscious, but his father was defiant. He glared at the High Priestess with eyes that were so swollen and bruised he could not open them fully.

'Cass!' he yelled. 'Don't do this. We were at school together. I was best man at your wedding. What's happened to you? This is insane! Stop this!'

She walked past him without a flicker of recognition.

'At least let Clarke go! You're his godmother! Cass! Cass!'

Drums started pounding and the audience began swaying in time.

'We have dwelt in the shadow of wickedness,' Cassandra declared. 'And allowed corruption to fester. We gave asylum to the outsider and behold where that arrogance and folly has brought us. The cancer we nurtured spread even to my own daughter. But one has come amongst us to show the way; he will lead us to deliverance!'

'Deliver us, deliver us, deliver us,' the crowd chanted.

'Whitby must be purged and made clean. Come, Queller! Guide us: we, your humble disciples, call upon you.'

'Queller, Queller, Queller,' the crowd repeated.

A chill wind blew in from the east. The torch flames bent before it and Cassandra's cloak billowed. The quarantine flag flapped wildly.

The people ceased chanting and they murmured in fear. A mewling cry sounded from the dunes behind and there was a scramble as the frightened audience sprang apart.

Two Rottweilers lumbered on to the pier, with Catesby perched upon one muscular back. Striding after, wrapped in tendrils of black mist, came the handsome Queller.

Cassandra welcomed him with outstretched arms and she tore the choker from her neck, disclosing a raw and angry-looking wound.

'Kiss me,' she begged. 'Let my hot blood be upon your cold lips.'

The dashing face smiled at her. 'Later, my juicy confection,' he said. 'First we must purify this accursed town.'

'We are still waiting on those you said would come.'

'They will be here,' he promised. 'All is unfolding in accordance with my design.'

Whispers of consternation rippled through the throng.

Queller grinned. 'And here is punctuality itself,' he announced.

Dennis Thistlewood turned his head to see this new arrival and his split lip bled again when he cried out.

Jack Potts emerged from the astonished crowd. Both eyes were flickering. Verne's rucksack was strapped to his back and the eleven-year-old's body was in his arms.

'Master Dark,' his metallic voice called. 'I am here at the time appointed. I bring the child who dared keep the Nimius from you.'

'Dead?' Queller asked.

'Upon the path,' the robot replied.

'Tie the little pig to the other pyre,' Cassandra ordered.

Two members of her coven stepped forward to take Verne and they lifted him on to the waiting bonfire.

'What of the girl?' Queller asked.

Jack Potts removed the rucksack and reached inside. His metal hands scattered broken china fragments.

'And here,' he said, 'is the box of watercolours.'

He passed it to Cassandra who stroked it reverently and placed it on the altar.

Jack Potts took out the last thing in the rucksack.

The firelight danced and flared over the sumptuously decorated Nimius and the assembled followers voiced their admiration. It seemed to shine with a light of its own.

Queller gazed at it. 'The marvel of marvels. Melchior Pyke's unrivalled accomplishment. Soon it shall be mine.'

'You are the rightful guardian and master,'

Jack Potts declared. 'The Nimius belongs unto you, Master Dark.'

'And what of you?' the phantom asked, his piercing eyes glittering. 'The mechanical man with such refined scruples and sensibilities, and the strict piety of a Puritan? How many times have I sensed your resolve and loyalty waver these past days? Are you now of one mind?'

'Most assuredly so.'

While they were talking, Catesby had been flicking his ears, and his whiskers quivered. He rose into the air and flew silently between the flaming torches. With a thrust of his wings, he plummeted down and swooped over the sand. There was the briefest of struggles, then he came racing back and deposited a small furry bundle on the ground at Queller's feet.

'They say the nicest gifts are in small parcels,' the phantom said, peering down.

A mouse with pale blue eyes stared back at him.

'You disappoint me, Miss Cerise,' Queller addressed it. 'Sending a mouse on a witch's errand? There is nothing here you could hope to learn by spying that I would not have gladly told you in person. Come and join us. Such a warm reception awaits.'

The mouse closed its eyes and covered its face with its tiny paws.

Queller signalled to Catesby. The cat pounced, then chewed and crunched the small bones with relish.

'Mister Potts,' Queller commanded. 'In case our guest of honour proves reluctant, go fetch her. Midnight is nigh and I would conclude my part of the contract as soon as I may.'

The automaton bowed low and placed the Nimius upon the altar, next to the paintbox. 'As you desire.'

Marching from the pier, Jack Potts headed over the sand to the East Cliff.

'I would be gone from this blighted sewer,' Queller uttered, leering round in disdain. 'Clad in a new, untwisted body.'

The drums beat faster and the violin and flute joined in.

Cherry Cerise stared sorrowfully at the empty cage and ran her fingers down the bars.

'I'm sorry, Ziggy,' she grieved. 'You was the best private eye a gal could ever wish for.'

She gazed into her full-length mirror. She had put extra effort into her appearance that night and she waited for her escort to arrive.

The window slid open and Jack Potts dropped into the room.

'It is time,' he said.

'So, Pottsy, you feeling all pleased with yourself now your little game is payin' off? You really had us fooled.'

'I could do no other, Miss Cerise. I must serve the master of the Nimius, to the best of my abilities.'

Cherry reapplied her glitter lipstick and checked her false eyelashes.

'Did you have to serve him up to Mister Dark though? You sly son of a coat hanger?'

'Trust me, it was the only way to keep him safe. Master Verne is in no danger now.'

'Unless someone gets match happy and lights them bonfires too early. You're taking one huge risk there.'

'The stakes could not be higher.'

'Guess so. I had Ziggy look in on Lil too, by the way. You think anyone's capable of working out that brain baffler you left? Why not just write a note instead of being so cryptic?'

'I dared not, in case it was discovered by one of Madam Wilson's followers.'

'The broken china was a neat touch on the pier.'

'I fear Madam Thistlewood will not be pleased that I deliberately smashed one of her ornaments. But the deception was necessary. Mistress Lil must have more time. We must buy her that at whatever cost.'

'Why'd you think I'm slappin' all this on? I gotta be dazzlin' tonight. Gotta stall them as long as we can.'

'Are you quite ready?'

'Is a turkey ever ready for Christmas?'

'You look spectacular, if I may presume to say so.'

'It's the foxiest best this old broad has looked in

years. Just wish I had an extra gimmick for when I make my entrance, give it some extra pizzazz.'

'Miss Cerise,' Jack Potts declared brightly, 'have I ever shown you *my* bona fide party piece?'

16

Lil passed a hand over her brow. Her head was aching. She turned over and reached for Sally. Her little dog was not there. Thumping drums and fluting music drifted through the window. Her face clouded and Scaur Annie's voice began to murmur.

> *'Does I love a bonnie sailor, or shepherd?*
> *No sir.*
> *Did I kiss the brave young soldier lad I met at Scarborough Fair?'*

Lil snapped awake and sprang up.

'No!' she snapped defiantly. 'You can't have control! I'm stronger than you!'

'For how long?' the voice echoed in her mind.

'As long as I have to be.'

She stared around the room, recognising it as Verne's, and tried to remember how she had got here.

The last she could recall was a blinding white light and a locking of her limbs. Then nothing until she thought she heard Verne calling her name.

She looked at the window. Why was it so dark outside?

On the chest of drawers, a paraffin lamp was burning and, by its light, she saw several objects had been carefully laid out.

There was a crochet hook, a ball of dark blue wool, a tea bag and, to her amazement, the final watercolour block – *Warrior Blue*.

'Potts,' she said, recognising the tea bag as one of his radical innovations. 'What's he done this for? Is it a message? What am I supposed . . .?'

She picked up the pigment, then reached for the wool. A smile of understanding spread slowly across her face.

'Oh, you metal genius!' she said.

Fifteen minutes to midnight.

There was an atmosphere of expectation and revelry down by the pier. The crowd were giving themselves to the rhythm of the music, but were impatient for the fires to be lit.

So too was Queller. Cassandra was feeding the altar bowl with incense and Dennis was gazing at his sons in anguish. Clarke had finally passed out and was slumped forward, only the ropes binding him to the central pole of the bonfire preventing him from falling.

Verne was slowly coming to. His head was nodding and his mouth was twitching. Dennis couldn't believe this was happening to them.

Catesby was perched high on the rail that ran round the lantern room of the lighthouse. His bright yellow eyes scanned the dunes that lay over the town. Shapes were moving beneath the sand. Spreading his great bat wings, he flew down to his ghostly master.

At that moment the drums faltered and the frenetic primal dancing stopped.

Jack Potts walked between them, head held erect and balancing a vinyl record on his middle finger, carrying it at shoulder height like a French waiter with a tray. Stepping out on to the pier, he waited for total silence. Then his finger began rotating at forty-five revolutions per minute and he raised his other hand until its little finger made contact with the spinning disc.

There was a slight crackle from his tea-strainer mouth. Then the immediately recognisable opening bars of 'You Sexy Thing', a famous seventies song by Hot Chocolate, came blasting from both it and his ears.

Sashaying to the funky beat, Cherry Cerise made her entrance like she was venturing on to a dance floor and owning it completely. Her body worked that tune like it was plugged into her hips.

The colour witch was dressed in her disco best.

Thigh-length lace-up boots, purple neon tights, hot pants encrusted with large pink sequins and a stole of citrus-orange faux fur. A long fuchsia wig flowed over her shoulders and a pair of rhinestone sunglasses practically covered half her face.

Reflecting the firelight, the sequins acted like a mirror ball and threw bright, shimmering circles around her.

Cherry promenaded on to the pier with enough confidence and glamour to shame an ostentation of peacocks. Even the Rottweilers tilted their heads from side to side. Cassandra was outraged, especially when Cherry sidled close and gyrated a bare shoulder at her.

Cherry boogied between the three bonfires and flicked her nylon tresses at an astonished Dennis as she took a good look at Verne. Then she danced back towards the altar where the ghostly Queller was glaring at her.

With one hand on her hip, she raised the other and wagged a disrespectful finger.

'Enough!' he bellowed.

Catesby flew to Jack Potts and raked his claws across the record, snatching it and spinning it through the air. It splashed into the sea. The sudden absence of music was startling.

'Aww,' Cherry said, disappointed. 'I was diggin' that. You need to mellow out some.'

'Take her to the beacon,' Cassandra instructed her coven.

'A moment,' Queller said. 'It is midnight. Let her see the final humbling of her beloved Whitby.'

Casting a despising glance at Cherry, Cassandra swept to the altar and ran her hands over the antique box of watercolours.

'Say, honey,' Cherry said quickly. 'Gotta tell ya, that hairdo really doesn't suit. You look like a yard brush died on your head. Still, old Dark there, he ain't choosy. Can't afford to be with that face.'

Cassandra had half opened the lid. She closed it again. 'His name is Queller, and he is the most attractive man I have ever seen.'

'That what he told you? No way! He's scammin' you, sugar. He's bad old Mister Dark and that ain't his real face neither.'

'I'm not listening to your lies.'

'Open your peepers, sister. Take a good long look at him. Here, let me help. I'm an expert at illusions; think my gorgeousness is natural?'

Cherry cupped her hands and a sparkle of pink light formed in her palms. Before anyone could stop her, she blew it at Queller.

It shot into his shadow-wrapped form like a star into a storm cloud. He snarled and twisted and let out a furious roar that made the Rottweilers jump off the pier on to the sand. The handsome face sagged and distorted and his neck buckled as a fused knot of vertebrae pushed sideways. Finally a long scar split his face.

'Well, hello there, gargoyle features!' Cherry exclaimed. 'That's the real him, Cassy. That's what you've been making cow eyes at all this time. Course, that wouldn't matter a bean, if'n he weren't twice as repulsive on the inside, but take it from me, Mister Dark is one hundred per cent monster.'

Cassandra stared at the misshapen man. 'I don't care,' she said simply. 'I love him. He has given me what I've always wanted, the gift of magic. When he is alive once more, I shall take care of him.'

Mister Dark let out a foul laugh and stepped up to Cherry. His ghostly fingers closed about her throat and he wrenched the sunglasses from her face.

'Know when you are beaten, hag!' he spat. 'Now watch what happens to the town you were supposed to protect.'

Turning to Cassandra, he told her to reveal the last watercolour.

Mrs Wilson raised the lid and stared in confusion at the open box.

'Why hesitate?' Mister Dark demanded. 'Drench all the stinking vermin in *Warrior Blue*!'

'I can't – the box is empty! There's only the brush.'

Mister Dark thrust her out of the way. He snatched up the box and shook it.

'Where?' he raged. 'Where is it? The contract must be fulfilled!'

He glowered at Jack Potts.

'You, metal man. You did this. Where is *Warrior Blue*?'

'I am not at liberty to answer that question.'

'So the machine with scruples was still dishonest enough to lie. You will tell me or your young friend burns.'

He signalled to the coven. They pulled the flaming torches from the sand and stood ready by the Thistlewoods' bonfires.

'The runt roasts first,' he said with a foul leer.

'You cannot harm Master Verne,' the robot replied calmly. 'He is the safest of us all. He has the best protection from your violent hatred there can possibly be.'

A flicker of doubt snagged Mister Dark's scarred lips. He stared at the boy on the bonfire.

'What have you done?' he demanded.

'This lowly robotic drudge has put a stupendous

spanner in your nasty works, Mister Dark. I have ensured that no one except Master Verne can ever operate the Nimius. Their fates are bound together.'

'Another lie!'

'Test it and see.'

Mister Dark glared at him then began to cackle.

'But the final pigment has not been triggered, so the pact is incomplete. The Nimius will not be given to me anyway. The boy might as well scorch and bake.'

He gave the order. A torch was thrust into the wood under Verne.

Cherry sprang forward to kick the burning timbers away, but the coven seized her and others grabbed hold of Jack Potts.

Dennis Thistlewood strained on his ropes, but they wouldn't give. He could only watch as flames began to lick upwards.

Smoke rose into Verne's face. He coughed and raised his head.

'Stop!' a voice cried out. 'Stop! You want your lousy paint block? It's here!'

Lil Wilson pushed through the crowd, holding *Warrior Blue* aloft.

Mister Dark gestured to the robed figures. They released Cherry and Jack Potts and the robot rushed to cut Verne from the bonfire. Cherry dragged him clear and held him in her arms.

He was groggy and disoriented.

'Cassandra, my dear,' Mister Dark drawled, 'your deplorable daughter has something belonging to us.'

Mrs Wilson took the ritual dagger from the altar and paced menacingly towards Lil.

'Give the pigment to me,' she threatened.

'Mum,' Lil began, 'listen to me . . .'

'You have no importance, girl. Give me *Warrior Blue*.'

'I brought someone with me. I went to the hotel before I came here. Look.'

She turned and beckoned a man forward.

Her father shambled on to the pier. His face was gaunt and sallow and his hair was plastered to his head with sweat, but he had found the strength to leave his sickbed. He leaned on Lil and stared at his wife in dismay.

'Cass!' he said. 'What is this? What the hell have you become?'

'Mike?' Cassandra murmured, confused. 'Is it you? I thought . . . I thought you'd gone . . . somewhere?'

Mister Dark called to her. 'You don't need either of them any more, my dear.'

'That's right,' she said, tossing her head. 'Me and Queller . . . no, Mister Dark, are together.'

'You and that dead nightmare?' Mike cried. 'Cass! Snap out of it!'

There was a rumble in the distance and the crowd

shifted uneasily. The sands around Whitby were quaking. Catesby slunk around the back of his master and hissed, scratching the stone with his claws. Down on the sand, the Rottweilers caught a strange scent and rushed up the nearest dune.

The humped ridge erupted and a beetle the size of a truck burst into the night air, its antennae thrashing. A sputtering roar blared from its dripping mouthparts and an acrid reek gusted across the sand. The grotesque head angled down and the dogs barked ferociously. The vast bulk sledged down the slope, then reared up on great, bristling legs.

The Rottweilers raced across the desert towards the East Cliff to escape, but the immense insect pursued them. Their yelping lasted only moments as the mandibles scooped them up. The giant beetle rocked unsteadily on its massive limbs, then it turned and the compound eyes bulged at the people gathered on the pier.

Panic and terror fuelled Cassandra's followers and they scattered into the labyrinthine dunes. The huge insect went barrelling after.

Lil and the others watched in horror. The horrific beetle crested the dunes and plunged down the other side. They heard people screaming. Then they saw countless sand blizzards break out as other segmented legs burrowed up and more beetles came crawling on to the surface to go hunting. Cherry hung her head.

'We didn't win, did we?' Verne uttered blearily.

'No,' she said. 'I lost.'

Laughing callously, Mister Dark advanced towards Lil.

'It would have been droll to observe the simple-minded swine destroy one another, emblazoned in blue warpaint. But this is far greater sport. What a week of diversion it has been. Watching my colourful poisons hatch out each day has afforded me much gratification, and I'm sure the Three beneath the waves would say the same. Yet now the merry gambols are almost ended, in fear and suffering. Hand the pigment to your mother.'

Cassandra was not aware of the devilish panorama unfolding across the town. Only the wishes of Mister Dark mattered to her. She brandished the dagger at Lil.

'My new love is aching to be flesh and blood once more.'

Shaken, Lil turned an angry face to her.

'There is no *Warrior Blue*,' she told her flatly. 'Jack Potts taught me a wonderful lesson. Any change is possible if you try hard enough. His speciality is tea bags; mine is wool. His fancy bags could make sawdust taste amazing. But my knot magic can have an even more awesome effect, 'specially on enchanted blocks of paint!'

She reached into her pocket, pulled out the small pouch she had crocheted just half an hour ago and slotted the watercolour inside. Pulling the drawstring, she tied it securely.

'At first I was going to change it from *Warrior* to *Navy Blue*. But that wasn't right either; this isn't a town for warships. Whitby has always been about simple fishing folk – the bravest heroes in the world, battling everything nature can throw at them to bring the catch home. So now, when this touches the water, it will be *Gansey Blue* – the colour of those fishermen's jumpers!'

Cherry watched her protégé with proud tears in her eyes.

'Sock it to 'em, Lil!' she cheered.

Lil grabbed hold of her mother's fist and wrested the dagger from her. The blade clattered to the ground and the girl darted off. She ran along the pier to where the unnatural sand gave way to the sea and flung the paint block as far as she could. It sank beneath the waves without a splash.

Standing on the edge, she waited to see what would happen, but a robed figure grabbed her and she was hauled back towards the altar.

A profoundly deep, bass boom sounded many leagues below. A vast spout of seawater was hurled into the air and a tremor ran through the pier. The lighthouse shook and timbers fell from the beacon. Lil staggered. The coven fell on their faces, Cassandra went sprawling, Mike fell backwards and Cherry and

Verne clung on to Jack Potts. The vibration rocked inland, where the gigantic Carmine Swarm tottered on the shivering sands and their prey stumbled.

Lil regained her balance and ran to help her father.

Mister Dark applauded. 'I really must express my gratitude. Your naive and clumsy tampering will not have invalidated the terms of the contract; quite the contrary. All the colours have now been spent. There remains only the question of the final clause. That shall be addressed without delay.'

He turned to Cherry Cerise and his scarred face split into a gloating grin.

'Take this witch to the beacon and burn her,' he ordered the coven. 'Let the Lords of the Deep know I have fulfilled my part.'

The hooded figures were picking themselves off the ground. Rising, they shook themselves and removed their robes. Underneath those velvet cloaks, each of them, including the women, was now wearing an old-fashioned fisherman's gansey and oilskins. Their faces were bronzed and cracked by years at sea and their hands were calloused. Staring at the tormented town, their weathered features set hard and they pulled the sturdiest lengths of wood from the unlit bonfires. The timber stretched in their grasp and steel spearheads grew out of their tips. Without a backward glance, they marched off to the dunes to defend their homes.

Throughout the length and breadth of Whitby it was the same. Those who were still able-bodied, even the children, had taken the form of doughty mariners from the town's glorious past. Leaving the emergency medical centres, church halls, schools and guesthouses, thousands trooped out on to the sands, bearing cruel implements used in the old whaling industry: barbed, arrow-headed or toggle harpoons, boarding knives, lances, blubber hooks, mincing knives, ropes and chains.

Under the uniting command of police inspector Brian Lucas, who appeared as a staunch, grizzled sea captain, they courageously advanced on the huge insects. Whaling guns fired and the battle to bring them down began.

'Never underestimate what the folks in this town are capable of,' Cherry said warmly. 'They just need the right kind of nudge and the right kind of leader.' Her gaze strayed to Lil.

Trumpeting screeches blared across the dunes and crimson founts sprayed into the air as harpoons bit deep. Luminous streams of acid squirted in high arcs, but the whalers dodged them easily. Rushing in, they hacked the tree-trunk-like legs and chopped them through. The first of the giant beetles toppled and crashed on to the sand.

Mister Dark turned away, displeased. Rain clouds were gathering on the horizon, moving rapidly towards the town. He knew they heralded the end of the paintbox's reign. When the last marauding insect fell, the downpour would wash the sand and the sickness away, and the whalers and porcelain people would be restored.

He had wasted too much time. He cast his cruel gaze around the pier. Without the coven, there was only Cassandra and Catesby to assist him. They were more than enough.

He rubbed the fingers of both hands together. Blue sparks formed into gobbets of crackling energy and he flung them into the bonfires where Dennis and Clarke were still tied. Flames took hold at once.

Jack Potts dashed to cut them free.

Mister Dark signalled to Cassandra and Catesby then strode towards the unlit beacon at the far end.

'Pottsy!' Cherry yelled. 'Look out!'

The mechanical butler glanced round in time to see Cassandra swinging a plank of wood at him.

It struck with sickening force. There was a snapping of metal. The brass pipes of his neck were torn from their brackets and the bicycle chain ripped away. The tin head flew from his shoulders, crashing to the ground at Lil's feet.

'NO!' she yelled.

The lights behind Jack Potts's eyes flickered a final time and died.

His decapitated body buckled and fell and the

bellows on his chest ceased pumping.

Cherry stared at it in shock, but there was no time to mourn. Flames were leaping around Dennis and Clarke.

Seeing the ritual dagger, she snatched it up and began cutting their ropes.

With Verne unprotected, Cassandra seized him roughly by the hair and dragged the boy after Mister Dark.

Lil chased them, but Catesby swooped down and attacked her father, slashing his face. Doubling back, she smacked the winged cat away. Catesby spat, then flew to the altar, took the Nimius in his four paws and raced to the beacon.

'Dad, you OK?' Lil asked desperately.

'Go get Verne!' Mike said, clutching a bleeding forehead. 'And Lil, save your mother. That's not our Cass. You know that.'

Lil kissed his hand.

Cherry had successfully freed Clarke and laid the unconscious boy down, away from the flames, but she was struggling with Dennis's ropes.

'Help me!' she called to the girl as she ran by. 'Quick!'

'Doesn't matter about me!' Dennis protested. 'Help Verne!'

'Verne's too important to Mister Dark!' Cherry told the pair of them. 'He needs him alive. He's in no danger. But you're gonna be a human doner kebab real soon. Quit strugglin'. Lil, tag in, my hands ain't as strong as they used to be.'

The girl took the dagger and jumped in her place. Black smoke flooded into her eyes, blinding her. Mr Thistlewood's clothes were beginning to singe and he clenched his teeth, twisting his head away from the rising flames. Then the final rope was cut. He lurched off the burning pyre and rolled on the ground. His clothes were alight and he yelled in agony. Thinking quickly, Lil pushed him off the pier on to the sand, jumped down and threw great handfuls over him, quenching the flames.

'It's OK,' Lil told him. 'I don't think it's too bad.'

Dennis raised his head and looked the length of the pier, to where the beacon was waiting to be lit.

'Please,' he begged. 'Save Verne.'

Lil promised. 'Me and Cherry won't let anything . . .'

She looked around her. Where was Cherry?

The moment Lil had taken the dagger from her, Cherry Cerise had run off. Clearing the lighthouse, she saw Verne pinned against the stacked timber of the beacon by Catesby, who was perched on his chest and mewling threateningly.

Cassandra had removed her cloak and stood with her head back and eyes closed, enraptured. Mister Dark's crooked, shadowy shape was looming over her. His hand reaching for her exposed throat.

Cherry steeled herself. She could do this. She had to. It was her job. 'Wait!' she called out. 'Let her go.'

His heavy-lidded eyes glinted back her.

'Don't give me the raised monobrow routine. You knew I'd be here. We been tippy-toein' around this all night long.'

'Blood is the bridge. I will have life again.'

'Fine! But not hers. She might be a witless dabbler with an overinflated opinion of herself, but she's got a kid that needs her. As she herself pointed out, I got no one. Take your hoodoo off – have me instead.'

'You?'

Cherry stepped forward.

'Like you didn't set this up from the start. The last clause of the pact still needs tickin'. You have to kill the Whitby witch, but you were never just gonna burn me. Waste all that funky witch blood? No way. You were after the two for the price of one deal. My death and your new life, wrapped up in one well preserved and still pretty darn knockout package, if I say so myself.'

'No!' Cassandra blurted. 'Mister Dark is mine! We belong together.'

'Pipe down, sweetheart, I'm tryin' to save your neck – literally.'

Cassandra was about to protest again when

Mister Dark passed a ghostly hand across her face. She fell silent.

'Wanted to do that to her so many times,' Cherry muttered.

'You must care for her daughter very much,' Mister Dark said with a revolting leer.

'We got ourselves a deal? Let this one go – and Verne too. You can keep the Nimius. Wear it as a medallion for all I care.'

'The boy stays with me. The Nimius is useless without him.'

'Then the deal's off. I'm outta here and you don't get to fulfil your contract with the three big bads. You think they're gonna be pleased about that? It'll be straight back to the deep cold for you, but this time there won't be no chance of parole.'

Mister Dark glowered at her. 'I'll kill so many more before that happens.'

'Oh, I know you will. So take what I'm offerin' and go from here. You know it's a great deal.'

A hideous smirk pulled at his scar.

'Very well.'

Cherry held up her wrist.

'Swear it on this,' she said, displaying the bangle with the three ammonites.

'My word alone is not surety enough?'

'I'd sooner skinny-dip in a pit of cobras.'

'Then I, Mister Dark, swear by the Rule of the

Three that I shall adhere to my promise. From this day forward, the boy Verne will be neither hindered nor harmed nor forced to do my bidding and I shall leave today.'

The ammonites in the bracelet glowed briefly, binding the oath.

'Catesby, release him,' Mister Dark said. 'Don't sulk – you've already had one mouse this night.'

The cat snarled. He unhooked his claws from Verne's clothes and flapped his great wings.

Verne stumbled to Cherry and she hugged him tightly.

'Go,' she urged. 'Whatever you do, don't look back!'

The boy stared into her pale blue eyes.

'Don't do this!' he implored, terrified. 'There's got to be another way.'

'Scram, kid.'

There was no dissuading her. Verne staggered past the lighthouse. High above, Catesby followed silently.

'Now Lil's mom. Lift your control.'

Mister Dark laughed cruelly. 'She was such an eager victim. Another lost soul, searching for meaning. There really are too many of them in this modern age. There is no jolly in it.'

Leaning in, he pressed his phantom lips against Cassandra's. She wilted and sank to the ground.

'And now,' he said, turning to Cherry, 'I would have my fill of witch blood. I am eager to obtain new life.'

'Gimme one minute. I need to speak to her.'

She knelt before Cassandra and clasped her shivering hands.

'Hey, you OK, Mrs Wilson?'

Cassandra stared at the witch with unfocused eyes. She swallowed fearfully and drew away.

'Don't be scared, it's all gonna be swell. I know your head is full of the fuzzies right now, but they'll clear. Your husband is waitin' for you right along there.'

'M . . . Mike? Is he all right?'

'He's just fine.'

Cassandra glimpsed Mister Dark waiting impatiently close by and she quailed at the remembrance of the things she had done.

'I'm disgusting!'

'Weren't you, not your fault.'

'But it was! At the start. Lil – I said . . . did . . . terrible, unforgivable things. I was so jealous of the magic you two had.'

'Want to know the truth, lady? I was the jealous one.'

'You? Jealous of what?'

'Of you.'

'I've got nothing!'

'You really do need a boot up the bustle. Don't you realise you got more magic in your life than I'll ever know?'

'Me?'

'You're a mother: that's the strongest, most

ancient magic there is. It's what created our whole universe. And look what you created – your little girl is amazin'. *She's* your magic. I won't never know anythin' like that.'

Tears ran down Cassandra's painted cheeks.

'She won't want anything to do with me now. I know I don't.'

'Hey, you conjured that spell real good. It's mighty strong and true. Just keep believin'. It's gonna dazzle you.'

Overhead the storm clouds rumbled and a curtain of heavy rain began moving down the Esk Valley. Whitby began to smudge and dissolve like a watercolour painting. The dunes dribbled away and the river flowed through the harbour once again.

'No more talk,' Mister Dark declared.

'Go,' Cherry told Mrs Wilson.

Cassandra gathered up her cloak and covered her bare shoulders. Sobbing, she staggered towards the lighthouse.

Cherry breathed deeply and closed her eyes in preparation.

'I was none too shabby,' she told herself. 'Didn't disgrace the sisterhood.'

She turned to face Mister Dark. His face was savage, like a demonic mask.

Tearing along the pier, Verne ran into Lil, hurrying towards him.

'Help!' he shrieked in terror and panic. 'Mister Dark's going to kill Cherry! I think . . . I think he's going to eat her!'

A petrified scream cut across her stunned reaction. Lil's heart pounded.

'That was my mum!' she cried.

Rushing towards the lighthouse, they reached for one another's hands. A figure came teetering into view.

Cassandra leaned against the stonework for support. She was visibly shaking.

'Lil!' she wept. 'I'm . . . I'm so sorry!'

The girl hung back from her.

'Where's Cherry?' she asked.

Cassandra clutched at the wall and glanced fearfully over her shoulder.

'Don't go back there! He's a devil! A devil!'

A horrendous dread clawed at Lil's stomach and she began walking towards the beacon. Her mother caught her arm, but she pulled away angrily.

Verne was too afraid to go with her. He covered his ears and started backing away. Cassandra summoned the tatters of her courage and went after her daughter. She caught her by the shoulders and spun her round.

'Let me go!' Lil yelled.

'I won't let you see that!'

Behind the lighthouse there was a flash of blue light and the beacon roared into flames.

Lil tore away from her mother and ran to the end of the pier.

Verne moved further and further away. He saw the beacon burn high over the lighthouse lamp and knew exactly what it meant. Squeezing his eyes shut, he cried for Cherry Cerise.

He couldn't bear it. He wanted to run away from this hollow pain in his chest and never stop running.

When he turned around, he was confronted by Catesby. The repulsive winged cat flew before him, barring his path.

Verne lashed out to ward him off. Catesby clawed his hand and battered the boy's face with his leathery wings.

'Have a care, my pet,' a silken voice said. 'We don't want to injure our young friend – at least, not his hands. I have need of those.'

Verne whipped about. A tall, handsome man with raven hair and a rakish grin was standing behind him. His clothes were from another age and in his hands he held the Nimius. There was a fresh bloodstain at the corner of his mouth and his lips were a vivid red.

'Mister Dark?' the boy spluttered.

'I rather think my new non-disfigured flesh deserves a more aristocratic title. Baron Queller, perhaps, or some combination of the two.'

'You murdered Cherry! You're a vicious killer!'

'And if you wish me to do the same to your friend Lil, I shall be more than happy to oblige.'

'No!'

'Then do as I instruct and I won't tear her throat out, pretty though it is. You're going to operate the Nimius for me.'

'But your oath! I heard you swear!'

Mister Dark laughed. '"From this day forward" is what I said, but we're not going forward, we're going back. I was never going to remain in this abominable future with its infernal weapons and machines that vie with the destructive force of the Nimius. Besides, possessing the power of one was never going to be enough for me. There is such an easy way of doubling its might. Now, follow my instructions exactly.'

The rain had reached the harbour. The avenue of torches had gone out and the downpour hissed in the beacon's towering blue flames. Lil's head was in her hands and she took faltering steps when she came away. She had seen what Mister Dark had done and was consumed by grief and horror.

Cherry was dead, murdered by Mister Dark. The sight of her lying on the ground, lit by raging blue flames, was seared in Lil's mind. The most incredibly alive and most amazing person she had ever known was gone and Lil's world would never be as colourful again.

'Sisters in witchery,' she wept desolately. 'Oh, Cherry!'

She thought she was going to faint. Cassandra tried to comfort her, but Lil pushed her away.

Hearing angry voices up ahead, Cassandra gave a cry of despair.

'It's him!' she said. 'It's that devil! And he's got Verne!'

Lil looked up to see a tall man smacking Verne across the face, then grabbing him roughly by the collar. With his other hand he held the Nimius aloft. A purple light shone from it and a glowing track appeared at their feet, stretching along the pier towards the town.

Dragging a struggling Verne with him, Mister Dark stepped on to the eerie, radiant road. Catesby flew to his shoulder and shook his wet wings.

The rain battered down. Lil dragged a sleeve across her tearful eyes and anger creased her face.

Hatred for that foul man blazed within her,

hotter than the beacon, and it gave her the strength she needed.

'Take your bloody hands off my friend!' she yelled.

'Lil, no!' Cassandra wailed as her daughter charged after them.

Lil reached the glowing path and stared ahead. Mister Dark and Verne were nowhere to be seen.

'Where are they?' she cried furiously. 'Where are they? Verne! Verne!'

She stared at the ground. The strange purple light was fading. If she ever wanted to see Verne again, she knew what she had to do.

Desperately calling her name, Cassandra hurried up to her.

'I'm going after them!' Lil said vehemently. 'Don't you dare try and stop me.'

Cassandra embraced her quickly.

'I won't,' she said. 'You go get him. Bring Verne back.'

Lil stepped on to the flickering track.

'I love you!' her mother called.

Lil didn't look back. The shining path vanished and so did she.

Cassandra was alone, and the rain teemed down.